THE SUMMER SACRIFICE

Book One of the Master Game Series

Holly Hinton

Edited by Joel Sams
Cover illustration by David Revoy
Interior illustrations by Holly Hinton

www.hollyhinton.com

The present world is often terrifying to a sensible adult. Hinton reflects its effect on youngsters in a powerfully imagined world that hums with poetry. In its pages, in the words of Yeats, a terrible beauty is born. Herein lies empathy, barreling adventure and an iconic heroine, Jamie Tuff.

—Charles Bane Jr., author of *The Chapbook* and *Love Poems*, and nominee as poet laureate of Florida.

The Island's Chart of Ages

0	Baby				
1	Toddler				
3	Mini Manshu				
6	Manshu				
13	Juvenite				
20	Hansum				
30	Human	=	Ripe		
60	Shamun	=	Overripe	=	Underground

Contents

Chapter One

Dancing Ledge

Jamie smelt fish. The tang of decomposing
ocean caught her throat, as stars glinted in
the night and waves danced in the light of
a swollen moon. She flicked her eyes up,
down and sideways, but the view didn't
alter. There was nothing before her but the
Blanket of Stars and the deep Great Sea.

A rush of noise filled her head. Chatter
drowned out the ocean's whispers, and not
the gentle, bubbling kind of chatter but the
voluminous, cresting kind, the kind that
crawls into your ear and then wriggles and
chomps. Jamie felt her head spin, and the sea-view was hurled
out of sight and was replaced with another view that revealed
her location.

She was standing on a giant tongue of rock which jutted out
from limestone cliffs and thrust into the ocean. And she wasn't
alone. Fifty of her schoolmates bustled about her, dizzy with
excitement. The moonlit slab was alive with expectation as the
juvenites waited to hear from the Great Goddess.

Most of the juvenites had dressed up for the midnight Taking
and wore colourful gowns and doublets. A few had dressed with
less regard and one or two were even wearing pyjamas. But some
way across the Ledge, Jamie spotted a boy who was none too
polished or laid back. He had spiky hair and the sweetest smile,

7

and Jamie's tummy flipped when he waved at her. She'd have waved back if she *could*.

So I'm back at Dancing Ledge, she thought. *But whose body am I in?*

Last month she had ended up in a boy who was a dead cert for a Taking. She'd been terrified what would happen to her soul if he died, though thankfully he hadn't. She wouldn't relax until she identified her host.

As if heeding her call, legs carried her forwards a hundred yards to the tip of the Ledge and eyes not her own peered into the Great Sea. Through the sea-foam slipping back and forth, Jamie spied mustard pyjamas, dark skin and candyfloss hair. Good friend Charlotte was her host! A conscientious student and Transparent as they came. The Great Goddess would never give *her* to the Ancient Spectre. She'd never be Taken to the Under-world.

As relief washed over Jamie, a light wind blew out to sea and a tingle crept up Charlotte's spine and into her heart. Quite suddenly the whole world was beautiful and full of a love so strong you could only stand amazed and soak it up. The wings of the Great Goddess were upon them. Every juvenite thrilled at the bliss of Her embrace.

With the full moon now at its height, the crashing waves made shards of light that exploded into fragments of rainbow delight. The waves splashed and the stars flashed and the crowd cricked their necks to the sky and oohed and aahed.

Then came the Music.

It sank into Charlotte's skin, the swell of the waves swelling the music, the pulse of the tide becoming the beat. The Music was different for each who heard it; Charlotte's was lyrical and stringed. And though Jamie received a diluted version, she could hear the joy and heartbreak in it.

Euphoria flooded Dancing Ledge.

The juvenites closed their eyes and began to dance. Jamie enjoyed being rocked inside Charlotte, feeling fluid and free. The juvenites' dance grew ever more wild, until the Ledge itself seemed to shift in sympathy.

And then,

Splash!

A wave hit Charlotte in the face. She opened her eyes.

Flash!

A blinding orb of light erupted from the sea in front of her. It shot out of the water as fast as lightning and sailed up to the sky, only to dive back from where it came. Then came another and another. Jamie found the arcing of the orbs, heavenward and back, indescribably beautiful yet unbearably sad.

Charlotte took a small step forward and raised her arms in wonder. Her toes now dangled over the rock-edge. Jamie willed her to step back from the brink: only the Great Sea lay before her and its tides were fierce. But it didn't work that way. Charlotte did, however, turn her head.

Jamie hoped her eyes deceived her. Familiar figures were shuffling towards Charlotte, but these weren't current school friends but friends of old; juvenites who'd been Taken last month or many months ago, juvenites Jamie had never expected to see again. They looked sad, hopeless—no, worse than that: empty. And as each reached the edge they threw themselves into the Great Sea. Its swirling tides pulled them under, and orbs of light shot out of the water.

Splash! Flash!

The embrace of the Goddess left Charlotte. She stopped dancing.

Pain.

Something dug into Charlotte's back, turning her spine to jelly. That same something spun her round and pushed her towards land, through the dancing throng. Her school mates'

9

eyes remained closed. They were still consumed in ecstasy, ignorant of what was happening to her or their old friends.

Then the pressure on Charlotte's spine lifted, bringing her to a jerking halt.

A lady with hip-skimming ebony hair and a dangerous-looking ruby mouth swept past, drowning Charlotte—and therefore Jamie—in a cloud of musk. Poured into a long silver gown, the lady strode across the Ledge, moonlight reflecting off her contours. She was a thing of breathtaking beauty. Could it be the Great Goddess Herself?

No, thought Jamie. She didn't have wings. And something about her was decidedly ungoddesslike. In fact, there was more of the Serpent than the Eagle about her.

The lady approached the boy with spiky hair. He too had spotted the flying orbs of light and was staring out to sea. His sweet smile was gone. The lady whispered in the boy's ear and lodged a scarlet talon in his back. The fear left his face and was replaced by an awful blank stare.

Billy! Jamie wanted to scream and shout and cry and kill something. Charlotte was re-stabbed and propelled towards the cliff. Both girls were preparing to hit rock when, inches from impact, the nail in Charlotte's back stopped digging. A square of stone dropped back from the cliff-face, revealing a secret entrance. A figure emerged from within.

The man was tall and pale, and muscles rippled beneath his blue satin suit. Jamie had never seen a more beautiful creature. But he had the saddest eyes she'd ever seen.

Charlotte's captor grabbed her shoulders and swung her round. He too was towering, and his perfectly twirled tar-black moustache gleamed in the moonlight. Jamie recognized him at once. It was the Island's chief Doctor.

He stared into Charlotte's eyes. Only he wasn't looking at Charlotte. He was looking *through* Charlotte. At Jamie.

"Troublemakers need to be re-educated," he said, his soft voice full of violence. Then his focus snapped back to Charlotte. "After you, Child of the Underworld." He waved her through the door and into the cliff.

Sporadic fire-beetle lanterns lit the passageway's earth walls, giving it a dull, green glow.

The man with the sad eyes came towards Charlotte with a syringe. The Doctor presented her arm for injection. The needle went in.

* * *

"Owwwwww!"

Seveny jolted upright in her bunk and clutched her arm. She looked round the dormitory to see if she'd woken anyone else. No one was moving and the girl above her continued to gurgle. She was glad of this, for though the mysterious pain in her arm was subsiding quickly, she was in no state for idle chat.

Seveny had a powerful heart. Sometimes she worried its beats might shatter a rib. Right now it was beating so hard she could actually hear it. She concentrated on the girl above's gurgle, and the image that had seared her brain started to dissolve and her pulse began to settle. But it sped up again when she saw the empty bed opposite.

Charlotte wasn't back. She'd been Called to Dancing Ledge and she *wasn't back.*

Seveny eyed the cracked wooden door at the far end of the dorm. She'd been staring at it for the last hour or so, willing Charlotte's return. As though wanting something hard enough would make it happen.

But as she watched, the door began to open. The full moon powered through the muslin of the dorm's lone window and silhouetted a figure in the darkness. Seveny could just make out a small form, dressed in the Orphanage's compulsory pyjamas.

11

"Charlotte?" she whispered, trying not to wake the sixteen other girls.

The mustard-clad figure tiptoed nearer.

Please be Charlotte.

The figure looked at her friend's empty bunk, at the mattress's springs poking cheerily through the threadbare sheet. Its eyes were large, round, and wet-looking. "Where's Charlotte?" its small voice asked.

"At Dancing Ledge, Kai," Seveny whispered. "She'll be having the time of her life."

Kai sniffed, and his eyes skitted to Seveny's bed. He'd often sneak into the girls' dorm, past Mr Gribbin the warden, to join his older sister in her bunk. He was only six, seven years younger than Charlotte and Seveny, but though his sister was tiny and they could share comfortably, Seveny had to reorganize her long limbs to make space.

Kai jumped in, wrapped Seveny's arm round him, twisted a lock of her long golden hair round his hand, and sucked his thumb. Seveny felt pinned down and awkwardly folded, but she was glad of the company: with Kai in the way she couldn't see his sister's empty bed. And that gave her space to think.

Just before the pain had coursed through her, she'd seen a vision of Charlotte and Jamie at Dancing Ledge. Except, somehow, they were the *same girl*. Sort of... She could understand why she'd pictured Charlotte there: Charlotte was attending her Taking tonight. But she had no idea why she'd seen Jamie. Jamie had turned thirteen just a few days before Seveny. They'd attended the same Taking, seven months ago.

But dreams are dreams, she thought. *And dreams are strange.*

Except Seveny had not been asleep. She'd been staring at the door when the vision had stabbed her between the eyes.

Charlotte and Jamie had been one. Combined. And their mouths? Seveny shuddered. *Had both been open. Screaming.*

"Aaaaaaaagh!"

Jamie thrashed out and hit something warm and furry. It flew off the bed, thumped into a wall, and let out a miaow of indignation.

"Loopy!" She beckoned the black cat onto the bed and tweaked his long white whiskers. "You shouldn't even be up here! But I think you may have saved my life."

Jamie had thought she was a goner after what had happened, but though her claw-punctured arm was sore, her soul seemed intact and her brain alive.

She still wondered how it had all gone so wrong.

It was around seven months ago that her soul had started wandering. She figured it must be her soul because though she was asleep when it happened, when she woke up she wasn't in her own skin. The first time her soul travelled, it hadn't gone far: it had dropped into her dad's tired body, lying awake in the room just next door. The next time it went further afield, ending up in the slow-moving, slower-brained night-watchman who guarded the school. Last month's wander had been much more eventful. She'd landed in Dino Scarpel, a member of the notorious Tombland Gang, in the middle of a Taking. Dino was as spiteful, dishonest and rule-breaking as they came, and Jamie was sure her soul would be Taken with his, though Dancing Ledge had left them both unscathed. So finding herself in Charlotte had been a relief. Charlotte was a Transparent: a hard-working, rule-abiding, conscientious student.

But Charlotte had been Taken.

Taken.

Jamie's thoughts turned to tomorrow's assembly. The Headmistress made a Taking sound like an occasion for joy: a gentle passing of souls to the Ancient Spectre, the Lord of the Underworld. A divine event ordained by the Great Goddess for the greater good.

Well, it hadn't looked very divine to Jamie. It had looked like the Doctor was doing the Taking along with his two weird assistants, and they were snatching anyone unlucky enough to have woken up.

Jamie's stomach lurched as she thought of the juvenites drowning in the Great Sea. The Doctor had done something to them. *But what?* she wondered. *And what for?* She hadn't the faintest clue. But she knew the same fate awaited Billy and Charlotte.

This would hit Seveny hard: Charlotte had been like a sister to her. And something else worried Jamie, even more than her best friend's grief. One of her closest friends still hadn't been Called to Dancing Ledge. Ella's thirteenth birthday was next month.

Jamie scrabbled under her bed. She retrieved her satchel, got out a small book titled PITY ME SCHOOL DIARY Year: 300 and flipped to the lunar calendar.

Tonight's full moon: Sunday April 25th. A TAKING.

Next full moon: Sunday May 23rd. A TAKING.

The full moon after that: Monday June 21st. THE SUMMER SACRIFICE.

Jamie threw the satchel and diary back under the bed and disappeared beneath the sheets.

None of this is real, she told herself. *I might think I have the ability to drop into other people's bodies when I sleep, but I'm just dreaming.*

But a red rash was snaking up her face. She was a terrible liar, and she knew it.

Chapter Two

Pity Me School (for No Place boys and girls)

Jamie woke to the smell of burnt worms—a regular occurrence in the Tuff household. She dislodged Loopy and rolled out of bed, hitting the floor with a thwack. This achieved the desired effect: consciousness. She always started the day this way.

Shooing the cat from her shabby room, she careered down the narrow staircase, ran through the tiny, smoky kitchen, almost collided with her hulking father Geoffrey, and dashed out of the back door into their small, wild garden.

Chalk steps led through the overgrown grass to a roofless cubicle. Above it hung a huge bucket operated by a gnarly horsehair rope. Jamie chicken-danced towards it, avoiding Loopy who was intent on hunting feet. She dived inside and shut the door smartly to the plaintive mews of the ostracized cat.

She threw her threadbare nightie over the door and braced herself. A sharp jerk of the rope upended the bucket, and freezing seawater crashed down over her. Mouthfuls ended up in her throat as usual. She'd taken a dunk-wash every day since she could stand and still hadn't figured out how to avoid a saltwater gargle.

A pipe burped and the bucket refilled. One bucket did not equal a wash, but she couldn't bear another. Snatching her nightie and throwing the towel round her, she cold-footed it back to the house. Hurtling past her father and Loopy's hunting paws, she ran upstairs and slammed her bedroom door. She towelled herself dry, put on her school uniform, ran a boar-bristle brush through her pixie crop, and inspected herself in the mirror.

The older she got, the more she resembled her mother. She certainly had her features: slate-grey eyes, rich mahogany hair, a little upturned nose. Delicate features all, except for two large, pointy ears—the most obvious part of her inheritance.

Her mum had tried to hide her own ears under thick bobbed hair, but not so for Jamie. On the eve of her Juveniting and with some help from the kitchen scissors, she'd turned hers into a feature.

Normally she loved her short hair. It gave her some sort of distinction at school, a place where in most respects she felt unfailingly average. Today it only exposed the shadows of last night's fitful sleep.

As for her uniform, it promised boundless optimism… and spectacularly failed to deliver it. The blue shorts engulfed her knees, the long white socks highlighted her bow legs, the lemon-yellow tie drew attention to her sparrow neck, and the oversized apple-green blazer made her look like a pea-head. Of course it looked charming on everyone else.

For most of the students it was the uniform's material that

irritated. To cut costs, the school mass-produced it from the coarsest hemp cloth possible. And there, literally, was the rub: the fibres were itchy as hell. But hemp was easy to grow, and as Professor Goodhew the Head of Science never tired of saying, the only thing limiting a list of hemp's uses was the length of the hemp paper you were writing it on.

Jamie's tummy felt like it wanted to eat itself, but after last night she couldn't face breakfast. She tiptoed downstairs, passed her dad who didn't seem to notice, sneaked out of the front door, and set out for school.

Only the Island had survived the Great Storm. It was quite small and just a quarter of it was inhabited. That quarter was called No Place. Pity Me Town, where Jamie lived, was No Place's largest settlement and its capital. It was a couple of square miles in size, and home to about six thousand people.

Pity Me School taught all five thousand of No Place's children from age six to sixteen. Every morning, four tiny steam trains brought students in from the villages and carried labourers out to the fields and mines, then swapped everyone back at sunset.

The trains ran on wooden rails, were powered by hemp oil, and were neither fast nor comfortable. They were operated by Crackpots, or 'ground rats' as the No-Placers called them, a dangerous clan to the west with questionable morals. Jamie was glad that, as a local, she could walk to school and avoid them.

But she dreaded what the morning would bring.

After every monthly Taking there was a celebratory assembly. This morning, two of the assembly hall's empty seats would belong to Charlotte and Billy. Jamie knew she'd never see them again, and she couldn't bear the thought.

In an attempt to delay the inevitable she chose a circuitous route to school, out of town instead of through it, following the coastline. It took her away from Pity Me's sad identikit houses and endless rows of fences.

Soon she was strolling over the high limestone cliffs that overlooked the bay and through long grasses peppered with delicious red wolfberries, lethal black deathcherries, and spherical moonflowers.

The moonflowers, which looked like their namesake, were doing very well. Sunlight tended to char their flesh, but spring this year had been unusually dull, and the winter mists they loved still clung to the high places of the Island. Only when a thicket of the white spheres blocked her path did Jamie realise she'd gone too far. The moonflowers spilled over the cliff like a white waterfall down to Dancing Ledge.

Jamie stared at the Ledge sleeping peacefully in the ocean a hundred yards below. It looked so innocent in the morning light.

"Appearances can be deceptive," she muttered.

She retraced her steps and soon reached the coastal graveyard where the people before the Great Storm had buried their dead. It was a crumbling, desolate place, and the favourite haunt of the Tombland Gang, Pity Me School's resident thugs.

She walked briskly, not wanting to risk an encounter, and made for the barbed-wire fence that surrounded the school, the playing field and the Orphanage: a small building made of wood and tin, which was stuck to the school with a mess of concrete. Jamie looked at the concrete-joined afterthought, and felt for Seveny. Being trapped inside the barbed wire fence was bad enough during school, but orphans were only allowed out on school-free Sundays, and then only with permission.

Jamie worked her way round the fence and came to the giant entry gate. She lifted the latch and the gate opened smoothly, shutting behind her with an impressive clang. Entering the school grounds was easy. Leaving was not.

The school's architecture didn't fit with the rest of Pity Me, either in size or look. Unlike the town's small wooden houses or the red brick villas of the wealthy, it was built from grey stone which had been covered in concrete and then painted—grey. It was a giant cuboid of ugliness spanning five floors, with narrow slits for windows, devoid of pane or frame.

Jamie came to its main entrance: a huge steel door set in an imposing stone arch. The school's emblem—a winged wand up which crept a snake—was riveted to the door in copper plating. Beneath the emblem were engraved the words:

PITY ME SCHOOL
(FOR NO PLACE BOYS AND GIRLS)

The green of the oxidized copper lent the sign an even greater sense of decay and hopelessness than the words alone suggested.

The door was a contraption that opened and closed in reaction to *something*, but no one knew *what*. Its sheer unpredictability caused many a student's lateness, but the door was not an excuse for tardiness. Nothing was. Jamie worried that the door would fail her today, for in choosing the scenic route she'd forfeited time. And the punishment for lateness was steep: solitary confinement in the Chamber Upstairs.

But as she approached, cogs clattered, chains slackened, springs wakened, and the enormous door swung open. Jamie leapt through it, her relief slightly dampened by the anguished yelp of an unfortunate pupil caught by the door on its close.

Pity Me School had no reception. There was an oak door opposite the main entrance, flanked on both sides by dusky stone corridors. The corridors looked like they went into the bowels of hell, which in a way they did: one ended up Down the Line, and the other corkscrewed up to the Chamber Upstairs. Both smelt of sorrow.

Jamie dashed through the oak door and into the Grand Hall.

The Grand Hall was the only building to have survived the Great Storm. Though encased in concrete, its interior remained untouched: it was a beautiful fossil, buried in a repugnant stone. Oak beams arced in intricate webs across the ceiling, and faded mosaics covered the floor. Its windows were stained glass, and even though the concrete casing dimmed their glory, they still gave off the odd glint of hope.

At the front of the Hall was a stage. Above it, a stuffed eagle hung from a long chain. A crispy-looking adder dangled from its talons in a sad, stiff spiral.

The Grand Hall held over five thousand cherry-wood seats arranged in a square, seventy-two by seventy-two. Most of the students were already seated. Solemn characters in crow-black gowns circled them, checking names chalked on the giant slate boards which lined the walls. Occasionally they crossed a name out. Jamie watched the caped teachers closely.

Her study was interrupted by a wildly flapping tent. It was the Head of English, Jamie's form tutor Miss Humfreeze, her oversized gown billowing as she waved. She was warning Jamie to sit down. Fast.

Jamie Tuff's chair was near the back, where the Scarpels sat. They were a large family with blond hair and permanent scowls. All of them were members of the Tombland Gang. Her seat was directly behind Dino's enormous older brother Blake Scarpel and directly in front of Blake's huge girlfriend Rosacea who— thank Goddess for small mercies—hadn't yet arrived.

Jamie squeezed past the more punctual students and wedged herself in. The rows were so narrow that even with her sparrow frame she had trouble fitting. But the lanky boy who sat next to her really struggled. And because of this, Jamie enjoyed even the dullest assembly. Billy's legs often ended up in her foot area, and then they'd practise a kind of courtship with their feet. She looked at the empty seat next to her. There was no Billy now.

She tried to spot her other close friends. Max Lively (Nine

Lives to those who knew him) was missing, but he was always inexplicably late for school. She saw Ella at once: the ash-blonde bounce of her hair was unmistakable. And Seveny and George were right at the front: she could just make them out through the sea of bobbing heads. But there was no hope of seeing tiny, kind Charlotte.

Jamie was shaken from her melancholy by something enormous thudding into place behind her. Rosacea had landed.

At the front of the Hall, Seveny was glaring at the stuffed eagle. She was sure she could smell it.

"Why do I have to sit right in front of that monstrosity?" she said in a low voice, which nevertheless echoed dangerously around the Hall's stone walls.

The boy next to her gulped. "Because that's your chair."

"Helpful George, helpful."

"And if the Great Goddess could hear you, I don't think She'd be best pleased."

"If the Great Goddess could see that," said Seveny, pointing at the hanging bird, "She'd send us an even Greater Storm than the last one!"

"Seveny..."

George glanced nervously to the rear of the Hall. The Establishment had arrived.

"This is the symbol of the Great Goddess's dominion over the Ancient Spectre? The triumph of good over evil?"

"Seveny please..."

"Symbol my arse. That, George, is a dead and stinking bird, attached to a dead and stinking snake!"

There weren't many pluses to being George 'bright as a button' Button, but one was his name following Seveny's in the register. In his estimation, Seveny Brown was pretty much a real-life goddess. Golden-haired and statuesque, she looked older than her years. George got kudos points just for hanging out with her. In fact, merely by association, she undid all the minus points he accrued by himself with his big nose, his mousy mop hair, and worst of all his boffin brain.

Like him, Seveny was a strange creature, but whereas George felt like some sort of gnome, Seveny seemed to him a sylph of the heavens, born of the winds. Her reckless bravery awed the other students, and their friendship left George mostly free of the Tombland Gang's assaults. Mostly. But her mood was as changeable as the Island's weather, and his seat could be the safest in the Hall or the most dangerous. Right now, he thought it deadly.

Seveny's amber eyes flashed with fire as the Establishment reached the front of the Hall. The men wore blood-red silk, the women emerald-green crushed velvet. Each carried three objects: an iron crook, a ledger and a quill. Like the school emblem, the crook had wings at the top and a serpent coiling up from the base. The ledger was bound in black leather, and the quill held indelible squid ink.

The Establishment ruled No Place. They spoke of tradition this and tradition that, and boasted of how they protected their people with fences just as they'd protected the Hall's walls with concrete. It seemed to Seveny that pretty much all they stood for was tradition, fences and concrete walls.

They gave off an atmosphere as ancient as the Grand Hall itself, as though they'd grown like fungus from cracks in its skin. Yet they looked ageless: there wasn't a wrinkle among them. But some laboured to heave themselves onto the stage, and a few even used their crooks as mobility aids.

The last Governor took his place: Phosphor-Jones, the Deputy Head and Head of History. He was built like an ox and his face was as red as his reputation was fierce. Nobody liked him. Seveny watched with glee as he struggled to fit his huge bulk into his wrought iron chair.

The final member of the Establishment came in by himself,

as though it pained him to be associated with the rest of the besilken, bevelveted herd. Unlike them, he had grace. He seemed to glide down the aisle and onto the stage, and he used his crook strictly for ceremony. He sat down and twirled his carefully curled black moustache.

With the Doctor seated, the Pity Me Perfects took to the stage, holding assorted wooden instruments. A voluptuous middle-aged woman stalked her way up the stairs after them, her wondrous behind encased in a figure-hugging skirt, her sky-high heels clicking as she walked. She launched herself onto the central podium at the front of the stage, bowed in deference to the Establishment, and tossed her head to the complete indifference of her frozen red quiff. Facing the Perfect Orchestra, she raised her baton and the music began. The so-called Music of the Earth.

The Pity Me Perfects were students selected by the Establishment to help them rule, both in school and out. Officially, they were selected for their objectivity and fairness. Really, they were selected from the ranks of the wealthy, who lived in the hills above Pity Me. And they were as unfair and biased as the Tombland Gang were criminal and violent.

They were by no means selected for their musical skills.

The Perfects puffed and twanged and bashed their instruments without pitch, tone, rhythm, or harmony. And the students sat, buttocks clenched, smiles fixed, willing it to end.

When the ghastly performance finished, the Perfects bowed to rapturous applause. Even the smallest manshu—the youngest children—knew you had to pretend. Pretence was a big part of staying out of trouble at Pity Me School. Indeed, it was entrenched in the ethos of No Place.

With satisfied smiles and cocked noses, the Perfect Orchestra left the stage. The conductor stayed on, a grin clawing its way across her makeup-caked face.

"Today, we have some newcomers to the school. Precious little manshu!"

She looked into the crowd. Small, frightened faces peered back.

"My name is Funnella Fitzgerald. I am the Headmistress of Pity Me School and the Head of the Establishment. But you probably all know that. At least, you *ought* to..." For a moment her eyes became pools of acid, before the smile re-found its place on her thin, red lips. "Now let us talk of Dancing Ledge. Imagine the music we just heard, filling your bones..."

"That'd be torture," Seveny whispered.

"That music, only a thousand times more wonderful."

Seveny snorted. "A million times would be just about bearable."

A bead of sweat dropped from George's brow.

"Music... of the Earth." Funnella Fitzgerald waved her hands about and sniffed the air like a chef. "That is what will soak into your souls at Dancing Ledge. The Music and the Dancing are what make a Taking a thing of beauty. Now after me... Hear that and we can die happy!"

"Hear that and we can die happy," said everyone, glumly.

Seveny mouthed the words. She was being watched. They all were. The Establishment's quills were poised to record the noteworthy, and the caped teachers circled, watching for disturbance.

The older manshu, nearing their teens, eyed the empty seats around them with grave suspicion. Their time to Dance had yet to come. The juvenites, thirteen and over, had the glazed look of survivors listening to a tale they'd experienced first-hand and heard told many, many times. But the newest students softened, enjoying at least the Headmistress's theatrics.

"On Dancing Ledge," said Funnella Fitzgerald, "the Great Goddess chooses whom the Ancient Spectre Takes. Those she chooses are Children of the Underworld. Like children born out of Wedlock, or—" Funnella mouthed the next word "—twins. Their souls are rotten. Their rightful home is with the Ancient Spectre, the vast and evil Serpent who sleeps beneath the ocean.

"However. If you are nice, honest and obedient, your souls will remain beautifully Transparent. Transparents are *never* Taken. And such is the kindness of the Great Goddess that even Children of the Underworld die without pain."

"Excuse me?" said Kai, his tiny voice wavering. "If the Great Goddess is so good, why would she feed anyone to the Ancient Spectre?"

There was a collective intake of breath. The Establishments' eyes were fixed on the small boy sat in the front row. Their squid-ink quills began to scratch menacingly across their ledgers.

"Bad souls rot society," said Funnella sharply. "The Great Goddess must pull out the weeds to make way for the flowers. Dancing Ledge is the purest form of natural selection."

"But my sister was much better than the most best!" cried Kai. "She was Transparent! So why was she Taken? Why was she Taken when she was all I had?"

The scribbling stopped. The Establishment put their quills behind their ears and snapped their ledgers shut.

"Accidents *will* happen!" said Funnella. Her brows, always pencilled high on her forehead, found a new position in her hair.

"But why do they happen all the time?" Kai shouted. "Charlotte!" he screamed. "Charlotte, come back. I miss you!"

Seveny's heart threatened to break through her rib cage. She wanted more than anything to comfort the boy, and was about to do something highly punishable when the Hall descended into chaos as other manshu began crying in sympathy with Kai. The Perfects tried to shush them, but the dam had burst. The wails of the manshu were supplemented by strange shrieks and shouts as members of the Tombland Gang seized the opportunity for undetected mischief. The crow-black figures stopped their slow

25

circling and walked one way, then the other, then *into* each other, and finally started to flap.

TAP! TAP! TAP!

An iron crook hammered on the stage. Deputy Phosphor-Jones' jowls trembled. He pointed his crook at Kai and headed for the stairs.

Miss Humfreeze was portly, but she had the reflexes of a whippet. She scooped up the little boy, slung him over her shoulder, and was out of the Hall before Phosphor-Jones was even off the stage. The room exhaled in relief.

The Establishment conferred. The Great Goddess's wisdom had never been questioned before. They furrowed their brows, waggled their crooks, reset their glasses, and adjusted their hair. The Headmistress finally resumed her place on the podium. She looked more than usually strange.

"Kai is an orphan," she said at last. "You all know orphans are unbalanced. Just look at the Tombstone."

The students stared at the giant grey tombstone fixed to the Hall's back wall. Thirty names were engraved on it.

Every so often, a troubled child jumped off the cemetery's cliffs. They were called Tombstoners because of where they leapt from, and because of the inevitable result. They were *always* orphans.

"What a shame if Kai were to suffer in the same way," said Funnella. "Someone must take him in hand. He shall come and live with me."

No! Seveny wanted to scream. Making Kai sit beside his sister's empty chair the day after her death was a torture of the cruellest kind. But that was nothing compared to living with Funnella Fitzgerald. Who knew what she might do to him?

Seveny gazed up at the hanging eagle.

"It would land on the Headmistress," George whispered.

"What?"

"The eagle. If the chain broke, it would land on her..."

From her seat at the back of the Hall, Jamie's eyes were fixed on the Headmistress. Something was wrong with her, and she couldn't figure out what. After deciding to house Kai, Funnella hadn't just recovered her composure, she looked positively delighted. That was, until the Doctor left his seat and whispered in her ear, his elegant moustache twitching as he spoke.

Funnella's face hardened. She stamped her heel on the floor for silence.

"Charlotte was pushed!"

Five thousand chins dropped.

"You know Dancing Ledge is out of bounds. No one goes there unless they are Called. Right?"

"Right," the children chorused.

"Wrong!" said Funnella. "Someone... un-Called for was there last night. Someone flouting the rules. And that someone was seen."

Eyes walked the room, eyes full of suspicion. Most landed on the Tombland Gang, especially the Scarpels, who coolly scowled back. It was Jamie who felt the heat.

The Headmistress can't be talking about me, can she? I haven't been there—at least, not in person...

The rash began to climb her neck.

"Dancing Ledge is sacred ground," said Funnella. "It's an altar where sacrifices are made, and must be treated as such. We can't have snoopers snooping on the Great Goddess, can we?"

"No!"

The Hall trembled.

"Remember what happened the last time humans interfered!" Funnella pointed at a boggle-eyed manshu sucking its thumb. "What happened?"

"...the Great Storm?"

"And why did it happen?"

The little girl stared unblinkingly at Funnella, completely frozen.

27

"Because people didn't know their places!" a plummy voice called out. It belonged to Edward Illustrious-Banks, one of the Perfects.

"Continue," the Headmistress growled.

But instead, a ginger girl stood up, Perfect Sylvia Scythe-Crawley. "They ignored boundaries and wanted what wasn't theirs!"

"So the Great Goddess sent the Great Storm—" said Banks.

"To destroy those who would pervert her Work!" a second boy concluded. Herbert Snodgrass, a Senior Perfect, was the oldest of the three. He was tall and thin, with a lollipop head.

"Precisely, Herbert!" said Funnella, gazing at him as if he were her own son. "Three hundred years ago, before the Great Storm, people didn't know their places. They tampered with the weather, seeded clouds, lasered lightning, poisoned rivers, attacked each other with tornadoes. And things went wrong. Well they were taught a Great lesson! We need to know *our* places, or the Great Goddess will wipe *us* out!"

The Hall was a sea of open mouths.

"We in the Establishment save lives through the boundaries we create. Our boundaries are your protectors. And trespassers will be punished."

Jamie's tie felt like a noose round her neck. The rash burned on her face.

"Do you, or do you not, want to be *wiped out?*" Funnella's teeth were bared, and her nose had begun to sweat.

"We do not!" cried the Pity Me Schoolchildren.

"Then I suggest you keep an eye out for troublemakers," the Headmistress said, calmly.

"Keep an eye out for them," the Doctor repeated, "before they ruin everything."

The entire hall followed the Doctor's gaze… and found Jamie and her bright red face.

They know! They know I was there!

A moment later everyone turned back round. Jamie was half-wondering whether she'd imagined them all staring at her when something flicked the back of her head, something undoubtedly real. She turned in her seat.

Rosacea Unvelope eyeballed her with menace. Her pudgy finger was poised mid-flick. "I'd be careful if I was you."

Jamie wanted to run, but she knew better than that. Assemblies were not something you ran out of—you'd be chased. Reluctantly, she turned back to the front. The flicking continued.

At the front of the Hall, Seveny was seething. Charlotte was gone, Kai was about to be kidnapped by the Headmistress, and Jamie... Along with the rest of the Hall, she'd seen the rash on her friend's face. But that meant nothing—Jamie would never have trespassed onto the Ledge. Except, she'd seen a vision of her on the Ledge last night... But Jamie wasn't a murderer!

Seveny was so furious that quite unconsciously she rose from her seat. Funnella Fitzgerald said something to her, but she was too angry to hear what. She only knew that the Headmistress was trying to make Jamie the scapegoat for something horrible and unexplained. Something that stank of rot and death.

Seveny's eyes travelled up to the eagle and serpent, and alighted on the heavy chain holding them aloft.

Then, everything went *strange*.

The taste of bitter metal filled her mouth and the eagle began to move—in tight, slow circles at first, but increasing in pace and breadth until it was whizzing in wide arcs high above the stage. The bird was flying. Flying again! Its path dizzied Seveny, as if somehow its flight were her own, and she dragged her eyes away, down past the spiralling snake, and back to the stage.

Then everything came crashing down.

Nothingness.
Consciousness.

Blood.

Seveny had bitten her tongue. The blood coursed warmly down her chin and dripped onto the floor.

The floor?

She looked up. George was leaning over her, trembling. The sound of rustling filled her ears. The Establishment's quills were scribbling furiously.

"What happened?" she said.

George's eyes flicked to the ceiling. The eagle was no longer flying. In fact, it was no longer there at all.

Seveny wrenched herself up and sat back in her chair, puzzled. Which was when she saw the front of the stage.

The eagle was no longer flying because, in a manner of speaking, it had come in to land. And in the very place George had predicted: slap bang on top of the Headmistress.

Funnella Fitzgerald was *very* horizontal.

Chapter Three

Birthdays and Deathdays

Jamie could tell her dad's state of mind by the smell of his cooking. What was wafting up the stairs didn't bode well.

She'd had four dunk-washes this morning and picked out her least baggy shorts for the dual occasion: it was Ella's birthday, and the anniversary of Gloria Tuff's death.

She slung on what should have been a tight white top, but which now hung loosely at her sides, and stared at her thin, tired form in the mirror.

It had been nearly a month since she'd last slept or eaten properly. Nearly a month since Charlotte and Billy were Taken, and *that* assembly. Nearly a month since the beginning of the Gang-flicking, pernicious Perfect prodding, and worst of all, the constant surveillance.

After *that* assembly, Funnella Fitzgerald and Herbert Snodgrass had taken to following her around constantly. Her friends joked nervously about her 'voluptuous shadow' and 'ant-shaped accessory.' But Jamie couldn't laugh with them. The surveillance was merely the symptom of a much greater ill.

She'd received the news after a long wait Down the Line.

Standing in the dark corridor, she'd listened as Phosphor-Jones caned Max for lateness in one room and Funnella Fitzgerald scolded Seveny in another.

From what she could hear, the Headmistress blamed Seveny for the eagle falling down. Jamie wondered whether Funnella was still concussed.

Seveny came out first, and two burly Governesses escorted her to the Chamber Upstairs. That ought to have been Max's punishment: missing an assembly was much worse than standing up without permission. But Max wasn't called Nine Lives for nothing. And besides, it seemed the Headmistress wanted someone to blame for her head wound.

A few minutes later, Max sauntered out of the Deputy Head's room, his hair hanging lazily about his cheeks. He brushed his thick, shiny mane back from his face and softly chuckled. His dimples grew deep. He had escaped the Chamber yet again. He never suspected that one of his closest friends had taken his place.

Then he'd seen Jamie.

"What are you doing here?!" he'd asked, too loudly.

His question was a worthy one. In all her time at Pity Me School, she'd not once been sent Down the Line. But before she could reply, she was ordered in.

The Headmistress's quarters were sumptuous, furnished in ruby-red velvet and emerald silk. Beautiful glass lanterns hung from the ceiling, illuminating Funnella Fitzgerald as she reclined on a golden throne, her red quiff blazing like fire. One side of her face was dark and shiny. As Jamie approached, she saw why: it was blood from the accident, waiting to clot.

Then the Headmistress had delivered the news.

Jamie was now officially on the Gifted and Dangerous Register. Funnella hadn't told her why, just that she *was*. You couldn't appeal an Establishment decision, in any case.

Being on the Gifted Register was applauded: most of the Perfects were on it. Being on the Dangerous Register was at least respected: all the Gang were on that. But being on the Gifted *and* Dangerous Register, *that* spelled disaster. *G and D* was for Extraordinary students. And no one Extraordinary lasted long at Pity Me. They disappeared. Not at once and sometimes not for years, but eventually, one morning, they didn't turn up at school. And you never saw them again.

The rumour was that they were sent Underground to the Dispensary for the Disenchanted, No Place's only hospital, for re-education. Given what the Doctor had said on the Ledge about troublemakers, and the fact that no one on *G and D* ever returned, Jamie suspected that 're-education' was terminal.

The thought of the Dispensary jogged a distant memory.

When her mum had become ill, she wasn't taken there. Her dad was adamant she stay at home. So Gloria Tuff had spent her last year dying secretly in the attic, a strange, crippling disease taking her by inches.

Her illness meant she could no longer work at the hemp mill, and when her ex-colleagues came to call, they weren't allowed to see her. With her dad at work and her mum in bed, Jamie usually had to answer the door and politely get rid of them. She'd harp on about how her father's promotion meant her mother no longer had to work. But nobody really believed her. Being a single-earning family was not just rare in No Place, it was virtually impossible. "Still... If we can do anything to help..." they'd say, and Jamie would answer with a friendly "No, thank you!" and close the door.

They *knew* she was ill. She could see it in their furrowed brows and pursed lips. But they didn't pass it on, the Establishment never came to visit, and her mother stayed safely hidden away under the attic's bows until eventually she expired.

"You're a fighter, Jamie Tuff!" her mum had whispered in her ear. Then there was a soft breath on her cheek and her mother was gone.

Four years ago to the day.

Jamie's thoughts, scattered as the junk around her room, turned to Ella. She couldn't bear the thought of losing her too. But it was possible: Ella turned thirteen today. Now she was a juvenite, she'd be Called to Dancing Ledge.

The next Taking was tonight. Mercifully, though Ella was eligible for it, she hadn't received an Opal Envelope containing her Call. With neither post nor school on Sundays, she'd definitely escaped. But the Call would come. Next month, or as occasionally happened, the month after. It would come. And Jamie dreaded this. She'd lost her faith in 'natural selection' and 'accidents.' And she wasn't alone. A nervousness had swept the school after the last Taking. *Who won't I see at the next assembly,* the students wondered. *Will the interloper strike again?*

Jamie, at least, didn't have to worry about the interloper. She was going to stay awake all night. That way, she couldn't end up in someone else's body.

Throwing on her jacket, she careered down the stairs.

Her father was already at the table, struggling through the charred remains of what had once been plump, protein-rich earthworms. Jamie sat down and, after a liberal sprinkling of sea salt and a squirt of mountain honey, started on her plate. Jamie studied her father as he threw the blackened worms straight down his throat.

Geoffrey Tuff's skin was etched with ashes and his hands were tough as leather from his work. He'd mined the lava flows of Boiling Rock Downs, and before that Hell Bottom Quarry, for twenty years now. Jamie wondered why the miners couldn't keep a little more of their haul given that No Place relied on the metals they unearthed. And they risked their lives every day: Charlotte and Kai had lost both their parents at Hell Bottom, and Ella had lost her dad that way.

Geoffrey was equally concerned about Jamie. These days, the damned cat looked healthier than his daughter. He knew that the school had put her on some sort of register and consequently her prospects weren't good, but what could he say? What could he do? He ran his fingers through his salt-and-pepper beard. "You ready, Jay?"

Jamie put down her artfully-sucked worms.

No formal services were conducted in No Place when a person died. The Establishment collected the corpse on behalf of the Dispensary and sent it Underground for disposal. It was up to the family to organize any gathering of remembrance. These unofficial funerals were usually conducted at Hill Drop. It was a popular spot for remembrances too, as it was less fenced-in than most places.

Geoffrey Tuff set the pace, walking with long strides like he had an appointment to keep, though Jamie didn't struggle to keep up. They jumped Spy-Barn Stile with ease, passed through the avenue of witch-hazels, and climbed the well-trodden path to Hill Drop. When they reached the top of the dandelion-capped hill, Jamie saw that they were not alone.

The woman was willowy with neurotic eyes. Beside her stood a short, round girl with highly sprung hair. Jamie had wanted to mourn the anniversary of her mother's death in private, but if anyone had to be up here with them, she was glad it was Ella and her mum.

As the Tuffs walked over, Mrs Violet Last patted down her long brown skirt and straightened her blouse.

"How are you?" said Geoffrey.

Violet fiddled with the wooden pin that held up her hair. "Oh, you know... you breathe easier each day, but it still hurts."

Harold Last had died early last year. A victim of Hell Bottom, he'd missed his step and gone straight into the lava. There had been no body to recover.

Jamie looked at Ella's bowed head, gravity accentuating her plump cheeks, and linked arms with her.

The two families sat quietly together, the girls occasionally blowing the tufts off dead dandelions, finding comfort in watching the seeds gently float up and away.

At last, Violet stood up and stretched. "My joints! I'm getting old!"

"You haven't changed a bit," said Geoffrey. (They'd lived next door as children.) "And you were lovely then!"

Violet blushed. "Can I have a word?"

Geoffrey nodded. "You girls go ahead."

Jamie and Ella started off at a pace, though Ella had a hard time keeping up as they ran down the grassy slopes. They had passed through the avenue of witch-hazels and were about to hop the stile when they saw the flame-red hair of the Headmistress.

Funnella Fitzgerald thrust an Opal Envelope over the stile and into Ella's palm.

"Open it!" she snarled.

Ella's fingers trembled as she took out the letter.

** Are you ready to Dance? * *

Ella Rose Lasky

this is your official Calling

DANCING LEDGE AWAITS

YOU!

Please arrive at 11.30pm sharp

for the midnight Taking

** Prepare to be enchanted! **

"Enjoy the experience," Funnella said sneeringly to Ella. She wrinkled her nose at Jamie. "And you, my dear, are being watched…"

Chapter Four

Stormy Weather

Blue Wood was named after the small clearing at its centre. It was filled with bluebells and forget-me-nots, and surrounded by golden oaks. In the middle of it, there stood an ancient granite sundial, rough-hewn but accurate almost to the minute, which Head of History Phosphor-Jones claimed pre-dated the Great Storm.

Jamie and Ella were lying quietly in the flowers, waiting for their friends to arrive for the birthday celebration, when something shattered the peace.

"Boom!" an excited voice, well, *boomed*.

Max loomed over them, his dimples dimpling, carrying what looked very much like a large round brain.

"What a magnificent *Labyrinthiformis*," said George, appearing from behind a nearby tree. Something laughed throatily in the branches above him. "Where did you come from!?" George yelped.

"I can be stealthy, too." Seveny swung herself down and landed at his feet. "And you just made Brainball sexy, George. *Labyrinthiformis*. Ha! Almost makes me want to play it..." She ran her fingers through his mop hair and kissed him on the forehead. "Almost."

George went a shade of lobster.

Max put the 'brain,' actually a type of local coral, at Ella's feet. "Pile in!" he yelled. There was a flurry of limbs, and Ella disappeared.

"Get off me!" she said, as her friends tickled her mercilessly.

"What, don't you like this?" said Max, continuing to tickle.

"No, Nine Lives, I don't!"

The pyramid of limbs unravelled, revealing the birthday girl. She was sobbing.

"I've been Called," she said. "Tonight."

"You'll be fine," Seveny said, too quickly. "Hell, if I could make it through..."

But George and the girls were silent.

"Brainball?" said Max, trying to lighten the mood.

Brainball was a much-played game in No Place. This year even more so, as the ocean had been burping up an unusually large number of the strange, light-as-a-feather orbs. Brainballs were still highly sought after, prized possessions: a fully mature specimen, with careful maintenance and regular shell-varnishing, could last up to sixty years. And Max was one proud owner.

Ella looked at the shadow on the sundial. "It'll have to be quick, it's nearly noon. Actually, I'll sit this one out."

"Me too," said Jamie.

"And me," said Seveny.

George admired Brainball more as a coral than as a game. However, the girls wanted to chat, and Max wanted to do anything *but*. He took up the gauntlet.

The game was simple enough: you had to toss the Brainball over another player's head, then catch it before it bounced more than twice. Each time you succeeded, you got a point. The match lasted until you were interrupted. Then you totted up the points and whoever had most, won.

As the boys started playing, the girls traipsed over to a large oak on the clearing's edge and sat beneath it. They beheaded some forget-me-nots and started making flower chains.

Eventually, Seveny broke the silence.

"We've seen them talking to you, Jamie."

"Who?" Jamie asked, knowing *who* very well.

"The Perfects."

Jamie flinched. Since going on *G and D*, the Perfects had attacked her every day at school, their words puncturing her like sugar-coated daggers. Today was a school-free Sunday, so it really ought to have been Perfect-free, too, but Seveny had brought yesterday's encounter flooding back. She'd been on her way to Geography when Sylvia Scythe-Crawley and Edward Illustrious-Banks had stopped her in the corridor.

"Billy was your boyfriend, wasn't he?" said Banks.

"No."

"Oh," said Crawley, "so he didn't feel the same way about you?"

"Well, never mind," said Banks. "He's gone now. And that's better for everyone."

"Billy had a dark soul."

"If he hadn't, he wouldn't have been Taken."

"We're here for you," they said together, smiling sweetly.

Jamie had wanted to throw up chunks of burnt worms on their polished shoes, but that would have got her in trouble. She couldn't have claimed she was ill: in No Place, you didn't claim illness unless you wanted to end up Underground. The Establishment would probably send her there anyway, but she had no intention of helping them do it.

"Think what you want, but I'm fine," she said. "Thank you," she remembered just in time.

And the Perfects, with almost-believable smiles of sympathy, gently shook their heads and went on their way.

Jamie was gripping her flower-chain so tightly she'd crushed some of the petals.

"The Perfects?" said Ella. "Born into the right families, more like."

"They are poison," Seveny spat. "And protected."

Jamie shrugged. "So who can I go to?"

Nobody, was the answer. In the Establishment's opinion, the Perfects could do no wrong. Breaking people's spirits was practically one of their jobs. And they never left marks—at least, not on the outside.

"Maybe the Tombland Gang could help?" Ella joked, though her laugh didn't quite reach her face. The Perfects and the Gang were far closer and had more in common than the Establishment let on, or the No-Placers pretended.

"You know the Gang hurt Charlotte?" said Seveny. "Before she got Taken. They made the little ones hurt her. And then they started on Kai."

"Yeah, I know," said Jamie, heavily. "The Gang recruit them young now."

The Tombland Gang had recently sworn in their fiftieth member and were now training manshu as young as eight. The juvenites in the Gang felt utterly invincible, having survived their Calling without being Taken. But it was the manshu who hadn't yet made a name for themselves who were the really deadly ones. And as the Gang's ranks had swollen, the number of Tombstoners plummeting to their deaths had also grown. This year two had jumped already, and it wasn't even June. As always, they were orphans.

The Establishment's coroner had concluded that both were tragic, unprovoked suicides: they'd been mentally unbalanced due to their lack of parents. But every student at Pity Me knew the truth. They'd witnessed the Gang beatings. They'd seen the Perfects whispering to the victims. But no one ever pointed the finger. Nor did they mention the bloodstains in the cemetery that appeared after every tragic, unprovoked suicide.

Ella stared at the Opal Envelope on her lap.

"They say that Dancing Ledge is the purest form of natural selection," she said. "That the Great Goddess has the Ancient Spectre Take those who would turn bad. But the Perfects and the Gang are about as Transparent as the charred rocks my father mines—used to mine."

She paused, just managing not to cry.

"And they always survive. Transparent means being honest, rule-abiding, nice and good. I'm all those things, aren't I?"

Her friends nodded reassuringly.

"But I don't see how that can count for anything! Because if anyone could be considered Children of the Underworld it would be *them*. And they aren't the ones being Taken!"

"It's a crock," said Seveny. "If the Great Goddess really chooses, then the Great Goddess has got no taste!"

Jamie's mind was whirring. She wanted to share what she'd seen on the Ledge, and this seemed like the perfect opportunity. But how could she tell them without sounding like a lunatic?

Yet the announcement in assembly about an interloper, and then her being put on *G and D*, seemed to prove she'd seen something real. If Ella knew what she'd seen at Dancing Ledge, perhaps she could avoid Charlotte's fate. And if she told Seveny, she'd surely help her fight the system... whatever the system *was*.

"What if the Great Goddess doesn't choose?" said Jamie, nervously. "What if someone else does?"

Her friends thought back to what the Headmistress had said in last month's assembly. About the trespasser.

Seveny's spine straightened. "Do you know something?"

Jamie didn't answer. A thought had struck her. What if her very presence in Charlotte had woken her? If she hadn't been there, might Kai still have a sister? And if she told Ella what she'd seen on the Ledge, would she cause her death, too?

"Well, um... No..." she backtracked.

But her tell-tale rash was climbing her neck. And Seveny spotted it.

"It was you! You were the interloper! You went back!"

"What? Where?"

"You know."

"To the Ledge? No, I..."

What had she been thinking? What would she have said? *Oh, I just happen to drop into other people's bodies now and then, but don't worry, I can't control it!*

"Not... I mean not in the usual way. I did—I didn't trespass. I couldn't help it!"

"You couldn't help what?" asked Ella.

"Did you do something?" said Seveny. "Jamie, did you do something to Charlotte?"

The rash burned. Jamie couldn't think.

"Well, yes. No! I mean... I'm—"

"*HELP!*"

The girls spun round at George's frightened shriek.

Jamie had never felt so glad to see a Scarpel. Let alone two of them.

Dino Scarpel had George in a headlock. His enormous older brother Blake was wrestling Max over the Brainball. For a few seconds Max looked, incredibly, as if he had the upper hand. But his luck didn't last. Blake dispatched him with a mighty punch to the gut, lumbered to his feet, and triumphantly thrust the grey orb in the air.

He had little time to gloat. Seveny's knee to his nuts was quick and vicious. The Brainball left his hands and sailed over Seveny's head. It bounced once, and Jamie caught it.

Clutching his crotch, Blake sank to his knees. The boy-mountain started to cry.

"That was for what you did to Charlotte," said Seveny.

"Your rotten little Charlotte deserved all we gave her!" said Blake through his tears. "Or have you forgotten the Spectre Took her filthy soul?"

Seveny lost it. She punched Blake in the head, cleanly laying him out, and ran over to George, whose head was still Dino's property. Dino looked as if he wanted to twist it right off.

"Fight *me!*" she said. "Go on! Or are you scared of girls?"

Dino dropped George: giving gorgeous Seveny a pair of pretty black eyes was a much more thrilling prospect. He'd just begun to curl his hand into a fist when he noticed his older brother lying behind her, blissfully unconscious amidst the bluebells and forget-me-nots. Attacking Seveny suddenly didn't seem such a bright idea.

He gingerly circled round her, and aided his brother's return to consciousness by kicking him in the shin. A concussed Blake staggered to his feet, and the brothers ran for the clearing's edge. The sound of the fleeing Scarpels faded.

Max whooped. "Did you see me smash it? Blake didn't know what was coming when I wrestled him to the ground!"

"Oh, *totally,*" said Seveny. "Nine Lives—you were devastating."

Max failed to grasp her sarcasm. He strutted about and puffed out his chest.

"Great job laying out Blake, Seveny," said Jamie. "Couldn't have happened to a nicer person."

Seveny pierced Jamie with her amber eyes. Jamie's bumpy rash hadn't yet retreated.

"Allergies?" said Max.

Jamie nodded."The Gang bring me out in hives."

"I think they broke my neck!" said George, waggling his head like a wet dog.

"You're fine," said Ella. "Thanks to a certain someone..."

Seveny bowed and the group all cheered. They drifted back to the middle of the clearing.

Which was when Ella saw the sundial.

"It's too late!" she cried.

"For what?" Max asked.

"The Juveniting Song!"

The Juveniting Song was a prayer of appreciation to the Great Goddess, and had to be sung at precisely noon on your thirteenth birthday.

The group clustered round the sundial. The gnomon's shadow was distinctly past the midday mark.

"I'm sure the Great Goddess has bigger fish to fry," said Seveny.

"I don't know..." said George.

"Please, let's get on with it!" begged Ella.

They linked hands round the sundial, and Ella started to sing.

> "You frighten us, enlighten us,
> Frown on us and sometimes drown us,
> Give us rain or droughts that pain us,
> Crashing, lashing Mighty One."

Suddenly, huge globs of rain fell out of dark, brooding clouds that hadn't been there a moment ago. Ella persisted, not wanting to risk the Goddess's wrath.

> "Your flashing, smashing, brash sun warms us—"

The sun shone brightly again.

"A rainbow!" Max yelled.

The group faced the rainbow and dutifully bowed, as the Goddess demanded of Her people.

> "—It gives us food but sometimes fails us,
> You're thunderous and wondrous,
> Life-giving-taking Mighty One."

45

Kaboom!

A crash of thunder ripped through the air. Ella jumped. She'd started the Juveniting Song late and the Great Goddess was clearly angry with her, but it would be even more disrespectful if she stopped half-way. She pressed on.

"You give us gales and sometimes hail—"

Whoosh!

A violent rush of wind knocked George to the floor. Ella sang very quickly now.

"—You make us quake with plates that shake,
And shock us with volcanic rock,
Oh stirring, whirring Mighty One."

To everyone's relief, Mount Venusius did not erupt. "Quick!" said George. "Tell her we love her!"

"—We love you though, in all your guises,
And are quite fond of your surprises,
Our love for you just grows and rises
Oh———————aaagggggggghhhhhhhhhh!"

A bolt of lightning struck the tallest oak on the clearing's edge, splitting it right down the middle. With a terrible groan, one half of the tree started toppling towards the blue flowers. Towards the group.

"*RUN!*" yelled Max.

They ran frenziedly for the woods as the tree crashed to earth, its topmost branches barely missing them as it hit the ground.

"Ha ha! That was brilliant!" said Max, as he sprinted past the rest of the group.

"Are you kidding? We were this close to death!" said Jamie, illustrating the point with her fingers.

"Isn't danger your thing?" asked Seveny, caustically.

"My legs!" said small, plump Ella, struggling with the sudden exercise.

"I am definitely going to come down with a cold," said George, running pigeon-toed behind.

They'd just got out of the wood when they were stopped by two shiny Perfects with two shiny perfect faces. Unlike the sodden group, the Perfects hadn't a drop of rain on them. Sylvia Scythe-Crawley spoke first.

"Dearest Seveny. It has come to our attention that you are not in the right place."

Seveny flicked her sopping hair away from her face. "The right what?"

"You are here, when you ought to be somewhere else," said Edward Illustrious-Banks.

"Does anyone have a clue what they're on about?"

Seveny's friends looked nervous. They didn't answer. Even Max's lips were buttoned.

"You're not at the Orphanage, silly!" said Crawley, as though she were cracking a friendly joke.

"It's a Sunday. That's the one day we're allowed out!"

"Oh, no," said Banks. "Orphans can't just be free to wander. Not without a responsible adult in charge. It's deeply unsafe! Why, the Tombland Gang could get you in those very woods!"

The two Perfects' eyes flitted in the direction of Blue Wood.

"So there's been a change of protocol," said Crawley. "From now on, Sundays will *also* be spent at the Orphanage, doing... orphan things."

"Excuse me?!"

"Rules are rules," said Crawley sympathetically, linking arms with her.

"That they are," said Banks, grabbing hold of Seveny's other arm and nodding sadly.

"Since when has this been a rule? And who made it?"

"Since now—"

"—and us!"

Crawley snatched the Brainball out of Max's hands.

"How kind. For the Orphanage."

And that was that. The Perfects led Seveny off to the Orphanage, and the remaining group schlepped back to Ella's house in silence.

Chapter Five

The Truth Hurts

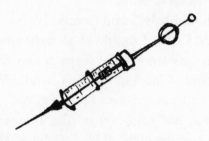

"What in the world happened to you?" asked Violet Last as a group of dripping wet juvenites burst through the front door.

"The Great Goddess cut our party short!" said Max.

"But you completed the Juveniting Song?"

"Um… No, Mum," said Ella, "we were nearly crushed by a falling oak, which sort of halted proceedings."

"Oh, dear." Ella's mum chuckled, though her cheek twitched. "But you're all fine?"

"Hey, they were with me! And they don't call me Nine Lives for nothing!" said Max.

"*We're* fine…" said Jamie, rather suggesting someone else might not be.

Violet Last cottoned on.

"Where's Seveny? Wasn't she with you?"

"She was," said Ella, "until the Perfects took her away. Rule change."

The group looked at their feet.

"Well, shoes off, and dry off upstairs," said Violet, deciding not to press them further. "There are clean towels in the cupboard. I'm not having anyone catching a fever. Not on my watch."

"I think I'm coming down with something already," said George, who suddenly sounded like his nose had been stuffed with wool.

"You do sound congested," said Violet, humouring him. "So up you go, dry yourselves off, and you'll come down to some of Sweet Cheeks' sweetest treats."

"Yes, that should help," said George, his voice miraculously clear again. "Yes, I think I should be all right after that."

As they ran upstairs, Violet leapt across the kitchen and shut the back door. Clasping the door handle for support, she exhaled. That had been close. Far too close. Jamie and Ella couldn't find out, not yet. Not on the anniversary of Gloria Tuff's death. Not on the night of Ella's Calling. The evening was already wrought with worries.

The Establishment thought people were being pushed off Dancing Ledge, and an insidious rumour was doing the rounds that Jamie was doing the pushing. Violet considered this an outrageous slander as, publicly, did all the mums who talked so animatedly about it. But it had been enough to put Jamie on the Gifted and Dangerous Register. And Geoffrey Tuff was devastated.

And as she laid out the birthday dinner, Violet kept on worrying. Ella hadn't completed the Juveniting Song. What an insult to the Great Goddess! It was well known that as She could nourish, so She could destroy...

When Violet looked at her hands they were trembling, but a nip of Moonshine soon shook off the shivers. The corn-whisky slipped down her throat, and by the time she called the children down she was wearing her best smile.

The juvenites' eyes lit up when they saw what awaited them.

Sweet Cheeks was the only confectionery shop in No Place. Violet Last had been saving her hemp mill money for months, and she had been generous with her purchases. The table was laden with Rainbow Brights, Volcanic Lips, Hard Rock Candy, Honeyspun Sweet-Spheres, Sugarcane Cages, and Sherbet Mountains. Other goodies included squid-ink straws, salted seaweed, scampi bites, and popcorn. The feast was topped off by a jug of non-fermented Honeydew, a sweet drink made from honey and apples.

Jamie hadn't eaten a proper meal in weeks, but the sight of the sugary treats did something. Hungrily, she scooped up sweets and shovelled them down. Only when her teeth began to throb and Max laughed at her lips, which were black from the squid-ink straws, did she step away from the table.

They passed a few hours hot-cocoa-slurping and ghost-story-telling before Violet came down to say that it was time for Ella to prepare for her Calling. It would only take half an hour to walk to Dancing Ledge, but she had to arrive in plenty of time for the midnight start.

The others changed into pyjamas while Ella put on her Dancing Ledge outfit: a white lace dress nipped in round her waist with a pink ribbon. Violet Last pinned a matching rose in her daughter's hair and checked that Ella had her Opal Envelope. She had to put it in a postbox on the Ledge: a safeguard the Establishment had thought up to make sure that the Called *went*.

Ella's walk to Dancing Ledge would be safe. No Place had a strict curfew: no one was allowed out after ten unless they were a night-watchman, a Senior Perfect, or, naturally, a member of the Establishment. So she'd be free from any altercations with the Tombland Gang. Only when she reached her destination would things become uncertain.

Violet Last was first to say goodbye. She gave her daughter a hug that to someone very intuitive might have appeared just a little too long and a bit too sad. Max babbled some excited nonsense and George bowed shyly. Jamie was last to say goodbye. She kissed Ella on the cheek. It was a kiss for being so understanding, for not questioning Jamie further about what she'd said in Blue Wood. Ella trusted her. It was a kiss for that.

Ella smiled nervously and stepped out of the house.

Violet Last closed the door. Her hand lingered on the handle as she faced her daughter's friends. "Time for bed."

Inside Ella's frilly bedroom the three got into their sleeping bags and tried to settle. No one felt like talking, which left Jamie alone with her thoughts.

She'd lost Charlotte and Billy last month, watched Max and George getting beaten by the Scarpels today and seen Seveny dragged off by the Perfects. She'd no intention of leaving Ella to her fate. Not if she could do something about it.

So she *would* go to sleep. And she would try her absolute hardest to get to Dancing Ledge and watch over Ella. Because even if the worst happened, at least she could see what was going on. And wasn't that the first step to putting a stop to it?

But as she hovered on the verge of sleep, Max's voice ripped through the silence.

"I feel weird having Ella's sleepover without her."

"Me too," said George. "Shall we stay awake till she gets back?"

"Yes, let's!" said Max.

No! Jamie inwardly screamed.

"Why not?" she said. "I just have to use the bathroom."

On the landing, Jamie assessed the situation. She had to be at the Ledge soon if she was going to watch over Ella. She'd have to go home to sleep.

She crept downstairs, passed through the kitchen, got to the front door, reached for the handle, and then—

A fingernail dug into her back. It found a spot between two vertebrae and twisted like a knife.

"Murderer!" said Violet Last. "Leave her be. I don't want you out there with my daughter."

Jamie's legs gave way and she fell to the floor.

Violet stood over her, frowning. "Jamie, what are you doing? You ought to be in bed!" She promptly pulled her off the floor and watched her go upstairs.

When Jamie reached the landing, she started to shake.

Could it be that Violet Last's a witch?

She had to escape, now more than ever, but downstairs was barred. So what to do? The bathroom beckoned.

She opened the door quietly, crept over to its narrow window, and looked for a way down. There was a drainpipe to her left and a shelf below the window. She swung her legs out, found the shelf with her bare feet, and, ignoring the temptation to look down, began working her way towards the drainpipe. She'd almost reached it when the bathroom door creaked open.

Jamie froze.

"Jamie! Are you still in the bathroom?!" she heard Max yell.

"It's me," said Violet Last. "Why, isn't she with you?"

Jamie made a side-lunge for the drainpipe, caught hold, slid down it, and ran.

Geoffrey Tuff wasn't particular about much—his house was as run-down and ramshackle as Jamie's bedroom. However, he *was* particular about doors and windows, and when Jamie arrived back she realized her quandary. The door was locked. Her dad would have to let her in. That meant questions and time spent answering them, and if she was to be of any use to Ella she needed to be in bed, asleep. But she didn't have a choice, so she banged on the door.

She soon heard her father's footsteps on the stairs. He grumbled something like "She's busy. You can't come in."

"It's me, Dad!" she said. "Your Jay! Let me in!"

Geoffrey fumbled with the lock and opened the door. He was surprised to find his daughter bare-footed and in her pyjamas. "What are you doing here?"

"I couldn't sleep."

Geoffrey stepped aside to let her in. "Does Violet know?"

"What?"

"Does she know you're here?"

"She knows I'm gone..."

"You ran out?"

"That's right."

"Because you couldn't sleep?"

"Yes!" The red rash snaked up Jamie's neck.

"Don't you realize how dangerous that is? For all of us? No one is allowed out after hours. If the Establishment found out... and in your position, on *that* Register..."

He couldn't even say the name of it. And then, as often happened, he started to cry. Jamie put her hand on him.

"Dad. If they're going to send me Underground, they'll do it whether or not I leave Ella's house after curfew. We should both go to bed."

She'd got to the bottom of the stairs before her dad spun her round.

"Don't you think about anyone else?" he said. "Poor Violet could get in trouble!"

"Poor Violet can be pretty hurtful actually!"

"So you fell out?" Geoffrey asked. It wasn't really a question.

Jamie thought this version of events would do. "Yes, but I don't want to talk about it. I want to go to sleep."

"She told you."

Told me what? That she thinks I'm a murderer? Yes!

Her father rubbed his brow. "Why didn't she wait? We were going to tell you and Ella together."

Tell me and Ella what? Jamie had to know.

"I... didn't believe her when she told me," she said, thinking quickly. "I had to hear it from you, too."

Her father sighed. "Well it's true, Jay. Violet and I are together. We're in love."

The next thing Jamie knew, she was on her bed surrounded by her sobs and the faint knocking of her father on the bedroom door.

Eventually, there was silence.

She got up and looked out of the window. The moon, high in the sky, illuminated the metal hands of Pity Me's concrete clock tower. Ten minutes to twelve. The Taking would be starting soon. She climbed back into bed. If she could just get to sleep... But she couldn't get to sleep. Minutes passed that seemed like hours.

Finally, the words *you are being watched* echoed through her head, she saw the flame-red quiff of Funnella Fitzgerald, and she drifted off, and out, and into...

* * *

She was definitely not in her own body, she knew that much. She felt strangely constricted.

She listened for the waves, the smell of the sea, the light of the moon, the sight of juvenites dancing. Drowning. But there was nothing. She seemed to be in a completely black, featureless room. She had just reached the conclusion that her host's eyes must be closed when she smelt a sweet, putrid odour, and...

Ow!

Someone stuck a needle in her host's face. It squirted something, and the skin around it thickened in response.

Her host let out a ragged breath. The needle withdrew, selected another area and repeated the process. Again and again and again.

Jamie was glad she was experiencing this second-hand: her host was moaning in pain. The caustic voice was familiar, but she couldn't place it. It certainly wasn't a juvenite's. Whoever she was, she wasn't struggling or trying to escape.

Whose body am I in?

The injections stopped and the chair she was sitting in began to spin. Her host's eyes opened.

Jamie was in a small, cube-shaped room hewn out of solid rock. A slab of black marble stretched along its walls serving as a lab desk, upon which shrivelled white petals lay in glass dishes. They were sweating out the remainder of their lives, filling the air with the sticky-sweet odour Jamie had smelt when she arrived. And there were clamps, tongs, cylinders, beakers, flasks and tubes. Many held liquids ranging in colour from deepest blue to palest yellow. They bubbled, dripped, fizzed, and in some cases steamed. In one corner was a tank full of live snakes; in another corner, a pile of dead snakes; and in a third, large sheets of snakeskin had been hung up to dry. A grandfather clock stood by the door, and Jamie's heart sank when she saw the time. Half past three. Dancing Ledge would have finished long ago.

Where am I?

The swivel-chair came to a rest. Jamie recognized the man before her, with his blood-red clothes and lacquered black curls.

The Doctor held two fizzing glasses of Honeydew—the fermented kind reserved for adults. He offered one to Jamie's host, raised her chin and looked deep into her eyes.

Jamie hadn't a clue what to do. The last time she'd been so near the Doctor, he'd spotted her—after what he'd said in assembly, she was sure of that. What would he do if he caught her spying again?

Instinctively she pressed herself against the back of her host's skull. Her view seemed to recede a little.

A plan suggested itself.

If I can change position, I wonder if I can shrink?

She could! She thought herself smaller and smaller until she was tucked in a corner at the back of her host's head. She could still see clearly, and felt much less cramped. She hoped she'd be harder to spot.

"Once the swelling goes down," said the Doctor, "you'll look quite divine!"

The woman giggled girlishly. "And here's to the most successful Dancing Ledge!" she said. They clinked glasses and sipped, and Jamie tasted bitter bubbles.

"Thanks to you. You Called Ella today. She has such a strong, sensitive soul. The Ancient Spectre will be pleased!"

Ella's been Taken?

Jamie's head swirled with sadness—and then she realized what the Doctor had said.

You Called Ella today...

Her host's grating voice sprang into focus.

"It was a pleasure," said Funnella Fitzgerald. "So what, my love, is the plan?"

Yes! What is the plan? From the sound of it, the Headmistress had been delivering up her schoolchildren directly to the devil.

"You, my love, are my perfect match! Always after the gory details!"

"You know me so well," she panted.

"But you must be patient, dear Funnella. The time will come when we won't have to hide our affair. When the Ancient Spectre shall reign as God, and I shall rule the world!"

The Doctor pulled Funnella from her seat and held her close. Jamie had never been so near him. He stank of bitter Honeydew and sweet rot. But there wasn't a hint of a wrinkle on his face, nor a glimpse of a pore.

According to her dad he'd been No Place's chief Doctor for over thirty years, which meant he must be nearly sixty. He was practically shamun age, yet his skin was baby-smooth. She got quite absorbed looking at it...

"Jamie Tuff!"

Jamie's breath hitched in her non-existent throat. *He's seen me!*

"That blasted girl Jamie is my only cause for concern..."

Jamie breathed out, to the extent one could when one was a disembodied soul.

"She's a Dreamweaver like me," he said. "And therefore dangerous. She's a meddler, too—her actions at the Last house are testament to that. If I'd not caught her, she'd have Dreamweaved to the Ledge again."

"What will you do with her?"

"Tomorrow, she'll be stopped."

Something of the serpent rippled in the Doctor's lagoon-like eyes. It was clear to Jamie what being 'stopped' meant.

But the Headmistress didn't seem the slightest bit concerned. In fact, as the Doctor pulled her to him, ready for their inevitable, dreadful kiss, Jamie's 'voluptuous shadow' convulsed with laughter.

And Jamie was shaken out of her host.

* * *

She woke with a start. The colourless light that preceded dawn shone in through the bedroom window.

She had been so desperate to get to sleep. Now, she wished wholeheartedly she'd stayed awake. She thought of the boys sat in Ella's bedroom and how much nicer it would have been to have stayed with them, waiting for Ella to return—at least, until realization seeped in. The boys would surely know by now that Ella wasn't coming back.

Jamie wondered what they thought about her sneaking out. Whether, like most of Pity Me's population, they'd now decided she was the cause of the recent 'accidents.' A Transparent slayer. Perhaps George, who liked to style himself as the school detective, had already opened a dossier against her.

And then Jamie stopped worrying. It didn't really matter what her friends thought of her now, or anyone else for that matter. Because today, somewhere, *somehow*, she was going to die.

But at least she'd die knowing she wasn't a lunatic.

She was a Dreamweaver.

Chapter Six

English

Some people are built like barrels and Miss Humfreeze was one of them.

The English teacher was nearing the shamun age of sixty. Her eyes looked like they could tell a thousand tales, and her wide mouth often told them. The manshu and juvenites loved her for this, lapping up her words like they were delicious drops of non-fermented Honeydew. But she was often reprimanded for going off on tangents when her teaching was Observed.

Miss Humfreeze hated Observations. And since *that* assembly she'd been inundated with them. Her decision to scoop up Kai before Phosphor-Jones could get him hadn't gone unnoticed—she'd interfered with the Establishment's Work. Every day since, Funnella Fitzgerald had come into her classroom and perched her generous bottom on a desk at the back.

Today, the Headmistress had chosen to Observe the first class of the morning. Her squid-ink quill scratched furiously across her ledger. As half the class were yet to arrive, Miss Humfreeze thought this was a little overzealous.

Those present looked pallid, which Miss Humfreeze well understood. This morning's assembly had been quite a shock.

Ten students had been Taken at Dancing Ledge last night. Ten!

It used to be the very occasional juvenite who didn't make it back. Three a year at most. But for the last few months they'd averaged five per Taking. And now ten in one go?

One of them came from Miss Humfreeze's form. She looked round the class to see how Ella's friends were coping.

George was sitting anxiously in the front row, pencil in hand. Miss Humfreeze picked up some chalk and started writing the Learning Objectives on the board for him to copy. Max hadn't arrived yet. That wasn't unusual: he was often late. Seveny was also absent, which *was* strange. And Jamie? Ah! She was coming through the door...

The girl was even paler than usual. But when she noticed Funnella, she burned a fierce red.

She has every reason to be scared, thought Miss Humfreeze. *Funnella's put her on G & D. One wrong move, and she'll be Underground.*

Her mind flitted to an ex-student who'd suffered the same fate. A boy who, she remembered, had been Seveny's best friend.

Tommy was a cheeky, charming Crackpot lad. That he'd come to Pity Me School in the first place was unusual: Crackpot children didn't normally attend. It wasn't that the Establishment *liked* them being home educated; they hated it. But Crackpots could get away with things no No-Placer could. Crackpots set their own rules.

The Establishment never explained why they allowed them such freedom. Miss Humfreeze thought it might have something to do with their rock-bullet guns: every Crackpot carried one. And they lived in a fortified city inside a mountain. And they ran the railway. And they produced most of the luxury goods on the Island. And they kept the Island free of snakes, which endeared them to the superstitious No-Placers, who thought snakes were made in the image of the Ancient Spectre.

The Crackpots were useful. Ordinarily, the Establishment left them untouched. But they made Tommy an example.

Tommy's arrival in a room was usually announced by a crash or a smash. His gift for breaking equipment was a constant source of staffroom moaning. But clumsiness wasn't a crime at Pity Me School. At least, not yet. No, like most Crackpots, Tommy said things as he saw them. And that set a dangerous example, one that other students had started to follow. The Establishment called an emergency meeting, and a smirking Funnella sadly decreed: "He *has* to go!"

So Tommy Crackpot, aged thirteen, was put on *G and D*. And one month later, he disappeared.

Since then, no other Crackpots had come to Pity Me School.

Some days Miss Humfreeze could almost convince herself that, after his time in the Dispensary, Tommy had gone back to live with his family. But it had been two years, and she still hadn't got up the courage to visit them and check.

Seveny crashed into the room in a temper.

Miss Humfreeze went on writing the Objectives on the board, hoping that ignoring the girl would calm her down. But it was no good. Seveny was on the warpath.

"I haven't done my homework!" she said, striding across the room and landing in the English teacher's face. "And..." she span round and glared at Funnella, "I don't give a flying Goddess that I'm late!"

Funnella stared straight back at her and kept scribbling. The message was clear: *This is an Observation, and I'm Recording.*

George tensed and Jamie's rash spread.

"Seveny…" Miss Humfreeze sighed. "Please go and wait Down the Line." With trembling fingers, the English teacher carried on writing the Learning Objectives. The chalk grated its way over the blackboard.

"That's right, turn your back on me!" said Seveny. "Turn your back on me like you did with Tommy! Like you did with your own children!"

Miss Humfreeze froze.

How does she know that? No one knows about my children!

"Stop ignoring me!" screamed Seveny.

Her eyes bored into Miss Humfreeze's chalk.

It exploded.

Miss Humfreeze almost fainted. Seveny looked terrified.

Funnella stood up. "It's back to the Chamber for you!"

She linked arms with Seveny and waltzed her out of the room.

The class looked peaky. Miss Humfreeze herself could hardly believe what she'd seen: the chalk had turned to dust before it had even reached the floor.

The English teacher knew—better than most—that there was rather more to the world than what the Establishment taught in school. But it didn't usually rear its head unless you went looking for it.

That girl was a *Mindmover!* Not a very adept one: she had plenty of energy, but little focus. But exploding things? That spoke of serious power in untrained hands, and if it got back to the Establishment…

The English teacher looked over her clammy class. They wouldn't say anything. They'd worry their imaginations would look too wild.

But Funnella would.

Last month, Miss Humfreeze had tried to convince Funnella, and indeed herself, that Seveny standing up and the eagle falling down had been a coincidence. The Headmistress wouldn't hear it. The mere *chance* of Seveny being a Mindmover had been enough to send her to the Chamber Upstairs.

But after today's chalksplosion, there'd be no doubt in Funnella's mind that the girl had intended to brain her with the taxidermy. And there was only one punishment greater than the Chamber.

She'll be put on G and D, like Jamie. And they'll both go Underground!

A rush of noise flooded the teacher's head. Miss Humfreeze gasped.

The Sight hadn't bothered her for a long time. She'd learned to tune out its chatter, after... the events to which Seveny had alluded. Events she thought she'd successfully lain to rest. But with so many students thinking the same thing, their words came through loud and clear.

If Miss Humfreeze had children, they thought, *what in the world did she do with them?*

Miss Humfreeze wanted to tell them that she wondered the very same thing. That not a day went by without her wishing she hadn't done it. And how often she imagined having lived a different life. A life in which she hadn't sacrificed her own children.

And to *him*.

Chapter Seven

Tombstoning

Seveny didn't struggle against the Headmistress as they walked arm in arm up the spiral staircase. She knew there was no way of getting out of a punishment. Especially not the Chamber Upstairs.

They reached the landing and came to an opulently embellished door. Funnella twisted the handle and pushed Seveny into the room. The door shut of its own accord. Seveny didn't bother testing the handle. She knew leaving was impossible.

The Chamber was the size of a broom cupboard and around seven feet tall. It had a tiny, hand-sized window and a slot in the door, and mirrors covered its floor, ceiling, and walls.

The Chamber offered not physical pain but mental torture. With all those mirrors, there was no getting away from yourself. And through the slot, Governors would whisper Observations precisely tailored to the student in their care.

How long you spent in the Chamber depended on your crime. It was rumoured that in the history of Pity Me School, some students had been locked inside for days, fed through the suggestion-slot.

Generally, it didn't take that long to break a child.

Seveny had the rare honour of being assisted in her personal development by the Headmistress. Funnella Fitzgerald's voice oozed through the slot.

"What do you see?"

Seveny saw pores like caverns, a mouth of wolf-like gnashers, and a nose that, somewhere, a crow was likely to be missing.

"Anything you'd improve?"

Everything! Seveny wanted to shout. But she didn't want to give the Headmistress the satisfaction, so she kept quiet.

"Do you consider yourself a cruel person?" said Funnella. "Because I do. I consider you a very selfish and hurtful young lady. Poor Miss Humfreeze! Invading people's private thoughts isn't very *nice*, you know."

Seveny flinched. How could the Headmistress know what she'd done? She hardly knew herself.

She'd seen an image, attached to a feeling, that somehow came from Miss Humfreeze. And suddenly she knew, if she wanted to hurt her teacher, exactly what to say.

And then the words were out there, hanging in the air. She felt horrible for saying them, but she hadn't expected anyone to take them seriously. And in any case they couldn't be true.

Could they?

"And why are you in such a hideous mood this morning?" said the Headmistress.

Seveny bristled. She had every reason to feel angry! From the moment Charlotte was Taken, her life had been on a swift downward trajectory. And last night's events had put the final deathcherry on the whole dung pudding.

The Perfects had dropped her back at the Orphanage and informed Mr Gribbin of the rule change: from now on, orphans weren't allowed out of the school grounds. Then they'd skipped off together, Max's Brainball still in their hands.

Though Seveny got on with the other inmates, the Orphanage was a lonely place without Charlotte or Kai. But this did give her space for a personal project. If orphans weren't allowed out... well then, she'd just have to invent a way *round*.

As usual, the lights went out at nine. Seveny had lain awake for ages imagining the preparations for Ella's Calling. Hoping her friend would return.

Then she'd had a vision, like when she'd seen Jamie and Charlotte at the Ledge the previous month. This time she saw the front door of the Last house. Jamie's fingers were clasped around the handle. Seveny had felt a shiver down her spine, and heard the voice of Violet Last cry "Murderer!"

But she didn't hit her *real* all-time low until this morning.

"Max and I waited up," George had told her before assembly. "Ella's gone..."

"You do know your friend was out after curfew?" said Funnella, bringing Seveny back to the room of mirrors.

"Obviously," she replied. "You Called her!"

"*Dear* Ella." Funnella's voice wasn't sympathetic. "But I was thinking of Jamie."

Seveny tried to put last night's vision from her mind. "Jamie was at Ella's house last night, with Max and George."

"Oh? I've heard differently. Still... your faith in your friend is admirable."

Seveny thought back to assembly and George's exact words. *Max and I waited up...* He hadn't mentioned Jamie! And in Blue Wood, before the Scarpels interrupted, she'd said that she'd done something to Charlotte...

...and now Ella was gone.

"Poor child. I think it's best you spend some time alone with your thoughts." The Headmistress's heels clicked their way down the staircase.

Seveny felt more alone than ever.

Is Jamie a murderer?

Trying to escape that thought, she turned her mind to escaping the room. Which was when she realized that even if she escaped the Chamber, even if she escaped Pity Me School, she could never escape the Island. Being the only place to survive the Great Storm, there was nowhere else to go.

The walls of the Chamber suddenly seemed to close in on her, and her skin felt much too tight. Her heart, which always felt too big for her body, began beating wildly in her chest. Afraid she was about to burst, she stared at her reflection and tried to slow her breath.

The mirror in front of her cracked. She jerked back, startled. There was a splintering sound behind her. She spun round. A shard of glass twisted free of the wall, flew upwards, smashed on the ceiling, and fell in pieces around her.

She had to get out. Now. But leaving the Chamber was impossible.

"*HELP!*" she screamed.

The mirrors around her smashed. Free of the wall, the glass shards shattered into thousands of tiny pieces.

Seveny beat her fists against the wooden door as the glass rained down. But it was useless. No one was coming to save her. Small splinters of glass sliced through the air and embedded themselves in the wood. She desperately rattled the door's locked handle, willing it to open.

It did.

She stumbled out onto the landing and caught her breath. It took her a moment to notice that her breath was all that she could hear. The mirrors had stopped smashing. When she looked back into the Chamber, she saw that there wasn't really much of them left to smash.

She looked down at her skin. There wasn't a scratch on her.

The eagle, the chalk, the mirrors. Truth dawned. *I really am a freak!*

Seveny ran down the spiral staircase. She had to get out of school before Funnella discovered what she'd done to the Chamber. She pelted down the corridor, heading for the fire exit at the back of the school. As she turned the corner she collided with Max, who was running in the opposite direction to get to English.

He picked her up off the floor. "Ella!"

"Is gone," she said. "I *know*. Unlike you, I made it to assembly. Why in the blazes are you always so late?"

Max didn't answer. But he didn't have to. Her freak mind did it for him.

An image snapped into her brain. Max had been looking for his sister. The one who'd got Fruitful out of Wedlock. The one who'd disappeared.

"Your sister was a slut!" she yelled, shoving Max out of the way and careering past him. She'd broken the Chamber. She didn't have time for visions.

The jibe worked: Max didn't chase after her. But someone else did.

Click, click, click.

Seveny sprinted down the corridor.

Click, click, click—

She burst out of the fire exit.

Click, click, click—

She ran across concrete.

Click, click, click—

She leapt onto the school field.

The clicking stopped.

Seveny raced across the grass and reached the barbed wire fence that separated the school from the coastal graveyard. She knelt down by a corner and found the spot: she'd hauled a small part of the fence out of the earth yesterday. Now, all she had to do was *pull*.

The wire tore at her fingers and one of the barbs dug under a nail, but a few rough yanks and the gap widened. Was it enough? It would have to do. She threw herself flat on the grass and started wriggling. Bit by bit, she worked her head under the wire. The wire tore at her blazer, but soon her shoulders were through, then her waist, then a hip. She was so nearly free when a hand grabbed her foot.

"You're pretty Extraordinary, aren't you?" growled the Headmistress. "Gifted, some might say. Dangerous, too. Never mind the Chamber... You're going Underground!"

Seveny bucked like a wild horse and kicked Funnella in the head, breaking the Headmistress's grasp.

The schoolgirl ran for the horizon, zigzagging round the crumbling tombstones as footsteps clattered after her. She risked a look back. Funnella was still in hot pursuit, her red quiff muddied, her green suit shredded by the wire.

And following in the distance were Max and George. And Jamie.

Jamie the murderer.

Their arms were flailing like corn in the breeze, and they kept on shouting something, but their words were snatched by the wind. They were pointing at something ahead of them, but she didn't know what.

Funnella Fitzgerald had almost caught her up!

"You have to stop Jamie!" Seveny yelled over her shoulder, quickening her sprint.

And then she disappeared.

Her friends ran wildly for the horizon and caught up with Funnella.

Together, the Headmistress and the schoolchildren inched their way to the edge of the crumbling cliff. They looked down at the crashing waves below.

The hopeful, candy tones of a Pity Me uniform lay bobbing in the Great Sea. An eagle hovered over them, looking forward to an easy lunch.

Seveny's friends turned green, their legs buckled and they forgot how to breathe. But when they saw their Headmistress they felt unimaginably worse.

For Funnella Fitzgerald looked pleased.

Chapter Eight

Sky Swimming for Supper

Plummeting towards the water, Seveny felt closer to freedom than she'd ever been. She could *breathe*. And she took one last breath before hitting the sea.

Her school tie choked her as the currents pulled her under. She somehow managed to remove it. Water flooded her lungs. She was sinking, but fighting. Struggling and losing. Then a sense of calm washed over her. Buoyed, hollow, lifted, she was floating in the sky. *Free.*

It was a while before she realized that a change had taken place. It happened when the hunger struck.

A mass of silver flickered in the depths below. Seveny tipped over and dived for the shimmering shoal. During her descent, she caught sight of her reflection in the ocean's moving mirror.

She was magnificent! Her size was imposing, her wings spanned several feet and her feathers ranged from chocolate brown to the palest gold. The gold ones hung like a cape around her crown, nape and wings. Piercing yellow eyes matched her hooked beak, and razor-sharp talons curved from her toes.

I'm beautiful!

Realizing the significance of her growing reflection just in time, she righted herself and hit the sea feet first as she'd done minutes ago. But this time the water didn't touch her; it slipped off her feathers. And nor did it choke her, for her nostrils had closed. Instinctively she closed her talons. Something smooth and oily wriggled in her claws.

She swoops she scores!

Her catch in her feet, Seveny thrust herself out of the water. As her wings beat the air, she reflected on her new mode of transport. *Flying is hard*, she thought. *Like swimming times ten.* But her heart, which always beat too strongly in her old self, now felt right at home. Even so, she was tiring. And her hunger was biting.

Her hawk-eyes spotted some cliffs in the distance. She set a course for them at once, her strong wings finding air currents she never knew existed. But even with a prevailing wind, she was almost exhausted when she arrived at the grass-topped white cliffs. Her first landing was inelegant, and she was glad no one was around to witness it.

She examined her catch. It was a large, juicy and very dead sea trout. She was so hungry that she couldn't care less about having to eat it with her hands. It was only when she tried to pick the fish up that reality hit. She had no hands. She was a bird.

A couple of hours ago she'd been a girl at Pity Me School. And now here she was, with no idea *where* here was, friendless, homeless and hungry. And most importantly, and deserving repetition, she'd turned into a *bird*.

I forgive you, nose! she thought. *I quite like you, face!*

To her astonishment, she felt her beak morph back into a nose—though she couldn't be sure it was hers, not without a mirror, or hands to touch it.

And as she thought about her hands, something happened in her wing sockets: a deep burning, right in the joint. Her feathers imploded inwards, and her arms and hands shot out.

But they were sprouting out of a hawk's body.

"All human, please!" she said to the heavens, and the rest of her figure returned. Seveny cringed at her nakedness, but she was glad to be back in her skin—even with its few barbed-wire scrapes.

She fiddled with the slippery fish and her fingers got ever more oily until she conceded that actually, for the purpose of eating, turning back into an eagle might be a blessing. She looked again to the heavens and called upon the Great Goddess who had saved her from the sea.

"I wish to be a fish-eating hawk again, please," she prayed. "Only till I'm done with dinner!" she added quickly.

And lo, she found herself with hooked beak, her eyesight powerful, her dinner magnified. She wondered briefly if fish bones might still choke her, but reasoned that if she could catch fish like a sea-hawk, she could probably eat like one.

Indeed she could. The fish was ceremonially flipped over and tossed down her gullet without pause for taste.

After dinner, she felt like a nap. Being human seemed preferable, despite the nakedness.

"All human, please!" she said, and her feathers turned to skin.

"What are you doing?"

The male voice rang out of nowhere. Seveny, embarrassed by her lack of clothes, looked anxiously around. She couldn't locate the voice's owner. She did, however, notice a large-leaved tree, which she ran behind.

"Nothing," she said. "Just sunbathing."

The voice chuckled. It sounded like a juvenite's.

Who is he? And how much has he seen?

"Do you know where you are?" said the voice.

"Of course I do," said Seveny, clueless. "Else why would I be here?"

"Oh, good!" said the voice. "Because I'm lost. Where am I?"

Tearing a huge green leaf off the strange tree, Seveny wrapped it round her for decency and stepped back out.

"I'm afraid you're up your own arse," she said. "Please show yourself before you disappear completely!"

A juvenite stepped out from behind the remains of a dry stone wall. He was a little older than Seveny. Laughter played on his lips and his almond eyes twinkled. Seveny, already pink with fury, now took on a ruby hue.

"Shouldn't you be at school?" said the boy.

"Shouldn't you be Underground?" Seveny shot back.

Both juvenites began to laugh.

"Where the hell have you been, Tommy?" Seveny demanded.

"What took you so long, angel-face?" was Tommy's bold reply.

Chapter Nine

Poisoned Arrows

Jamie sat in the Canteen and picked at her rubbery squid.

It was lunchtime, not even two hours since Seveny had plummeted, and she could already hear her friend's name being added to the Grand Hall's Tombstone. It was a distinctive sound, chisel on rock.

The Perfects hadn't found Seveny's body. Jamie imagined they hadn't looked very hard. Seveny was an orphan, and orphans sometimes Tombstoned. Fact.

Max and George entered the Canteen, caught Jamie's eye, then walked straight past her. They seated themselves at the other end of the room. Since Seveny's fall they'd both ignored her, neither bothering to ask her where she'd gone last night. It seemed they'd reached their own—or Seveny's—conclusion.

The Pity Me Perfects then turned up en masse. They wound their way around the wide, greasy room, delightedly spreading the news. Savouring the taste of a fellow student's doom.

"Seveny was extraordinarily troubled," they said, again and again. "At least now she'll rest in peace."

Students turned in Jamie's direction. Some shook their heads; others were crying. A few of the Tombland Gang pointed and laughed. Jamie chewed on her squid and tried to blot out the Gang and the Perfects. She was relieved when the bell rang for the beginning of the afternoon's lessons.

She exited the Canteen and made her way up the corridor to History, thankful she didn't share this class with Max or George.

Then she felt a hand on her arm.

It was Sylvia Scythe-Crawley, with Edward Illustrious-Banks. Fake concern drenched the Perfects' pinched features. As usual, they took it in turns to speak.

"Oh, *darling* Jamie!"

"What a *horribly* tragic thing to have happened to you!"

"Your mum dead, Charlotte and Ella Taken, Seveny drowned..."

"It's a wonder you have *any* friends left! Still, at least you have Max and George.

The two Perfects looked at each other.

"Only..."

"We couldn't help noticing..."

"They weren't sitting with you at lunch."

They let that sink in.

"It's almost as if you make the ones you love *disappear!*"

They wrung their hands in a display of sorrow and flounced off down the corridor.

The Perfects had wormed their way under Jamie's skin. A tear crept from her heart and crawled up to her throat. She managed to choke it back before it reached her eyes.

And then her knee gave way, and her skull met the floor.

A piggy face squinted down at her. Rosacea dropped a well-formed spit-blob onto her cheek, prodded her with a pudgy foot, and stomped off down the corridor.

Jamie picked herself up, dusted herself off, and was using the sleeve of her blazer to wipe off Rosacea's slime when the voice of Senior Perfect Snodgrass chimed down the corridor, clear as a bell.

"Pity Me poise!"

But Jamie couldn't lift herself any higher. She wanted quite the opposite: for the earth to swallow her up so she could simply disappear.

Jamie got through most of History without hearing a word Deputy Phosphor-Jones said. He'd garbled on in his usual fashion, not really caring who was listening. Only near the lesson's end did he catch her staring out of the room's tiny window.

"Dreaming," he said loudly, "is of little use, and *not* to be cultivated."

Jamie jolted up and tried to look attentive.

"Remember Rhyme Intrinsica!" he continued. "We must learn from History, so that we never make the same mistakes!"

Fifty years ago, Pity Me's neighbouring hamlet, Rhyme Intrinsica, was the artists' quarter of No Place. Now, it was a quarter-mile stretch of carbon and ash.

One dark night, the artists had burned their village to the ground, taking themselves with it. The cause? Imagination. Dreaming had sent them mad. When they'd seen the impossibility of their notions, they'd taken their own lives rather than wake up to reality. As Professor Phosphor-Jones said:

"Hopeless dreams never come true,
They never can and never do!"

The land was cordoned off and declared 'Contraland,' ground where No-Placers were forbidden to set foot. The Establishment had declared most of the Island Contraland.

Jamie thought the story smelt awfully fishy. Where were the witnesses? If no one survived the fire, who had told people what happened? She would have asked Phosphor-Jones about it, but History was not something you questioned.

"...and all of Rhyme Intrinsica's inhabitants were swallowed by fire." Phosphor-Jones, having recounted the sad tale, was now ready to draw to his moral conclusion. He stroked his chitterlings-filled belly and glared at Jamie.

"*That's* where dreaming gets you," he said. "Death by fire!"

On her way out of school, Jamie ran into her form tutor. Ignoring all protocol, Miss Humfreeze enveloped her pupil in a massive hug.

"I am so sorry about Seveny," she said.

The hug released something in Jamie, and the tear she'd kept back earlier escaped. She brushed it swiftly away on hearing the click of Funnella's heels.

"Jamie Tuff!" the Headmistress yelled. "Where do you think you're going? I have it on good authority you were out after curfew."

I bet that sneaky Snodgrass reported me! Jamie couldn't bear to wonder whether it might have been Max or George.

"This evening you will have a long detention," said Funnella, "and then I shall escort you home."

Jamie's breath caught in her throat. Seveny's death had completely ousted her own fate from her mind. But now she remembered the Doctor's words: *Jamie must be stopped.* She imagined 'detention' was more likely a code-word for 'death.' A desperate need to get away from this madwoman kicked in.

The main door was wide open, as it always was at the end of the day. Jamie bolted through it and made for the also-open gate, the quickening *click* of the Headmistress's heels following behind. But as Jamie reached the gate she heard a kerfuffle behind her. She risked a look back—and found Funnella in a headlock.

"After all that girl's been through!" Miss Humfreeze was hugging the Headmistress half to death.

"You don't understand!" squawked Funnella, struggling to get free. "Jamie must be stopped!"

Jamie dashed through the gate and out of the school grounds.

After a few minutes of solid running, she slowed to a walk. Where could she go? Normally she'd hang out with her friends, but that was no longer possible. And she couldn't bear the thought of going home. Breakfast with her father had been agony. It seemed plain that he had moved on from her mother— as, apparently, should she.

But Jamie didn't blame Violet for what she'd done last night. From what she'd heard in the Dreamweave, the Doctor had probably made her say and do those things.

Dreamweave. The word still sounded strange. Jamie knew she could do it. She knew what it was called. But she didn't know what it *was*.

Eventually, she went to the Gravel Pit.

The Gravel Pit was a small, deep pit at the end of a chain of inland chalk cliffs. The cliffs divided No Place from Crackpot territory. You never saw a Crackpot at the pit, though: the cliffs were quite unclimbable, and it took half a day to travel round them to Giddyfoot County.

No-Placers preferred using folk medicine over going to the Dispensary. Hot stone massage from Boiling Rock Downs, amber healing, Mugwort Moxibustion, Chuckleberries, hypnotherapy. The Gravel Pit's salts were thought to guard against exhaustion.

Jamie breathed in the salt-stone vapours at the bottom of the Pit. The rocks around her were as white as snow. She drank in her surroundings, and was enjoying being completely and utterly alone when something stabbed her left shoulder.

"Owwww!"

A large, sharp flint fell at her feet, its corner red with blood. A gust of wind had probably blown it over the Pit's side. Even so, Jamie's guard went up.

"Hello? Is anyone there?" Her cry echoed round the walls of the Pit.

Silence.

Jamie's mood to be alone had passed. She started making her way back up the slope when again something sharp hit her. This time, she saw the rock cut into her knee. She howled as a stream of blood flowed down her leg and collected in a pool at her foot, staining the white gravel crimson.

I'm not alone!

She ran across the Pit and had started up the opposite slope when something bit into her scalp.

She looked up, and saw at last who hunted her.

The Tombland Gang were standing in a circle round the edge of the Pit. They had her surrounded.

"What happened to your friends?" Rosacea Unvelope shouted down. She was holding a sharp stone, just like the one that had slashed Jamie's leg.

They were all holding stones.

"Seems you make *everyone* vanish!" Blake Scarpel sneered.

"Maybe she's a witch!" a familiar voice cackled—Perfect Sylvia Scythe-Crawley.

"If she's a witch, perhaps she can disappear!" laughed the plummy tones of Illustrious-Banks.

"She *ought* to disappear!" snarled a wolfish boy.

"Once we're done with her, she'll wish she had!" screeched a girl with rotten teeth.

Something cut into Jamie's arm.

"What's wrong with your arm, Jamie?" asked an angel-faced manshu.

The Gang's cries echoed round and round the Pit as they hurled their sharp stones.

"What's wrong with your knee, Jamie?"
"What's wrong with your arm, Jamie?"
"What's wrong with your face, Jamie?"
Jamie looked up to the sky. "Please, don't!"
Stone daggers rained from the heavens, and Jamie knew that she would die. But when the end came, it surprised her.
Everything turned white.

Chapter Ten

Rabbit Holes

Well, this is curious! thought Jamie as she fell down a smooth white tunnel. *Death's not how I pictured it.*

Then it occurred to her that dead people probably didn't feel things like vice-like grips on their ankles or chalk up their noses, or consider things to be curious. She considered that dead people probably didn't consider things at all.

I'm still alive!

The tunnel opened out, and Jamie dropped through space and into a cave and landed on a cushion.

"*Huuuuugh!*"

"*Aaaaaaaaagh!*"

"*Oooooooouuuuuuuuuch!*" the cushion yelled.

Jamie hopped off the cushion and staggered to the opposite side of the cave, avoiding its stalagmites and stalactites, the underground river running through it, and the pool at its centre.

The cushion came after her, its lanky form as white as the tunnel she'd plummeted down.

"A ghost!"

"Excuse me!" said the ghost. "I am not a ghost! I am a ha-

hansum. *And*," it said, puffing out its skinny frame, "I am a ha-ha-hansum *Crackpot* at that!"

He stepped into a shaft of light that shone in from the cave's main exit and grinned. His bared yellow teeth did nothing for Jamie's nerves.

She was alone, in a cave, with a Crackpot.

The Crackpot picked up something near his feet and rounded the pool with a few long strides.

"And I ha-ha-have to say that people in stone h-houses, shouldn't throw glass!"

"What do you mean?" said Jamie, trying to sound assured.

"I mean look at yourself before you go round calling other people ghosts!" He thrust a piece of glass at her. "Ha-ha-have a look."

She looked in the make-shift mirror. An enormous cave worm stared back. Jamie began to shake with laughter.

"You saved me!" she said.

The hansum turned red. Not that you could tell through all the chalk.

"Oh, it was nothing!" he said. "I'm Nesbitt Crackpot. What's your name?"

"Jamie Tuff. But how did you know I was in trouble? You couldn't have heard me down here."

"It was just... instinct!" Nesbitt looked at the cave's pool. "Just instinct."

The pool looked inviting to Jamie. It had been a long tumble down the admittedly smooth tunnel—she'd fallen right through the Giddyfoot Cliffs and into Crackpot territory—and her skin felt dry and sore.

"I feel all grimy," she said, pointing to the water. "I'll just—"

"Noooooo!" said Nesbitt, before seeming to think better of it: "Nooooooooo... problem!"

Wonky, thought Jamie. They definitely had that right. But otherwise, the popular description of Crackpots seemed rather skewed. There wasn't a gun in sight.

They went to the pool together and washed off the chalk.

Nesbitt had called himself a hansum, which meant he was at least twenty. But he seemed younger. His hair was brown and floppy, and he constantly had to move it away from his large puddle eyes. He wore a brown checked shirt and dark leather braces which hung about his knees. A belt held up his trousers. There was a holster on it, housing—Jamie's eyes widened—a small black handgun.

When Nesbitt saw Jamie goggling at the gun, he removed it from the holster and waggled it happily in the air.

Jamie stepped back in shock and fell into the cave's shallow pool.

"I didn't mean to scare you!" said Nesbitt. "I'll... I'll put it... over there!" He pointed with his gun to a part of the cave which formed a natural jetty, where a long, narrow boat was banked.

"Well *do* it then!"

Nesbitt climbed into the flat-bottomed boat and placed the gun between his coin-filled cap and his beloved violin.

Not that Jamie saw him do this. For as she said "Well *do* it then!" the pool grabbed hold of her and pulled her underwater.

* * *

She was falling again, down through the puddle, then down through the earth, down, down, down, then up, up up...

And out of an oak. *Whoosh!* She flew at breakneck speed through white sand...

jagged rocks...

an abandoned village...

a swamp full of reeds...

stone steps...

a farm...
a white farmhouse...
Silly Whim...
Wham! Something rammed into her and she flew backwards at thrice the speed of her forward journey.

farmhouse farm steps swamp reeds village rocks sand oak down down DOWN up up up UP...

* * *

Jamie sat up, took a large breath, and opened her eyes. She was back where she started, sitting in the shallow pool.

What in the blazes just happened?

It was almost like Dreamweaving, only she hadn't been asleep. She suspected it had more to do with the pool than her, and was about to ask Nesbitt about it when she saw the hansum's horrified eyes.

A ghastly red shadow was ebbing out of her and into the water, growing and spreading as she watched. The pool had cleared her wounds of chalk.

And the Tombland Gang had done some damage.

Chapter Eleven

Not the Only Freak

"No really, where have you
been?" said Seveny, woozy with
excitement. "And what have you
been doing?"

"Pretty much what you were
doing just now, only for longer,"
said Tommy.

"Talking to the Goddess?"

"No, the bit before that."

Seveny blushed. She'd been
feathered and then naked. What
had he seen? She wanted to
hide herself again behind the
enormous-leaved tree and was
about to do so when Tommy made
the change.

It happened slowly. First his
head disappeared, then his torso, then his legs and finally his
feet. As his human self departed, grey feathers, beak and talons
grew. Seveny found it funny to watch, and when Tommy finally
emerged in falcon form from under his empty shirt, she fell about
laughing.

"I'm not the only freak!" she whooped, punching her fist in
the air. "Thank the Goddess!"

Tommy stepped inside his shirt and changed back so quickly

that Seveny wondered whether his grey-feathered form had been merely a wild hallucination. She bit her lip.

"That really did happen," said Tommy. "And I love the way you do that—talking to the Goddess. It's sweet!"

"Sweet? Necessary, I think you mean. If I hadn't pleaded with her I wouldn't have got my nose back."

"How could you ask her for your nose when you didn't have a mouth to say it?"

Seveny was caught out. "I... I suppose I must have thought it."

"There you go! Intention is all you need."

"So I can turn into anything I want?"

Tommy doubled over. "Ha ha haaaaaaagh! Of course you can't, silly. That's the stuff of fairy tales! 'Can I turn into anything I want?' Pah!"

"Talking of ridiculous, what about you standing there looking like a cut-price Peregrine!" said Seveny. "I think your stuffed hawk-head would look great hung up in the Grand Hall! A taxidermist's and a teacher's dream!"

She instantly regretted her words.

Pity Me School hadn't been kind to Tommy. He didn't fit, he couldn't spell, and he had a large, unwieldy Gift. Professor Goodhew in particular wasn't too upset about his disappearance: conical flasks were an expensive outlay. And Tommy was a Crackpot. So many black marks against his name. And here she was, being horrible, when really she wanted to be anything *but*.

"I'm sorry," she said, quietly.

Tommy smiled. "Well, I am at times, as you observed, a Peregrine Falcon, or something of the like. Whereas you, with your taste for fish, are *almost* a Sea Hawk. But you have golden feathers. I guess you're a Golden Eagle, Sea Hawk mix."

"Not exactly pedigree."

"Let's just call you exotic."

Seveny realized she hadn't asked the really important question.

"What *are* we?"

"Messengers. Half bird, half human. The Farseers call us Halfhawk Mortals."

"Oh!" Seveny was none the wiser, but whatever she was, it was clearly *awesome*. "So what do we do?" she asked brightly.

But before Tommy's tongue could meet his teeth, Seveny dropped like a stone to the floor.

Chapter Twelve

Deliverance

 Bare-chested and filthy with mud, Nesbitt carried an unconscious Jamie through the dark stone passage. He didn't want to take her to the Dispensary. People who went in there tended not to come out. But she was too far gone for the surgeon in the Crackpot capital, Catacomb City.

He'd ripped up his shirt and wrapped the makeshift bandages round Jamie's worst wounds, but her wrist and knee were still bleeding very badly. So it was either certain death for her in Little Sea Cavern, or *un*certain death at the Dispensary. And a Crackpot always played the odds.

It was a long trek. He'd carried her through Come Down Passage for an hour at least, and he felt sick. His nausea was not helped by the giant crickets crunching under his feet, or the passage's fire-beetle lanterns highlighting the carnage left in his wake. For someone loath to swat a fly, this was torture.

And he missed his violin.

But when he looked down at his spindly arms, struggling under the weight of the unconscious girl, his heart swelled.

Little Sea had told him he'd find a girl Up Above, but not one in so much trouble, and certainly not one with such a Gift. He thought back to the pool. The girl didn't know its divining powers, yet Little Sea had practically welcomed her in.

Well, he thought, *I'll probably never find out why.*

They reached what appeared to be a dead end. Nesbitt pushed a small, smooth rock in the wall with his elbow. It moved back a couple of inches, there was a series of clicks, and the dead end yawned open.

He stepped into the ice-blue marble corridor encircling the Dispensary. The wall swung silently back into place behind him.

There was a door nearby. Its brass plaque advertised it as "The Ward of Extraction." It was locked. All the doors were, except—according to his mum—the main entrance on the opposite side. But the girl didn't look like she had time to spare. His hands full, Nesbitt kicked the door to get attention.

At last the door opened. Candlelight flickered inside the room. Nesbitt made out two silhouettes.

"Excuse me... " he said.

"You are excused." The lady's voice was all vowels and snakes. She stepped into the light.

She was monstrously beautiful. She ran her nails through her long black hair and opened her mouth. It was red and moist and full of small, pointy teeth.

"I have a girl he-here and h-h-h-h-her name is Jamie. She was in trouble and... she found h-herself in the caves. Dropped in, as it were!" Nesbitt tried to smile, but managed more of a grimace.

"Looks like the fall hurt her," said a husky voice behind the lady. Her partner stepped out of the shadows.

In one swift move, the man scooped Jamie out of Nesbitt's arms and nodded at him to leave. His sapphire suit entirely failed to hide the muscles lurking beneath it. Nesbitt was about to beat a hasty retreat when the lady spoke again.

"I think you also need looking over. For the shock. Yes! The shock." The lady's large tongue worked its way slowly around her lips before extending towards Nesbit. It was unnaturally long, and split at the tip.

Nesbitt jumped back.

"I'll be fine!" he said. "I ha-have this!"

He pulled a small tin from a pouch on his holster, raised it to his nose, and sniffed. His eyes took on a certain wonkiness.

The countenances of the man and woman also shifted: they'd seen what else the holster carried. Staring at the gun, they stepped back inside the room, taking Jamie with them.

"Best be on your way," the lady slithered.

The door closed with a bang.

The bang brought Jamie back to a confused state of consciousness. Shortly after, she was dropped on a hard, cold surface. But she didn't make a sound. Nor did she open her eyes. She had no idea where she was or how the creature had caught her, but she knew she was in danger. She could smell the animal's musky odour as it loomed over her. Knowing her life depended on the next few moments, she kept perfectly still until the creature moved off, at which point she risked opening an eyelid.

Instead of the monster's lair she'd expected, she lay on a table in the middle of a dark stone chamber, lit by a dribbling red candle. The creature, whatever it was, skulked in the shadows at the end of the room.

"The girl's alive," it hissed.

Jamie's mind suddenly sharpened, and she began to recall how she'd got there. The Crackpot called Nesbitt had scooped her up out of the pool and said "hospital," and then she'd conked out. *So this must be a room in the Dispensary,* she reasoned. *And that creature*—Jamie remembered its musky scent—*is none other than the lady from Dancing Ledge!*

The lady was talking to someone by the door. It was the tall, well-built man from the Ledge. Him with the sad eyes.

"The Tombland Gang failed!" the lady said. "I told Daddy, if you want a job done properly, do it yourself. Only Daddy wouldn't listen—that woman has his ear. She's probably wittering into it in his study, right now."

Jamie decided that 'that woman' must be Funnella Fitzgerald. *So Funnella masterminded the Gang's assault?*

"Daddy wanted the Tuff girl dead," the lady continued. "And I've not smothered anyone in ages! I've not even chucked someone in the Furnace since last year's Harvest..."

Jamie's view started to waver. She wanted, more than anything, to slip back into sweet oblivion. A feeling of peace stole over her. It would be *so* nice to drift off and—

No! You must stay awake!

"Oh please, Magnus, purleaaaaaaase!" the lady said. "She's pretty much dead anyway."

She turned back to Jamie, who shut her eyes just in time. The urge to sleep was stronger with them closed, but she held on. Just.

"Miss Amina!" said Magnus to the lady. "You know we should talk to Father first. Now he has the Tuff girl trapped, his plans for her may change."

And that was the last Jamie heard, for then the darkness took her.

"Fine!" said Miss Amina. "At least let me rid her of her soul. It can join the others."

"Of course. I'll get the anaesthetic."

"Magnus, I don't *want* to wait. I'm *hungry*..." Miss Amina leaned over Jamie and then jerked back. "She's dead!"

Magnus shoved his sister aside and picked up Jamie's wrist. He turned away from Miss Amina and stared at Jamie. His pupils dilated until, for just a second, his eyes went completely black.

"We must inform Father at once," he said.

Miss Amina licked her lips. "I'll stay with the body."

"No!" said Magnus. "We must tell him the news together. If it looks like you had something to do with her death, I shouldn't like to think what he'd do. He could even *expire* you."

"Are you flirting with me?" asked the sharp-toothed beauty.

"No. Don't be ridiculous."

Miss Amina looked disappointed. "Still," she hissed lovingly, "how can I refuse such a handsome man's request?"

And with that, she linked arms with her uncomfortable brother, and they left the corpse of Jamie Tuff.

Chapter Thirteen

Miss Mackadoo and the Brainticklers

I really am dead this time! thought Jamie, deep in the darkness.

No I'm not...

She tried to open her eyes, only to find that she couldn't.

I'm blind!

"Decamp!" something shouted.

An army of tiny, squishy, angular things swarmed across her face and dropped off her ears. Jamie opened her eyes. What she saw was rather disconcerting.

Standing on the tip of her nose was a tiny ginger-bearded man no more than an inch high.

"Now I hopes you don't mind, ma'am," he said, "only we had to set up camp on your eyelids."

Ah! Jamie thought. *I'm dreaming.*

"Why?" she asked the little man.

"Because we wanted you to See better!" a thousand voices replied.

Jamie looked down. Several thousand tiny people looked straight back.

"You wanted me to see better... so you clamped my eyes shut?"

"Yes," said the man on her nose. "You can only truly See in the dark."

Not frightened, but wanting out of the dream, Jamie went to pinch her arm. She couldn't. She'd been swaddled in white gauze.

"You was nearly dead!" said the man on her nose. "Folks is always *nearly* dying on us. But we knows tricks!"

The hope that this was a dream dissolved. The miniature folk were still on her. Still talking. Jamie looked around.

She was in a large cave with a low, domed ceiling. Overhead, hundreds of maggots the size of cats sat and pulsed on a network of vines. They had blue and green bodies and glowing red heads.

Jamie blinked a couple of times. The view didn't alter.

"I notice you is admiring our *Nocturluminous Lampi Gigantae*. They is Giant Glowfly babies!" said the man on her nose, proudly.

"I think they is quite beside the point!" said Jamie, whose niceties were exhausted. "Who, or *what*, are you?"

"Pleased to make your acquaintance, miss. My name is O'Brady."

He was big-built for a tiny person, and looked as strong as a teeny ox. His patched-up orange dungarees complimented his carrot mop of hair, furry eyebrows and generous beard.

"O'Brady by name, O'Beardy by nature!" said a mischievous boy sitting on Jamie's cheek.

"Ahem. Thank you," said O'Brady. "You can call me Sam. And we..." Jamie stared at the thousands of folk who were spread over her and the cave floor. "We... is what you call *Brainticklers*."

Sam O'Brady bowed.

"Now. What I is going to tell you is classified information, but seeing as you is with us now, and we has just saved you from the hands of the Doctor, and you is both eminently and imminently likely to be re-found by him, then I can't see that you is likely to get out anyways, in which case us telling you this is of little or no consequence, so to speak."

Great! thought Jamie. *Why save me in the first place?*

"Empu Miss Mackadoo's orders. She is not one to be ignored..."

Did I say that out loud?

There was a collective mumble of agreement as two thousand Brainticklers nodded and hummed.

Jamie wasn't sure which part of what she'd said, or indeed *not* said, they were agreeing on. But given that no one seemed to be saying anything important, or at least, anything that could be understood, she took the opportunity to have a proper look at her saviours.

She discovered that the Brainticklers were even more interesting to look at, and rather less human, than they'd first appeared. Until now she hadn't noticed how bird-like their faces were, as Sam's was mostly hidden under his enormous ginger beard. Some were owl-like, some rather hawkish, and some resembled sparrows. But there was a lot of variety within these main categories: it seemed that Ticklers loved to interbreed. There were hawk-nosed owl faces, owl-nosed sparrow faces, and sparrow-nosed hawk faces, with even more exotic birds featuring in the mix.

But after their size and bird features, the one thing that defined them was the look of tremendous concern they all wore. They had narrow-set eyes and a vertical furrow between their eyebrows. Their worried expressions worried Jamie, but she would come to understand that this was simply how Brainticklers held their faces, even Tickler babies.

Jamie was so busy studying them, she didn't notice *she* was being studied in return.

Sam O'Brady coughed and the lesson began.

Sam, it transpired, was the Brainticklers' official spokesperson. You could tell he loved his job. Jamie gleaned from his long lecture that Brainticklers looked after shamuns who the Establishment had deemed too old for Up Above. These shamuns were given the label 'Overripe,' and were sent Underground at the annual Autumn Harvest. This was something Jamie was well aware of: there was nobody on the Island aged a year over sixty. The Harvest saw to that. Jamie had thought the Overripe were sent straight to the Dispensary, but Sam said the Brainticklers cared for them until they expired.

He then detailed a Braintickler's duties. According to Sam, the problems of mass *age* could be combated with mass*age*. The most important Tickler job, therefore, was sitting on top of shamun heads and massaging their scalps. This was called Braintickling.

During a Braintickle, a thousand other Ticklers surrounded the shamun and chanted mathematical equations, scientific formulas and algorithms, all carefully designed to perk up their ancient brain. Sam said that the chanting was essential, but it was the Braintickling Teams who had the really complex task. Only the most skillful, athletic Ticklers were allowed on the Tickling Teams, and cups were awarded to those with the best technique. Sam puffed himself out a bit then and peacocked around. It emerged that he was Head Tickler. An honour indeed!

Sam then spoke about what Brainticklers did off-duty. Apparently, a popular Tickler pastime involved betting on each shamun's individual expiry date. When Jamie's eyebrows involuntarily raised, Sam said there weren't many perks to being a Tickler, that their hours were long and their consciences large, and that gambling was harmless.

"Right," said Jamie, who'd listened very patiently. "So where are your shamuns?"

"Umm... Sham*un*," Sam said. "We has *a* sham*un*. Singular. Solo. Just the one, so to speak..."

"What happened to all the others?"

"Well, ah, you see... We wasn't meant to have any in the first place!" Sam looked bashful. "We sort of... took liberties.

Kidnapped them from the Dispensary. And we hasn't been able to collect any new ones recently, and all our others is expired."

"So you're no longer stealing shamuns. I take it they're in the Dispensary where they belong?"

"Um, we calls it *saving*, not stealing, miss. You wouldn't calls it stealing if you saw how they was treated in the Dispensary. They was much happier here with us. But there is no shamuns in the Dispensary now. As soon as they arrives, they is *gone!*"

Jamie's skin crawled as she remembered Miss Amina's comment about chucking people in the Furnace.

"Would the shamun you still have possibly be called Miss Mackadoo?"

"Yes!" said the Brainticklers collectively.

"So where is she?"

"Empu Miss Mackadoo is the best Sooth Seer we've ever had!" said an enraptured little girl in a sickeningly sweet manner. "And..." she looked nervously past Jamie's shoulder.

There was a whoosh of air.

"She's behind you!" an old voice hooted.

Miss Mackadoo was lying on a bed made of rock which was carried by a thousand Ticklers. Jamie gasped at the old woman's crinkliness. None of her generation had ever seen anyone aged over sixty. Jamie's own grandparents were sent Underground when she was three. But here before her lay a shamun. And not just any old shamun—a *really* old shamun.

She had skin like veined marble, a gurgling stomach and whistling breath. Her eyes, which lay behind thick wooden-framed glasses, were quivering and shut.

Miss Mackadoo snorted. "It's rude to stare!"

"Oh, please excuse me!" said Jamie, trying to work out how Miss Mackadoo, through her closed eyes, knew she was staring.

Fifty thousand Ticklers covered their ears.

"You didn't let her finish!" said Sam. His bushy brows had knitted themselves together with worry.

"Finish? Finish what?"

The screeching started. It got louder and more piercing every second until it pinned many of the Ticklers to the cave's walls. Jamie had never heard such a sound.

"*CAN I DO ANYTHING?!*" she shouted over the noise.

Sam, though holding strong, looked a little wilted. "*NOTHING TO DO!*" he yelled. "*JUST LET HER CONTINUE!*"

Jamie waited patiently. For what, she did not know.

Eventually the screeching subsided, and as Miss Mackadoo calmed down, the Ticklers came out of their haze and those pinned to the walls were able to move.

"...I came to find you," said the shamun,
"But you have no care."

"Ummm. Sorry?" Jamie offered. She was petrified the screeching might return, but Miss Mackadoo just started to snore.

A Braintickling Team crept aboard the old woman's head and set to work on a vigorous massage. A thousand others crawled under the bed and carried it out of the room. They were gone in an instant. Jamie realized why she hadn't noticed Miss Mackadoo approach: Tickler transportation was strong, silent, and fast.

Once Miss Mackadoo had been carried off, the remaining Ticklers sighed with relief.

"Sorry about that," said Jamie.

"Don't worry yourself, girly," said Sam. "She used to live in Rhyme Intrinsica, where she was famed for her poetry and made an Empu."

"What's an Empu?"

"An honour, miss, bestowed on those that is considered masters of their craft," said Sam. "Since she was put Underground she's spoken only in rhymes. They burned her poetry

Up Above, see. So down here, if we doesn't let her finish... But you wasn't to know. And we *has* told the Empu that you can't tell if she's done if she doesn't speak in couplets, or takes too long a pause!"

Jamie wouldn't be jollied. She felt guilty for causing Miss Mackadoo trauma. And something else troubled her: her throbbing knee. When she looked down, she discovered one of the web-like bandages had come loose.

Within a second, she'd been transported to another, smaller room. A bed had been carved out of the rock and a moss mattress lay on top.

Once the Brainticklers had got her on the mattress, she was de-swaddled and her dressings replaced with fresh spider-silk bandages. (Sam said that spider-whispering and web-collecting were two other Tickler jobs.) To help her settle, the Ticklers gave her a couple of sugar-coated grubs dipped in mulled vine—a warm, green, sickly substance. Mulling was another Tickler job.

Jamie closed her eyes, and the Ticklers mounted her head.

First she felt a fluttering, and then the sensation deepened. The Ticklers were giving her a most thorough brain-brush complete with floss. And it wasn't long before they got right on her nerves.

Braintickling is a misnomer, she thought. *This isn't fun at all.*

Still, she fought the urge to flick the Ticklers off. It was their job, after all.

Soon after, the image of Seveny swam into her mind. Seveny as she'd recently been: alive, not dead. And Jamie let herself pretend, just for a moment, that her friend had survived.

The thought gave her comfort, and the Tickling became relaxing, and she drifted off into a much-needed, deep, Dreamweave-free sleep.

Chapter Fourteen

Star-Spotting

"Easy does it," said Tommy, as Seveny wrenched herself up from the bed.

Seveny's head was pounding. She put her back against the wall to steady herself and squinted her eyes.

She was in a rickety shelter, bare except for the bed she was lying on, a stove and a small window. A blanket had replaced the leaf she'd wrapped herself in. Tommy was sat on a chair next to her. Outside, it was pitch black.

"Where am I?" she said, weakly.

"Not far from where we met."

"We're still in Contraland?"

"Contraland is just land, like anywhere else—no matter what people might have you believe. Now, what did you see before you fainted?"

Seveny rubbed her forehead.

"Children snarling... sharpened flints... crooked teeth... blood—Jamie!"

Tommy nodded.

"Why am I seeing these things?"

"You have the Sight—as do all Halfhawk Mortals. Seeing is part of our Gift, part of our job. The Sight lets us receive important messages. It'll get clearer as you get used to it, but it generally arrives in bursts like that."

"The images are real?"

"You know they are."

Seveny's skin goose-pimpled. "Then Jamie's hurt!"

"But she's alive."

"I know, I can feel it."

"You mean, you have Seen it?"

"No, I can feel it." Seveny pointed to her heart. "Here."

"You *are* an exotic Halfhawk... I've never heard of that before."

Seveny couldn't cope with the intensity of Tommy's stare. She broke the gaze. "What do Halfhawk Mortals actually *do?*"

"That'll be easier to explain outside." Tommy reached under the hut's small bed. "These are for you."

He put a bundle in her arms. Seveny unravelled the gift eagerly, but when she saw the clothes her expression changed. They would be a welcome change to Pity Me School's itchy uniform and her mustard pyjamas, but...

"How did you come by them?" she said.

"I liberated them from Giddyfoot market in preparation for your arrival."

"That figures."

Seveny turned her back on him and put on the cheap, thin threads. Crackpot clothes.

When Tommy saw her in them, his eyes popped. Well, she'd never have chosen a bright pink halterneck and leggings for herself, but she had to admit she didn't mind their effect.

"Wait!" Seveny started. "You said 'in preparation for my arrival.' How did you know to expect me?"

"The Farseers showed me."

"The who?"

"Come with me."

"See the stars?"

Seveny looked up and saw diamonds twinkling in the indigo. "How can you miss them?" she said.

"We mortals, like those shining lights, are stars," said Tommy. "And like stars we make up constellations, on Earth and in heaven.

"All mortals are spirited. When we expire, our soul travels back up to the Blanket of Stars to continue on as part of the cosmos. Though our bodies die, our souls live eternally. No soul can be destroyed.

"Now most souls, when the body dies, make their home in the Blanket of Stars. But the most Gifted souls travel higher and settle in the Ocean of Emptiness above it. This Ocean is Nothing and yet everything, and the souls who make their homes there are Farseers. They guide and guard the world below."

Tommy checked to see if Seveny was still with him. Her lips were pouted in concentration.

"But recently," he said, "the Blanket of Stars and the Ocean of Emptiness aren't the only places souls have been going. Some of the dead have found a new home."

"Where?"

"In the Underworld."

Seveny's eyes widened. "Which souls are those?"

"The souls of the juvenites Taken at Dancing Ledge."

"So the Ancient Spectre *does* Take them! I thought the Establishment were telling us a whole load of hooey!"

"No," said Tommy. "I've had the Ledge under Watch. The Doctor Takes the juvenites one month, does something to them in his Dispensary, and releases them at the next full moon. They then march into the ocean and drown, and their souls travel

104

down to the Underworld instead of up to the Blanket of Stars. It shouldn't even be possible! Souls have an unshakeable instinct about where to go, and it's never the Underworld. The Underworld has to stay as empty as the Ocean of Emptiness stays full."

"So what do you think the Doctor's up to?"

"I've no idea. I've spied on the Ledge, but I can't spy on the Dispensary beneath it. The Farseers know more, of course. I'm pretty sure they know everything. But they're not telling." Tommy frowned. "They can be bloody elusive."

"But how can the Doctor be so powerful?"

"Because he's a Dreamweaver, like Jamie. When he's asleep, he can possess other people and have them do his will."

"Jamie's a... Dreamweaver? I thought—"

"Jamie's the one who'll stop the Doctor. The Farseers have told me that much."

Seveny's heart ached. She wished she could take back what she'd said about her friend.

"But how can Jamie stop him? She's hurt!"

"She's being looked after. And she will have our help. That's something the Farseers *have* shared."

"Right!" said Seveny. "So what should we do?"

"Nothing. Not till the Farseers drop us the hint. Otherwise we could be working against them and never know it. But that doesn't mean I can't start training you. You're a Halfhawk Mortal now. And you have lots to learn."

Chapter Fifteen

Death by Fire

Hot sands...   hard rocks... abandoned village...   scratchy reeds... Silly Whim!

Jamie woke at speed and catapulted herself off the moss mattress.

"Avalanche!" screeched the Brainticklers, somersaulting off her and out of the way.

"Sorry! Force of habit. I always wake up like that."

"No harm done, missus!" said Sam O'Brady, dangling from a nostril. "Miss Mackadoo wants a word with you, anyways."

Jamie picked him off her nose and put him on the floor.

"Can't it wait? I didn't Dreamweave last night, but my dreams were pretty tiring. I was hoping for a rest."

"Of course you were, my child,
That's exactly why you're here!"

There was a whoosh of air, and suddenly Miss Mackadoo was in front of Jamie, lying on a rock bed carried by a thousand Ticklers.

"All aboard!" said Sam O'Brady.

Before Jamie could reject their advances, her head swarmed with Ticklers. Miss Mackadoo cleared her throat and said:

"Look at me, my protégé
And do not close your eyes.
Dreamweaving while you look awake's
A wonderful disguise.
Enter my mind and try to find
The memories I'll show,
And see the tale they have to tell,
A tale from long ago."

Jamie didn't see how she could fall asleep with her eyes open. But the Brainticklers' massage swiftly brought on a strange, open-eyed slumber.

Vibrant colours flooded her mind. Oranges, reds and yellows, which slowly became an image, a beautiful painting into which she found herself transported.

* * *

She was in a high-ceilinged hall. Art dripped from three of the walls, and leather-bound books in grand bookshelves occupied the fourth. Unlike Pity Me's Library, which just had books on Geography and History and some pre-storm volumes kept locked in an iron safe, here she saw books of dreams and imagination. They had names like 'The Soul's Flight' and 'The Common Flame.' Gold lettering glinted on their spines.

A sea of faces stared at her across a giant oak table. They looked angry and fearful, and ranged from the newest born to the dangerously ripe.

"The Establishment are a bunch of ninnyhammers!" said a many-freckled man.

"It was a veiled threat, but one we should listen to!" argued a ball-shaped woman.

"They're trying to divide us because they fear us," came a calm voice.

Jamie's host turned to a dark-skinned man beside her who was polishing a raven-headed wavy sword.

"Because as long as we live," he continued, "we will create. And as long as we create, people will experience, and as long as people experience, they will *live*. And they won't just live: they will live with imagination, and their souls will fly!"

His eyes pierced the crowd.

"How many fences have gone up in recent years? We are being divided from our land. And for what reason? Control. We are not governed by the Great Goddess, but by the Establishment!"

There was a rumble of agreement.

Then Jamie's host opened her mouth, and out whistled the younger though still familiar tones of Miss Mackadoo. "Salim, I can't help feeling this is a distraction!" she said. "I don't think they wanted to divide us. They must have known we'd unite. I've seen this moment in my dreams. And next..."

"What, Brigid?" asked Salim, gently. He held her hand.

Yes, next what?! Jamie wondered.

"Fire."

The room began to crackle. Flames were licking at the windows, waiting to devour.

And all of Rhyme Intrinsica's inhabitants were swallowed by fire...

The air was thick with black smoke. It clogged Miss Mackadoo's nose and filled her lungs. Jamie felt all but drowned in it, when her host ploughed through the village hall's door. Miss Mackadoo glanced back at the blazing building, and then she was running, through Rhyme Intrinsica and towards Pity Me.

When she reached the town's welcome sign she saw a burly man lounging against it: a young Phosphor-Jones. She begged him to raise an alarm, to rally the people of Pity Me to help her go back and save the others. Phosphor-Jones nodded kindly and took her arm in his. And then Jamie felt his fingers dig into Miss

Mackadoo's smoke-burned flesh. He frogmarched her to Pity Me School. Jamie wasn't surprised to see that the school looked exactly the same.

Once they were through the fickle main entrance, Phosphor-Jones escorted Miss Mackadoo up the spiral staircase to the Chamber Upstairs, where the Establishment questioned her through the suggestion-slot. She insisted that since every villager had been in the hall round the table, none of Rhyme Intrinsica's inhabitants could have started the fire. After what seemed like hours of interrogation, the Establishment informed her that they'd carried out a search—and that she was the lone survivor.

They wanted to know why only she had escaped.

Miss Mackadoo wondered the same thing. But she couldn't speak to tell them: grief stopped her throat. The Establishment declared her hesitation a proof of guilt, and pronounced that *she* had started the fire.

She was sentenced to life imprisonment in the Dispensary.

* * *

Jamie woke with a gasp.

"You've been Underground all this time?"

Miss Mackadoo looked exhausted.

"Empu Miss Mackadoo has been Underground for fifty years!" said Sam O'Brady. "But she escaped the Dispensary a long while back. She'd Seen us Brainticklers in her dreams, and imagined us smuggling her out. And one day, so to speak, we did!"

Jamie didn't really understand, but she didn't feel up to another of Sam's lectures, either. She turned her attention back to Miss Mackadoo. "I think I'm getting the hang of this Dreamweaving thing."

Miss Mackadoo snorted.

"The experience you had
Mustn't get you too excited,
Of course you found it easy,
For you had been invited."

The shamun beckoned Jamie closer.

"Like me you are a Dreamweaver,
You can embroider life.
When you realize your Gift
You will deliver us from strife.
Your battle at the Ledge
Will be hard won,
But you can't avoid the fight
If you're to save the sun.
You will face the Doctor
On a mournful night.
My job is to prepare you
For the painful fight!"

"I'm afraid you've got the wrong person." Jamie inched away
from the shamun. "You've made a mistake!"

Miss Mackadoo breathed in with a whistle and grunted for
the Brainticklers to take her back to her quarters. She was gone
in a flash.

Jamie didn't feel like a hero. Like the Perfects said, the only
Gift she had was for making people disappear. Billy was Taken.
Charlotte was Taken. Ella was Taken.

And Seveny was dead.

Chapter Sixteen

Mindmoving

As Miss Mackadoo and the Ticklers terrorized Jamie into fulfilling her destiny, Tommy trained Seveny.

In the first night alone, he taught her how to use the wind for lift, spot rising thermals and make controlled landings. She discovered how to shape-shift in a fraction of a second and turn into any size hawk she liked—within reason. Finally, he introduced her to hawkthought: mind-to-mind communication. She excelled in all these pursuits, and two weeks later she'd mastered many of the skills a Halfhawk Mortal needed.

However, though her crash course had proven surprisingly crash-free, one skill in particular was still causing her difficulties.

"Do we *have* to continue?"

"Yes. Mindmoving is the most dangerous weapon in a Halfhawk's arsenal. You have to master it."

Seveny shook out her aching muscles.

Mindmoving was an athletic process. It involved bringing the energy of an object to life and then getting it to do what you wanted. It was fairly easy to bash something around or break it—Seveny remembered her bouts with the chalk and the mirrors—but moving things without destroying them was quite another matter. However, when properly channelled, Mindmoving could quite literally open doors.

The wooden door of Tommy's hut had been the object of her training, and it bore the marks to prove it. It was splintered and holey, as though it had been repeatedly punched.

"Right!" said Tommy for the hundredth time. "In your own time."

Seveny stared at the door and channelled the power up through her spine as he'd shown her.

Somewhere in her neck, it got stuck.

"Don't worry," he said, manipulating her shoulders to release it. "Concentrate."

She found his hands distracting, but they found the point of tension and set the power free. It shot up through her neck and buzzed around in her skull.

"Great stuff!" said Tommy. "Now focus your power into one line of force, as strong as you need it and as thin as a pin."

Seveny concentrated, and an invisible line of force extruded painfully from between her eyes. It danced all over the place: she could hardly keep it in front of her, let alone trained on the door. Every nerve jangled. The agony in her skull was nearly unbearable.

"Good!" said Tommy. "Now, release it with control."

His words—or perhaps just his breath on her neck—did indeed help Seveny find a release. Unfortunately, it wasn't very controlled.

She exploded the door clean off its hinges.

Chapter Seventeen

Expiration

In the fortnight Jamie had been Underground her wounds had almost healed. Only the welt on her knee remained. And though the Ticklers couldn't stop it bleeding, their surgical spider-silk greatly slowed the flow.

The Ticklers themselves were small-bodied but big-hearted. In the two weeks she'd spent in their company, many of them had fallen completely in love with her. She let them kiss her on the cheek when she went to bed, and she was fond of their squeaks of "goodnight and big dreams."

But her sleep was never easy. She was haunted by her trip through Nesbitt's puddle: the oak, the blistering white sands, the abandoned village, the wall of green reeds, the swamp, the farmhouse, the words 'Silly Whim.'

But even the worst nightmare, the biggest dream, couldn't compare to Miss Mackadoo's teaching. Jamie had grown accustomed to and even begun to enjoy Miss Mackadoo's temperament, but Dreamweaving was a demanding discipline. One that she would have to master if she was to duel with the Doctor and live.

Miss Mackadoo had explained that a master Dreamweaver could choose when to Dreamweave, whom to occupy as their host, or victim, and could even full-on possess them. And in the two weeks she'd been taught by Miss Mackadoo, Jamie was made to flex muscles she never knew existed. Muscles that weren't even her own.

Miss Mackadoo had the girl practise on her. Jamie was allowed to move the old lady's arms, head and torso, open and shut her eyes and (hardest of all) use her voice. But she was never permitted to move the old lady's legs. That would have been impolite: Miss Mackadoo had not moved them herself in years.

To begin with, Jamie's movements were far too wild for the old lady's bones. How the Empu ached after each lesson! Still, she let her keep practising, for the girl had to learn.

Other things came more easily to Jamie, like the all-important falling-asleep-instantly-whilst-remaining-standing-up. And she was commended on how quickly she could locate and drop into Miss Mackadoo, no matter where the Ticklers hid her. Staying put, that was the difficulty. At first, Jamie's soul was ejected from the Dreamweave whenever Miss Mackadoo made so much as a sudden movement—let alone when she actively tried to force her out.

To improve Jamie's stamina, Miss Mackadoo put her through exercises she called "the physical jerks," because that was in fact what they were. Jamie would Dreamweave in, and then had to hold on tight as Miss Mackadoo tried to cough, shake, and with the help of a Braintickler up each nostril, *sneeze* her out. At first Jamie was easy to eject, but little by little her soul-grip increased, and Miss Mackadoo's attempts to break her hold became less a matter of physical jerks and more one of soulogical warfare.

That was when the training moved from taxing to downright brutal. Miss Mackadoo had a hard, strong soul and she had no qualms about using it. Jamie felt almost relieved every time she was ejected. Which, Miss Mackadoo said, was absolutely the wrong reaction. Apparently a Gift was not a Gift unless you knew how to use it. And if you were getting thrown out, you did *not* know how to use it.

There were, however, occasions when it was safer to leave a Dreamweave before being discovered. Unfortunately, there were also occasions when leaving would be disastrous and you simply had to hang on. Jamie had to learn the difference.

Morning, noon and night, Miss Mackadoo tested her. Tonight was no exception.

Jamie was woken by a hoot. Miss Mackadoo, lying on a Tickler-levitated rock bed, demanded she Dreamweave into her at once. Jamie was to possess her, and then try to move her legs.

Miss Mackadoo wanted to walk.

This went quite against all of Miss Mackadoo's previous orders, but Jamie did as she was told. Quickly Dreamweaving in, she opened the shamun's eyes.

"Why does she wear these glasses when she rarely opens an eyelid?" she asked Sam O'Brady in Miss Mackadoo's hooty voice.

"Well miss, they'll be no use to her after she's dead!"

Jamie couldn't fault his logic. She looked around the cave to strengthen the Dreamweave. The glowing maggots pulsed brightly overhead, and the Ticklers scuttled around on the floor, curious to see if she could make the old woman walk. Finally Jamie looked at her own body. Her eyes were vacant, yet focused on the shamun.

When she'd first begun her training, looking at herself was a sure way to end up catapulted back. Now it didn't bother her at all. But it was still a curious experience, seeing herself through another's eyes.

With her Dreamweave strengthened, she got back to the task in hand.

She imagined Miss Mackadoo's tendons, joints, muscles and bones becoming her own. Then she imagined moving them... and the old lady moved. First her neck and head, and then her arms, which pushed her up to a sitting position. Jamie's movements were controlled and considered. So far, so smooth.

But moving Miss Mackadoo's legs proved tricky. Their muscles hadn't moved in years, and they'd forgotten how to do it. Jamie's imagination pushed and pulled to its limits, but the message wouldn't go through. Force clearly didn't work here, so she tried focus. She deepened and deepened her concentration, and at last was rewarded: Miss Mackadoo's toe twitched.

She laughed hootily.

As her confidence increased, so did her depth of focus. Instead of jerking Miss Mackadoo's limbs around like a marionette's, she wore her body like a second skin. She swung her legs off the bed and, after a minute, got her standing.

And then she began to walk.

Knowing that one false move would make Miss Mackadoo fall, she started slowly and gently, sensitive of the Empu's delicate bones and wasted muscles. The Brainticklers followed her, ready to catch her if needed. There was one close call, a minor stumble, but Empu Miss Mackadoo didn't overbalance.

Eventually, Jamie walked her host back to bed and lowered the old lady down.

When Jamie opened her own eyes she saw the Brainticklers jumping lustily into each other's arms, which was how they usually dealt with being very excited. Sam O'Brady, or at least the bits of him that she could see over his ginger beard, was pink with pride.

"You only went and did it, so to speak!"

But Miss Mackadoo's breathing was laboured.

Jamie's throat tightened. "What have I done to you?"

116

"I am just tired.
Nothing a long sleep won't cure;
But you are ready for your final test.
Of that I'm sure!"

"Final test?"

"Dreamweave into the Doctor now,
Find out his next move.
Seek not to control him,
For you've nothing more to prove."

Jamie couldn't think of anything worse. But she brought the Doctor's face to mind. The real one arrived behind the imagined one and she hopped across, keeping her mind quiet so he wouldn't notice her arrival. It was easier than she'd anticipated. His blue irises rippled like oceans as she passed through them—

* * *

—and when she looked back out, she saw a wide expanse of real ocean, glinting beneath the light of a waxing moon.

The Doctor was on Dancing Ledge. He was unsteady on his feet and stank of Honeydew—the adult kind.

She felt cramped and claustrophobic. Dreamweaving into Miss Mackadoo was like entering a well-kept pantry. Dreamweaving into the Doctor was like entering a... well, she didn't know what it was like, but it was deeply unpleasant.

"For too long the Great Goddess has been over-worshipped and over-fed! But soon, you and I will be the recognized rulers of this pitiful world!"

Off on a rant again, thought Jamie.

"I'm only sorry it took so long."

Who is he talking to?

117

The Doctor bowed unsteadily to the Great Sea. "I thought the Overripe would make perfect soul-food for you: too old and frail for life, and already Underground. Who'd notice if they went missing? And their frail bodies drowned so nicely. But their souls wouldn't go down. They all went up, up, up to the Blanket of Stars!"

He shook his fist at the sky.

"Do you know, the old are practically unteachable? Completely unreceptive to new experiences! And," he said darkly, "their souls remembered where to go.

"But Dancing Ledge was an inspiration! The perfect camouflage. And oh, how I love juvenites. Receptive, vulnerable, capable of change, they're the perfect students for re-education! When I've finished Turning them they jump straight off Dancing Ledge, and their souls go the *right* way. Down to you, my Lord!"

Splash! Flash! Jamie remembered the juvenites jumping off the Ledge and drowning.

"Of course the more we Take, the more get scared at their own Takings, and the more wake up. But that's all the better for us: the most sensitive souls are always the strongest. They're the most trouble to re-educate, but I'll have them all ready for the next Taking. And then, oh, how you shall feast!"

The Doctor was so enflamed with this idea that it seemed to flood out of every invisible pore on his wrinkle-free face. And then he thrust his head forward and roared a terrible roar, and a dark, bluish-black smoke spiralled out of his mouth. The smoke rolled towards the Great Sea, dived beneath the waters, and the waves crashed all the harder. Something giant and dark and sinuous moved in the deep.

The Ancient Spectre had come, for He had heard His servant's call.

The neck of the Serpent smashed up through the water and streamed into the sky, its waxy scales gleaming in the light of the half-moon as the brine poured from them. It was impossibly vast. Its head alone had to be a hundred yards long.

The Ancient Spectre's real?!

Jamie had always believed in the Spectre, but in much the same way as she believed in Justice or Death. Or, come to think of it, the Great Goddess. They were all more force than form. Sure, the Goddess existed, but She didn't flit down from heaven on sky-spanning wings and strike up a conversation with you.

The Serpent roared.

"WHY DO YOU WAKE ME FROM MY SLUMBER!"

Its voice was so deep it made the Ledge tremble. It reminded her strangely of the Doctor's. Evil, she supposed, was alike all over.

A mile out to sea, something swayed in the moonlight: the Serpent's tail. The Doctor fizzed with excitement at the sight of the Spectre and clapped his hands with glee.

"My, how you've grown! You need only one more batch of souls, and then I shall rule the Island!"

The snake hissed and lunged at the Doctor, who was too slow, or drunk, to remember not to flinch.

"IF YOU RULE, PROUD MORTAL, IT WILL BE AT MY SUFFERANCE!"

The Doctor cowered. "Of course... of course... at your sufferance! I will make you a symbol of worship. I have fed you souls and made you strong! Now you live in water as easily as the Underworld. But wouldn't you like to live on land? I can give that to you. The souls will keep coming. The threat of being eaten by you will help me rule. And while I rule, you will be fed. That will be your reward."

"NOT REWARD, MORTAL! TRIBUTE!"

"Yes—yes! Tribute! I shall make you a God!"

The Ancient Spectre nodded in approval.

"THE BARGAIN IS ACCEPTABLE."

The Doctor grinned.

"THOUGH THE GIRL SEEMS NOT TO LIKE IT."

The Doctor stopped grinning. "Girl? What girl?"

Jamie hid as Miss Mackadoo had taught her. But it was too late. She was no match for the Doctor even when he was drunk. And now he knew who to look for, he spotted her at once.

"Jamie Tuff!" he screamed.

He seized hold of her soul with his, and *squeezed*.

The pain was worse than anything Miss Mackadoo had inflicted on her in training. His soul was dark—so, so dark, and it choked and choked her. But she held tight. This seemed like a situation where she ought to hold on.

The Spectre's eye-slits widened.

"HER SOUL IS STRONG."

The Doctor's body joined in the soul-struggle. He'd stopped his drunken swaying and was resorting to the physical jerks. He was rhythmically arching his back like a cat ridding himself of a furball. "She's a trifling nuisance, no more than that. Soon, she will be dead."

"NO! YOU WILL TAKE HER ALIVE, AND DELIVER HER TO ME. OR IS SHE TOO STRONG FOR YOU? PERHAPS I SHOULD BE TALKING TO HER INSTEAD. YES... PERHAPS YOUR SOUL SHOULD TAKE HER PLACE AT MY FEAST."

"No, my Lord!" The Doctor's voice was strangled. "Her soul shall be yours!"

"VERY GOOD... MY PRINCE."

The Spectre's tail swayed. It opened its jaw in anticipation, and sank beneath the waves.

The Doctor tightened his soul-grip on Jamie. He'd show her who was the master Dreamweaver!

But the girl had already fled.

*　*　*

Sam O'Brady was re-bandaging Jamie's leg. Not realizing she was back from the Dreamweave, he kept talking.

"...and she'll be leaving us today, I'll stake my cup on it!" he said.

The other Ticklers flibbertigibbeted. "Shhhhhhh! She's awake!"

"Oh, deary me," said Sam, fussing with Jamie's one remaining bandage. "It's still not healing, so to speak."

Jamie looked down at her leg. The bandage was soaked through with blood.

"It's three in the morning," said Sam. "We'll finish changing your bandage, miss, and you can get some sleep."

"No!" she said. "I've Seen quite enough for one night!"

A whistling filled her ears.

Miss Mackadoo was lying as she'd last seen her: prostrate on her rock bed, eyes shut, wood-framed glasses on her nose.

"Fear is not your friend," she warned,
"T'will only make the monster grow.
If you bow down to the Doctor,
The Ancient Spectre's sure to know!"

How can she know what I've seen before I've told—The penny dropped. It *had* been a claustrophobic Dreamweave.

"You were there with me!"

Miss Mackadoo nodded.

"And he didn't spot you?"

Miss Mackadoo raised an eyebrow.

Jamie was amazed and cheered. The Doctor might be powerful, but he couldn't hold a candle to her teacher! Not even the Ancient Spectre had noticed her. Suddenly the situation seemed more hopeful.

Miss Mackadoo waved the girl over.

"You will fight the Doctor
On a moonlit night.

His soul is black, but yours is filled
With Golden Light."

"I *might* be able to beat the Doctor with your help," said
Jamie. "But the Ancient Spectre's the Lord of the Underworld!"

Miss Mackadoo, her eyes firmly shut as usual, shook her
head.

"The Doctor and the Spectre
Are one and the same.
Only when you see this
Will you win the Master Game."

"The Master Game?"

"When Sacrifice is made
On Dancing Ledge,
You must reject the Image
At the water's edge.
And when the Fiend's upon you
Do not fight!
But flood it out, your soul ablaze
With Golden Light."

Jamie looked at her web-wrapped knee. "How can I fight
anyone in this state?"

Miss Mackadoo grabbed Jamie's hand. For the first time in
the girl's company, the Empu opened her eyes.

"Poisonous thoughts are but rot!
Do not make real that which is not!
Within you lies the Golden Light,
In that you must believe,
Far to the North lives Creaky Nan,
There lies your way, now lea—

ea—ea—
u-u-u-u-u!!!"

The Empu jerked violently. She struggled to breathe, taking in air in short, sharp gasps.

"Miss Mackadoo? Miss Mackadoo? Please don't die, *please!* I'm not ready! I need your help!"

Somehow, Miss Mackadoo found the strength to heave a full breath into her lungs. But all that came out was a long, drawn-out screech.

The Ticklers could hardly keep their balance. Even sturdy Sam O'Brady was pinned to the wall.

"*JAMIE, DO WHAT THE EMPU ASKS!*" he yelled, pointing at one of the many tunnels out of the dwelling. "*YOU MUST FIND CREAKY NAN! THERE LIES YOUR WAY!*"

Petrified, Jamie ran from the cave and up the dark tunnel. The screeching of Miss Mackadoo's death-throes rang out behind her.

And then, as suddenly as the screeching had started, it stopped.

Ignoring Sam's instructions, Jamie returned to the room, desperately hoping against all hope that her teacher had recovered. That perhaps she'd finish her rhyme.

But there was no comforting gurgle of Miss Mackadoo's stomach, nor the gentle whistling of her breath. There was only her old friend's glasses, hovering above the rock bed.

"On your way!" said Sam O'Brady gruffly, peering out from underneath the wooden frames.

Jamie left the cave once more, her heart full of lead, and started trudging up the rocky path that would take her to the surface. She could hardly see the way ahead, her eyes were so full of tears.

She had lost Miss Mackadoo.

But perhaps she would find Creaky Nan.

Chapter Eighteen

Ghost Hawks

Tommy schooled Seveny by day. By night they patrolled the skies, waiting for the Farseers to communicate the next step of their plan.

After a harrowing day of Mindmoving practice Seveny was completely exhausted, so Tommy let her skip the patrol and turn in early. She ate a meal of fried fish and green tea, then went to bed.

She'd hardly got to sleep when she was woken up by something landing on her chest.

So she did what came naturally and punched it.

There was a pained squawk and something thumped to the floor. Seveny peered sleepily over the side of the bed. The culprit peered back up at her. Its head was human, the rest was bird, and its wings were akimbo.

"Tommy!"

Tommy shifted shape.

"Ow." He rubbed his head.

"Sorry!" Seveny winced. "What's with the wake-up call?"

"I just got the message we've been waiting for."

"From the Farseers?"

"Yes. I'll fill you in on the way."

"On the way to where?"

"We'll be seeing your friend George."

"Agh!" Seveny jumped out of bed. "I can't wait! But George is a scaredy-cat—he'll think I'm back from the dead."

"So don't scare him. And don't punch him. Come on, let's go."

"Now?" Seveny looked out the window. "It's not even morning!"

"By morning it'll be too late to deliver the message."

"What is the message?"

"That Max's sister is alive and living in Contraland in a secret village called Little Breedy."

"Ha! I knew Maria was alive! So *did* she give birth to a mutant?"

"Oh Goddess," said Tommy. "I have a lot of explaining to do."

Two hours and a great deal of hawkthought later, Seveny and Tommy reached Pity Me.

George's house looked like all the others in town. But it could easily be identified by the cacophony of crashes, smashes and shouts that issued from the ground floor.

"Do you know which window's his?" Tommy hawkthought.

"Yes."

Seveny had never actually been to her friend's house as his dad didn't allow visitors, but she could tell which room was

George's easily enough: it was the one with all the stationery hanging from the curtain rail. George *really* liked stationery.

Seveny flew at the window and knocked her beak against the glass.

Tap.

No reply. She circled back and flew at it again.

Tap, tap, tap.

The window opened, and George's generous nose poked out from between two pieces of paper and a ruler. He spotted the golden eagle hovering outside, looking straight at him. Confused, he closed the window and returned to his desk.

Seveny couldn't understand why George, normally so drawn to mysteries, would ignore this one. She had to remind herself that eagles didn't tend to knock on windows. That wasn't so much mysterious as just plain weird, and it was bound to be unsettling, even for Pity Me School's finest (and indeed only) amateur sleuth.

She kept hovering and tapping.

Tap, tap. Tap-tap-tap!

She was about to give up when the window opened again. She zoomed through it and crashed into George, who doubled over and smacked his jaw hard against his desk. Once he reached the floor he fainted, Seveny thought more from surprise than the table's unexpected uppercut. She took the opportunity to shape-shift, and swiped the blanket off his bed for coverage. When he stirred she put her hands over his mouth.

He tried to scream, but luckily it was drowned out by his parents' rather louder shouts. George wilted to the consistency of soggy lettuce. Seveny let go.

"Oh my Goddess! What *are* you, and what do you want from me?"

"I might have been gone a fortnight," Seveny said, "but I didn't think I was *that* forgettable."

"You're Seveny's ghost?"

She pinched him on the arm, rather brutally.

"Do I feel like a ghost?"

"I don't know what ghosts feel like, but I do know Seveny's dead!" His bottom lip trembled.

"Oh, George! That's really cute. But I'm not dead, I'm changed."

Seveny morphed back into hawk-form to show him. As she ruffled her feathers, George started shaking again. So she shape-shifted back.

"I hit the water and then this happened."

George remembered the hawk he'd seen hovering over his friend's floating uniform. He started bouncing with excitement.

"You're alive?" he said. "You're alive!"

That was much more like the welcome Seveny had wanted. "I'm more than just alive. I'm a Halfhawk Mortal. I receive messages by way of visions from—well, Tommy calls them Farseers."

"Farseers? No, wait, Tommy? Who's Tommy? Tommy—"

"—Crackpot. You remember him. He's just outside."

George looked out the window. Another bird was sitting on the tree outside his room. When the bird saw him looking, it waved a wing cheerily.

George blinked. *"That's* Tommy Crackpot?"

"You'll just have to trust me. Can you do that?"

"Yes I can!"

"Good, because Jamie and I need your help."

"Jamie's alive too?" George resumed his excited bouncing. "Where is she?"

"Underground."

George stopped bouncing. "She's in the Dispensary?"

"No, she's somewhere safe." Seveny spied his compass on the desk. "Best you pack that for the trip."

"Oh Goddess!" said George. "Where do you want me to go?"

"Into Contraland."

"But—"

"You're going to Little Breedy."

"What's Little Breedy?"

"It's a secret village inside Strip Limpets Wood. The people who live there ran away from No Place rather than send their newborn babies Underground."

George's brow furrowed. "Max's sister disappeared. Could she be there?"

"The one I called a slut? Yes. Tomorrow you'll find Maria."

"But... but... I'll be surrounded by mutants!"

"Oh, George!" said Seveny. "There are no mutants in Little Breedy. Just families seeking sanctuary away from the Establishment."

George rubbed his chin. "So are you telling me this is a Quest?"

"Well, it's a *request*," said Seveny, "but call it what you like. Just so long as you tell the residents of Little Breedy whatever you discover at Askerwell, which is to be your first stop."

"Askerwell?" George remembered the manshu rhyme about visiting that place, which was buried deep within the Great Forest. "If I go to Askerwell, I'll be dragged down to hell!" He paused for thought. "Can I take anyone with me?"

Seveny laughed. "I was going to say you should bring Max."

George looked at the rows of self-written detective stories stacked neatly on his bookshelf.

"All the best detectives *do* have a right-hand man," he said. "And they *are* normally of slightly inferior intelligence. And blundering. Max is the obvious choice!"

"He also happens to be your best friend, and I expect he'd like to see his sister again. It's agreed, then. Today you're skipping school."

George's knock-knees clunked together. Quests were all well and good, but skipping school was not something you did. Even the worst members of the Tombland Gang, though they might be tardy, never dared to truant.

"Do you know how much trouble I'd be in if I skipped school? Not just there, but at home?"

Seveny looked at his desk. "George, it must be four in the morning and you are still doing homework."

She pointed at his bedroom floor. Underneath it, George's parents were still screaming at each other.

"And if you can put up with *that* and still get As, you can do anything!"

He blushed. "Well... I suppose I could give it a go."

Seveny kissed him on the forehead.

"Wait!" George looked hopeful. "Will you be travelling with us?"

"I wish I could. But according to Tommy, I still have some training to do."

Seveny rolled her eyes, then made the change and flew away.

George watched the two birds fly off before picking up the blanket Seveny had dropped as she'd changed.

"Wow," he said.

He paused for a few moments in quiet contemplation. And then, in his methodical way, George started packing for his Quest.

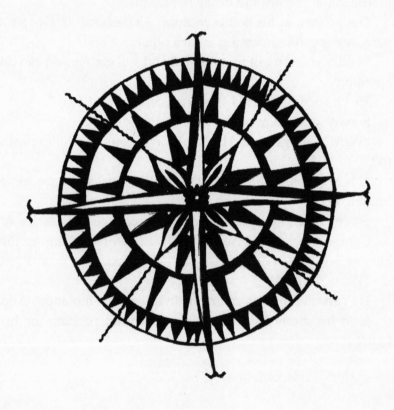

Chapter Nineteen

Journey into the Unknown

Jamie spent the rest of the night trudging through the tunnel. Whatever its destination, it certainly wasn't a direct route to the surface. At last the floor sloped up, and three hours later Jamie stepped out of a hollow oak.

It was dawn. The sky in the east was a pale pink, and a tired-looking sun rose by Mount Venusius, illuminating a scorched and barren landscape. Jamie was surrounded by a flat desert of sand, blasted white by time and the elements. Somewhere in the distance she could hear the cry of crows. She sat down on a rock by the oak and gazed at the ocean sparkling on the southern horizon.

Miss Mackadoo was dead. The Brainticklers had cast her out. And she had to find someone called Creaky Nan. But she hadn't the slightest notion how.

She could tell from the sun's position that she'd surfaced somewhere in the Uninhabited West. But she recognized neither the miles of flat, white sand surrounding her, nor the jagged rocks to the north, nor the...

Hollowed-out oak she'd stepped from...

The trip through the puddle!

Jamie couldn't believe what she was seeing. The journey was right in front of her. *If I head north*, she thought, *past those jagged rocks, there should be a village, then reeds and a marsh, and after that a white farmhouse, and then, perhaps I'll find Creaky Nan.*

Not understanding how, but knowing she'd been shown the

way, Jamie set off through the hot white sand.

The huge bell of Pity Me's concrete clock tower rang out, proclaiming the official beginning of a new day. The pain in George's jaw seemed to ring in answer.

He looked into the small mirror above his desk and inspected the damage. A kaleidoscope of colour swirled from chin to ear. But in spite of the bruise he couldn't stop grinning. A real-life Goddess had put her Mark upon him and sent him on a Quest!

"You've missed a bit!" George's father shouted from the next room.

Given that his mother was in the kitchen and his father was in bed, George found this judgement wildly unfair. But as he listened to his mother's wilful scrubbing and his father's piggish yawns, his eyes twinkled. Things might be the same for his parents today, but *he* was skipping school!

George dashed downstairs, scooted through the kitchen past his mother, dunk-washed himself, and was out the door half an hour early, his compass in his pocket and his school bag on his back—though it wasn't filled with schoolbooks.

"George!" his mum called from the kitchen. "You've forgotten your tie!"

He reluctantly returned to his mother, who surprised him by pressing him to her bosom.

"What did he do to you?"

George saw where her confusion lay. He'd gone to bed fine, yet woken up with this bruise. George wasn't his father's preferred target, but every now and then…

"Nothing, Mum." George prised her off and pointed to his jaw. "This is a gift from a Goddess. Now, if you'll excuse me—"

And before she could stop him, George flew past her and ran down the street.

"Your tie, George! Your tie!" his mum shouted, waving desperately from the doorstep. "Oh my Goddess, and your breakfast! You'll never get through to lunch!"

George slowed. He couldn't very well have packed a lunch, given that he had school dinners. And who knew how long it would take to reach Little Breedy? His tummy did funny things when it wasn't being fed. But one had to endure such hardships when one was on a Quest.

"I'll be fine. Just fine!" he said, before running away.

George's mum was all out of kilter. Her boy was bruised but laughing. Since the day Seveny Tombstoned and Jamie disappeared he hadn't even smiled.

"Thank you, Goddess, for giving my boy a rainbow," she said, looking up at the sky. "It needn't have been on his face," she muttered. "But I give thanks, nonetheless."

"Shut that bloody door!" her husband bellowed from inside.

The Lively household was a ten minute walk in the wrong direction for school. Max's dad answered the door.

"Good morning!" said George. "I wondered if Max and I might walk to school together?"

Max's dad frowned. "He left ten minutes ago, same time he always leaves, to go to your house, as he always does, so you can walk to school together, like you always do. Isn't he with you?" Reality dawned. "He isn't with you."

George shook his head.

"Do you *ever* travel to school together?"

"Not exactly. I often have an extra morning class, and Max is well, um..."

"Often late?"

George nodded, embarrassed. He hadn't meant to snitch on his best friend. Snitching was for the likes of Senior Perfect Herbert Snodgrass.

Max's father sighed. "I've a feeling I know where my boy is. Check for him at the Library. When he's at home he talks of nothing else. Actually, I'd appreciate it if you *did* check. I know you call him Nine Lives, and now I understand why, but—" his shoulders slumped. "I just don't want my son to get in trouble with the Establishment. Lives run out."

"Right!" said George. "The Library. I'll try him there."

George was perplexed. Why had Max been using him as an alibi every morning for what sounded like yonks? What was he up to?

With no other leads, he headed for the Library.

"Woh-wa-woh *wooooooooooohhhhhhhh!*"

Max toppled down the front steps of No Place's bleak, slate-covered Library. He hit the bottom with a thud. Something landed on top of him.

"Oh, um, sorry!" said George, climbing off and helping Max to his feet. "I needed you to stop and I didn't want to attract too much attention."

This was skewed logic, thought Max, especially for a thinker. "Nice tackle, but a simple holler would have done!" he said, brushing himself off.

"Quick!" said George. "We have to hide."

"From what?"

A round head, balanced on a tall, thin neck popped out from behind the Library.

"Snodgrass," George whispered, dragging Max away.

"Why? We haven't done anything. And if we keep this pace up, we won't be late for school."

George looked around. Confident no one was following, he walked Max back in the direction they'd come. "That's not where we're going!"

Max boggled as George marched him back past the Library. "You? Bunking off?! And what the hell happened to your face?"

"Seveny."

"Wha—? Right," said Max. "Talk."

As they walked, George described last night's visitation.

"Are you telling me Seveny's turned into a bird and Jamie isn't dead?" said Max.

"There's much more to it than that. But essentially, yes."

A look of disbelief was etched in Max's face. "And Seveny's sent us on a Quest? For what?"

This was the moment George had been dreading. "She's sent us to find Maria. Your sister lives in a secret village called Little Breedy hidden inside Strip Limpets Wood."

For a few moments Max couldn't speak. Then he nodded. "Right," he said. "We'd better get going."

Around an hour later they were in open fields and heading north, far away from Pity Me. Max still couldn't get his mind round George's story.

"So Jamie's Underground?"

"Yes."

"And Seveny's a bird?"

"She calls herself a Halfhawk Mortal. But yes, she can turn into a bird."

George could see that Max didn't believe him. Nonetheless, he was certainly eager to accompany him to Little Breedy.

Max's spine suddenly stiffened. "There's someone behind us!"

George had to agree. He could hear footsteps.

Max risked a look back. "Guess who?"

"Not Herbert Snodgrass!"

"Yes, Herbert Snodgrass."

George panicked. Though Snodgrass looked like an ant he could sting like a scorpion. "Well then, we're for it! If he finds us this far out of Pity Me and sees us heading for Contraland... What do we tell him?"

Max shrugged.

The two boys stopped to face the snitch. But though Snodgrass glanced in their direction, they couldn't get his attention. The Senior Perfect looked quite panicked himself. He was foraging around in the shrubbery looking for something.

"Well, let's not wait for him," said Max. "Let's get out of here while we still can!"

So Max and George went on their way. But even after they'd left Snodgrass far behind, they were still haunted by imaginary footsteps.

In another hour, they reached the stile that separated fenced-in No Place from the southernmost tip of the Great Forest, the start of Contraland proper.

Leaving No Place for Contraland was as simple as hopping the stile. But no one ever did—at least, no one who ever wanted to come back. Not with the punishments the Establishment gave deserters.

Now that they'd actually reached the border, George felt less adventurous. Knowing one had a Quest was all very well; setting foot on its path was quite a different matter. Especially when it went straight through Contraland. But if Max had second thoughts, he didn't show them. He put his foot on the stile, hopped it with ease, and set off into the Great Forest.

He got twenty yards before he realized that George wasn't following.

"Hurry up!" he said. "What are you waiting for?"

"Oh, I'm not sure... I mean, now that Snodgrass has seen us, we'd be foolish to—"

"What? Find my sister? Didn't you just say how even being *headed* for Contraland would get us in trouble? We might as well enter it!"

"I don't think it's sensible."

Max strode back towards George, jumped over the stile, and grabbed him by the collar.

"Listen to yourself!" he said. "You talk about things being sensible? You think Seveny's a bird! I hadn't planned on leaving today, but I was going into Contraland anyway. And I'll be fine by myself. I stole a map from the Library!"

Max unearthed a flimsy sheet of paper from his pocket and pointed out a spot in the upper middle of the Island which he'd circled.

"There! Strip Limpets! You see? I don't care if there are mutants there. I've had enough of No Place. All our friends are either dead or disappeared, and if you're not coming with me then I've had enough of you, too!"

Max was about to jump back over the stile when something small and fast leapfrogged over him and ran madly towards the tree-line of the Great Forest.

"Kai? *KAI!*" George and Max shouted, as the small boy entered the dark woods.

Max looked at George. "Well?"

George sighed. "I'm with you."

Seveny sat on the hut's little bed and glared at the door. If it could, it would probably have glared right back. At this point it was hardly a door at all, though yesterday, after two weeks of trying, she'd finally Mindmoved it back and forth without blowing it off its hinges. But this wasn't enough for Tommy. He'd woken her just two hours after they'd got back from George's house in order to continue her training.

Now the sun had reached its height, and she'd mastered the push-pull technique and could repeat it at will. But she was tired.

"Right!" said Tommy. "Now let's try something harder. It's easy to move a big target—" Seveny could have hit him "—but let's see how you do with the latch."

"Really?" said Seveny. "You *really* want me to fiddle with a latch when we could be helping our friends find Askerwell?"

"The boys will be fine. They've a compass and George's brain. *You* must learn to control your power. Mindmoving without intention has the potential to kill."

Seveny flicked her hair and got off the bed. Standing opposite the door, she stared at the metal latch and extruded a line of force. She grabbed the latch easily, and willed it to lift.

It did.

Unfortunately, the latch lifted so sharply that it broke free of the door and hit the roof with a clunk. The latch wedged itself into the wooden ceiling, stayed there for a second, then hurtled back to earth.

"Your thoughts are with your friends, aren't they?" said Tommy.

Seveny nodded.

"You miss them?"

"Yes. Just as I missed you when you were gone. My friends are my family."

Tommy gazed at Seveny.

Her eyes dropped to the floor. "Do you know why I was abandoned? Do you know who didn't want me?"

Mr Gribbin the warden had found her in cubicle seven of the Orphanage's toilets when she was just a baby.

"I don't," said Tommy. "You could ask the Farseers to give you an inSight. Have they introduced themselves to you yet?"

"No."

"Oh. Then you're probably not quite ready."

Seveny crossed her arms. "For what?"

"To say goodbye to your old life."

Seveny flipped. "You know *nothing* about me! Two years is a long time to go missing, don't you think? Since you left Pity Me, both you and I have changed." As if to prove her point, she shifted shape. Her golden eagle sea-hawk looked particularly fierce.

Tommy stared at her. "You're right. But I think our friendship has stayed the same. If anything, it's stronger."

Seveny's bird-face softened.

"Listen," he said. "How about sacking off the training today and going for a nice relaxing fly? We could even look in on how the boys are getting o—"

Seveny was out the window and heading west before Tommy had finished his sentence. Shape-shifting at once, he flew after her as fast as his wings could carry him.

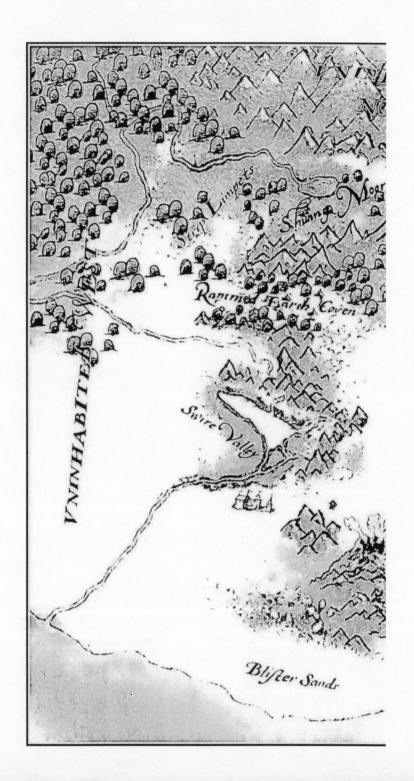

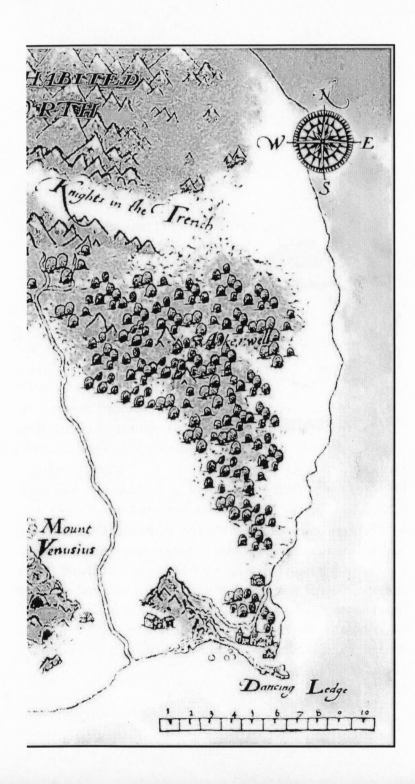

Chapter Twenty

Askerwell

It didn't take long for the boys to catch up with Kai. He'd waited for them behind a tree.

The boys asked him all sorts of questions. "Why are you here?" "Were you following us?" "How did you escape Funnella Fitzgerald?" "What was it like living with her?" But Kai wouldn't answer. He hadn't spoken a word since he'd gone to live with Funnella Fitzgerald, and even now he was out of her clutches he wouldn't talk. So, in near silence, the three of them headed for Askerwell. George had the compass, and Max held the map.

The trees of the Great Forest were dense and thorny, but Kai had an eye for seeing how best to pass through them. Without a peep he'd show them where the branches got sparse. Every so often, George would stop to examine the soil, and comment on some startling species of hairy snail, velvet grass, or noxious weed. Mostly the wildlife indicated they were going in the right direction, but sometimes, in spite of the map, it showed they'd veered off course.

It was a long four hours to Askerwell.

The ancient well was so abandoned and overgrown with

vines that the boys almost missed it. They tore the vines back and trampled them with their sandals until they had space to stand.

Max folded the aged map and put it in his pocket. The boys stared into Askerwell's depths.

"So what do we ask it?" Max said.

"Nothing?" said George, hopefully.

Nobody knew how old Askerwell was, but a legend about it dated from just after the Great Storm:

Once upon a time, a boy was born who was ailing and feeble. His parents went to every medicine man and woman on the Island, but each time the answer was the same: the boy was sick, they didn't know why, and there was nothing they could do.

Seven years passed and their babe, now a manshu, was still frail. At last, the couple turned to Nature in search of an answer. The mountains rang with their sobs, the wind matched their wails, and the sun reddened with their anger, but their little boy grew ever more weak.

One day the father found himself in a wood filled with vines. He hacked them back with his axe, and discovered an ancient well.

The woodsman loosened his purse, poured all his hard-earned coins down the well and sang:

"Askerwell, Askerwell, answer I pray,
For I've given you all that I've earned today.
Askerwell, Askerwell, hear my plea,
What future awaits my family?"

At once the well flooded over, and his coins floated back to the surface. They formed graves in the water: a small one in front, and then two larger ones behind. Askerwell was showing him that he, his wife and his son were all going to die.

"But when? Tonight?" the father asked—and the coins formed a crescent moon in answer to the man. Then the water fell back down the well, and took his money with it.

The woodsman ran home, and he and his wife organized a send-off, welcoming in their neighbours to say their goodbyes. And then, as the well predicted, early in the morning their son died.

The whisperings began.

"How did they know when he'd die?"

"Poison!"

The tale swept the Island. The couple protested their innocence in vain.

"But it told us the future! The well! Askerwell!"

George sang the rest of the rhyme under his breath.

> "'Then drown yourselves in it!' the neighbours jeered,
> They did, and the Islanders crowed and cheered.
> So never dare go, child, to seek Askerwell,
> Or the Spectre will carry you straight down to Hell!"

Max rolled his eyes at the manshu rhyme and looked into the well. "All right, Askerwell. How do I find my sister?"

Nothing happened.

"What a shame!" said George. "Nothing to see!" He trampled back through the vines and had got right out of the clearing before he stopped and had a word with himself.

Call yourself a detective? Where are your nerves of steel? Why aren't you trying to make that well talk?

George rootled around in his shorts for loose change and stomped back to Askerwell. Before Max could stop him, George had dived into his pocket, grabbed his savings and tossed them into the well along with his own.

Askerwell looked troubled as the glinting coins pierced its water. But it didn't speak.

"What did you do that for?" yelled Max. "Do you know how many Sweet Treats that could have bought? And for what? I'm no closer to finding my sister! All these years of looking for her—of being sent Down The Line. All my beatings!"

Max started to cry.

George gaped—he'd never seen Max shed a tear. Kai's eyes had also become saucers. But he wasn't looking at Max.

Water was running down Askerwell's ancient walls.

The astonished boys peered in. The flooding well soaked them right through, but they didn't care. They couldn't believe what they were seeing. Swirling in strange patterns on top of the geyser were their coins!

The coins stopped dancing and formed an image. A hawk.

"My sister's in a hawk?" Max said. "My sister *is* a hawk? Like Seveny? Are we *all* going to turn into hawks?"

The image disappeared and the coins swirled again in hypnotic waves and spirals. George wondered if that meant they could ask the well a further question. One sprang to mind, though his voice quavered as he asked it.

"Will we find our missing friends?"

The coins formed a horizontal line, then pirouetted this way and that.

"They're dancing," said George. "Dancing... Dancing Ledge! We'll find our friends on Dancing Ledge!"

Kai peered into Askerwell's waters. "What's going to happen to them?"

George and Max were gobsmacked. Kai hadn't spoken for weeks.

The coins formed a face. It had a twirly moustache.

George gasped. "The Doctor!"

The moustache became a coiled serpent. It started to writhe.

"The Doctor's a snake?" Max asked the well.

But Askerwell decided they'd had their money's worth. The fountain of water fell back into the depths as quickly as it had risen, taking the coins with it. There was a distant splash.

The boys were quiet for quite some time.

Finally, Max spoke.

"Well, that was disturbing. But given we've no idea what to make of it, can we get back to finding my sister?"

"Let's see the map, then," said George.

Max delved into his pocket and retrieved it. But as he tried to open the map, it dropped in a soggy lump to the ground. The overflowing water had soaked it right through. Max hurriedly picked up the soaked paper—which led to its complete destruction.

"Now what?" he said miserably, wiping yellow pulp off his hands.

"We still have the compass." But as George said these words, he realized how little they'd used it and how much they'd relied on the map. "Oh, I don't know."

"I thought you knew everything," said Max, his voice full of spite.

"Might I just remind you that *you* were holding the map? My compass is still intact!"

Max didn't bother to reply. He wrestled George to the ground.

Crunch.

The boys stopped fighting and looked down at George's shorts. George excavated his pocket.

What had been a compass was now splintered wood and glass.

Kai began to cry.

"I'm so stupid!" Max shouted. "My one chance to find Maria and I've ruined it!"

"Look," said George, "maybe we don't need the map. Little Breedy is in Strip Limpets Wood, we know that. And Strip

Limpets is near Shwing Moor. That's on the other side of Knights in the Trench Valley, which will be directly ahead of us once we clear the forest. In the meantime, I can keep us on track by checking soil and plants!"

"Well," said Max, "there's no point in staying here."

They were about to leave Askerwell when they spotted something hovering above them. A golden hawk. It cocked its wings, dived straight for them, then flew off in the opposite direction from the one they were about to take.

"That's Seveny!" said George.

Kai stopped crying and waved at the hawk.

The hawk circled back, now accompanied by a less handsome but bigger-built friend. Now both birds dived for the boys. The force of their wings almost knocked them over.

"And that grey bird's Tommy!" said George. "Let's follow them!"

Max shook his head. He wasn't about to let two birds get them lost in the Great Forest.

"Askerwell showed us a hawk," said George. "That's how we'll find your sister, remember? And either we follow these birds, or I spend hours on all fours examining topsoil."

"That is pretty persuasive," Max admitted.

The eagles dived again. And this time, the boys were ready for them.

Chapter Twenty-one

Village of the Sick and Itchy

The sad-looking signpost was nailed to a sun-bleached stake. Burnt into the wood were the words 'Blister Sands.' They were painfully apt: Jamie's feet were scorched after hours of walking through the desert, even through her leather sandals.

Minutes later, the sand was replaced with smooth yellow pebbles and dark jagged rocks. Jamie had to use every ounce of focus not to slip or twist her ankles. She'd been walking for several hours when the land finally smoothed.

Cracked earth stretched in front of her as far as the eye could see. It was wonderfully flat and firm. She found a comfortable patch and sat down for a break.

The trek had taken its toll. Her mouth was dry as toast and her bandaged knee stung terribly. She loosened the top of her dressing and looked in.

Grains of sand had snuck inside the open cut, and as she'd struggled over the terrain they'd danced around. And without the Ticklers' constant applications of fresh spider-silk, the bandage was soaked through with blood.

Feeling increasingly woozy, she stared up at the sun. It was late afternoon. She couldn't remember when she'd last had anything to drink or eat. It was before she'd Dreamweaved into the Doctor. Before Miss Mackadoo had told her she must find Creaky Nan.

I must reach the farmhouse!

Jamie got up and ran.

Her pace meant she had no way of preparing for the harsh descent when it came. She tumbled down the earthy slope and just managed to stop short of colliding with a barbed wire fence. When she got up, she almost fell down again with surprise. Past the fence were cobbled stone paths, and houses far larger than those permitted to the inhabitants of Pity Me. It was the village of her dreams.

In her sleep, she'd entered the abandoned village with ease. In reality it would be more difficult. The fence was too tall, and the gaps in the wire too small for her to climb through. She looked up and down its length and spotted a darker section. She walked over to it and found a rusting metal door. Years ago, someone had splashed red paint across it, spelling the words:

VILLAGE OF THE SICK AND ITCHY
→ CONTRALAND!
DO NOT ENTER
DANGER OF DEATH

Her history lessons came flooding back. Two centuries ago, a few hundred people left No Place and built this village beyond the Western Mountains. It was somewhere they could live freely, far from the Establishment's reach, and worship the Goddess as they wished.

Except just after they finished building it, the village was taken sick with a fevered pox. Every last settler died, a punishment inflicted by the Great Goddess for building pridefully and on unhallowed land.

She'd never really believed the tale, but here the village was, just as Phosphor-Jones had said: the cordoned off land, the empty brick houses...

Looking at the dreadful sign, Jamie thought about circling round the village. But what were the risks of straying from the path she'd been shown?

She pushed against the rusting door. It didn't budge, so she threw her whole weight against it. The locks stayed put, but the door's corroded hinges gave way, and she tumbled into the village.

Jamie's delight at getting in was short-lived. Now her knee was not just stinging—it was starting to itch. *If I run*, she thought, *perhaps the itching sickness won't catch me!* She pounded over the cobbles and passed a triangular-roofed building which had once, perhaps, been a village hall or school.

The field behind the building was a sallow green and in the middle of it was a giant mound of earth covered with brilliant red poppies. Something about the mound made Jamie feel very uneasy. She kept running.

One of the village's larger houses had a big cross nailed to the door. Underneath, an empty crib rocked in the breeze.

Then Jamie clocked something in the distance. She raced towards it like a blinkered horse.

The large well's triangular roof was rusted yet elegant and its belly was full of promise. Jamie peered thirstily in. The water was covered in snotty bubbles that smelt of rotten eggs. A gap in the scum revealed a glutinous brown fluid out of which popped a tiny, bloated sparrow's head.

Jamie turned away in revulsion—only to find that the village had vanished! Out of nowhere a dense white mist had descended, leaving her no clue which way to go. Confused and defeated, she sank to her knees.

"I'm in the middle of a dead village, and I am going to die here, alone!"

"No you're not," said a young voice from out of the mist.

"You're not," agreed a kind, wise voice. "We'll help you on your way."

She could just make out the outline of a small boy walking through the mist, holding a man's hand. As they neared, she realized it was not the mist that made them hard to see. Father and child looked as gentle as the wispiest cloud—and were just as transparent.

Other shapes in the mist also resolved into figures, until a sea of see-through people, all oddly dressed, bustled around the well.

"I'm dying, aren't I?" said Jamie. "You're ghosts. And you're taking me with you."

The little boy giggled. "You've got one thing right!"

His father nodded. "We are dead."

Jamie hauled herself up. Terrified as she was, these spirits did not seem malevolent. If anything, she felt sorry for them. Now that they were close, she could see that the father's neck and joints were unnaturally bloated, and his son was covered in large red spots.

Jamie looked at the surrounding crowd. One woman's neck was so swollen that her whole spine was bent out of shape. Another young girl was consumed by a rash. They all had red-raw hands, feet and noses, and apart from the localized swellings were grotesquely thin.

"Oh Goddess!" said Jamie. "What happened to you?"

"We got the pox," said the boy.

Jamie's skin began to prickle. "I thought the Establishment were lying. Just like they did about Rhyme Intrinsica."

The father's brow furrowed. "Rhyme Intrinsica?"

"Oh, of course, that would've been long after your time. The Establishment burned it down and claimed the villagers had done it. That their dreaming had turned them mad."

"I see," the father said. He didn't sound surprised. "And what do they say about us?"

"That the Great Goddess sent you a pox as punishment for building on unconsecrated land. That the village is still dangerous to enter. That the fence round your town is there for our protection."

"We died of the pox all right," said the man. "But the Establishment gave it to us."

Jamie scratched at her sore knee. "What do you mean?"

"On land the Establishment called uninhabitable, a few hundred of us built a farm. We found that far from being useless, the land was full of promise. We could live self-sufficiently, away from the Establishment. Word spread, and people volunteered to build, farm, and teach. A doctor came to help the ill. The settlement was ready sooner than we'd dreamed.

"We'd feared the Establishment would try to stop us, but they kept quiet. A few weeks after we'd settled they asked to see what we'd done with the place. We welcomed them to our village. Our children performed a play, and then we had a fête.

"Halfway through the play, a member of the Establishment whispered in my ear. We were pioneers on this land, he said, and he didn't want to see us come to harm. Could he please check our water? I asked if it could wait, but he was quite adamant. I thought he was worried we'd given him unclean water to drink. I offered to come with him but he said he knew where the well was.

"I thought no more of it. The play was well received and the Establishment, though they remained suspicious of our food and water, enjoyed the fête. They left our village in the highest spirits. My wife was the first to fall."

The man looked at the woman beside him. She had delicate bone structure, but her eyes bulged horribly.

"A week after the Establishment's visit, Lucy got a headache so strong it felt like her brain was being crushed and her eyes squeezed to bursting. Next came the fever. She burned so hot she was painful to touch. Then large swellings broke out. Vomiting followed. Six hours later she was dead."

Jamie started to shiver.

"More and more began to fall. Our doctor was one of the first."

A man with a curly grey beard and spectacles bowed.

"Some succumbed quickly to the pox," the father continued. "Others, like Charlie, it took weeks to kill." He ruffled his son's hair.

"After Charlie died, I remembered the conversation during the play. With a few other survivors, I went to this well. It didn't look bad but I noticed a smell. I poked around with my fishing rod while the others drained it, and I speared a large, rotten rat. Such rats do not live here. It couldn't have got here without help."

"The Establishment!" said Jamie.

The father nodded. "The water was contaminated and the disease could incubate for weeks. Even before the first of us fell, we were all condemned to death."

Jamie's skin started to burn, as though she'd been rolled in nettles. But she was cold, oh so cold. Her teeth started to chatter.

"But the bug is long gone. You are not ill."

Jamie's stomach spasmed, causing her to retch. Now bent over double, she furiously scratched her bandaged knee.

"You are horrified, hurt and hungry," said the father, "but soon you'll find relief."

Jamie continued to wretch and continued to scratch—and then his words sunk in. She realized how long she'd been travelling without sustenance. Now the man had explained it, the pain in her stomach left. She ripped off the bandage and felt immediate relief. As Jamie's fever departed, *Do not make real that which is not!* hooted through her head.

And then the mist started to dissipate, taking the ghosts with it.

"Wait!" said Jamie, as the spirits sailed up towards the heavens. "Am I going the right way?"

The little boy, Charlie, looked back and smiled, before fading away. Only his father remained.

"Towards fighting the Establishment and the Doctor?" the man said. "Yes."

He too became vapour, and the last of the mist cleared, revealing a road that terminated not in barbed wire, but in a wall of green reeds.

Chapter Twenty-two

Forbidden Fruit

After leaving Askerwell, Kai had unearthed a packed lunch from his backpack, something Max and George found curious given he had free school dinners. They had salivated when he produced seaweed-seasoned crisps, squid-ink straws, red wolfberries and fresh tomatoes. But when Kai silently offered to share, the boys declined— they did not want to steal food from a mouth younger than theirs. It was a decision both of them now regretted.

Seveny and Tommy had taken them through Knights in the Trench, a dry valley full of black deathcherries and not much else, and they were ravenous by the time dusk approached and they reached Schwing Moor.

Shwing Moor floated over water. As they walked across its thick peat, the land moved with them and the moor's golden willows swayed.

"This is wicked!" said Max.

George felt seasick. Kai skipped along in a world of his own.

An hour later the land solidified. The hawks guided them to a heart-shaped clump of silvery trees with weeping branches and dark purple leaves. The tall birches seemed to hug each other.

Max whooped. "We've reached Strip Limpets!"

156

"How can you be sure?" said George.

"I've been doing my research. Have been since Maria disappeared."

The boys made their way through the embracing trees.

George cleared his throat. "What happened to your sister?"

"Almost two years ago, she disappeared in the night. She'd become Fruitful. Everyone said she'd been taken to the Dispensary. I knew that wasn't so: her boyfriend Jason went missing the same night. So I read her diary. Turned out, a couple of her friends had also become Fruitful out of Wedlock. They played by the Establishment's rules and went to the Dispensary. They didn't return."

"With child?"

"At all."

George gulped. "What made you think Maria would be in Strip Limpets Wood?"

"Her final diary entry just said 'S.L.' I figured the initials must be important. I couldn't link them to anyone she knew, so I started thinking geographically."

George was caught between being supremely impressed at Max's detective skills and being a little bit rankled.

"Weren't you worried about getting in trouble?"

"No," said Max. "Some things are more important than the Establishment. Or a Down The Line beating. Ah, see that light up ahead? That must be Little Breedy!"

Something rustled nearby. Two hawks were perched on a branch above them. They nodded at the boys and flew off into the night.

Max stared after them. "This hawk thing's weird!"

As the boys got closer to the light, the trees changed. Gone was the silver birch; now green apples hung from lush boughs above their heads.

"Hungry?" said Max.

Kai shook his head.

"Starving!" said George.

Max leapt in the air and plucked one of the shiny fruits. "I'll be your official taster!"

He'd just taken a bite when someone screamed.

"Hey! Stop! Don't eat that! Drop it! *Now!*"

A woman ran out of the trees in front of them. She was carrying a bucket full of apples.

"He didn't know the apples weren't for picking!" said George, turning white.

Max faced the screaming banshee. She had wild hair, and wore leather trousers and a midriff-exposing top. Amber stones dangled from her ears and wooden beads hung from her neck. An embroidered belt was slung round her hips.

The chunk of apple fell from Max's mouth.

The woman dropped the bucket. "Max, you great pranny! You could have been killed!"

Maria catapulted herself into her brother's arms and bathed him in kisses. After Max had been sufficiently loved, she inspected his friends.

"George! What happened to your jaw?"

"It really *was* an accident..."

Maria went in for a hug. As she looked over George's shoulder she discovered a crouching little boy.

"And your name is?"

"Kai."

Max and George stared. Maria had got more of a response out of Kai than they'd managed all day.

Maria grinned. "Good to meet you, Kai. But what are you all doing here? You've skipped school, you're in Contraland—Max, did anyone see you?"

"Yes. Funnella's right-hand Perfect, Snodgrass."

"Then I've done you a disservice." Maria looked at the chunk of apple lying on the ground. "At least *that* expiration would have been quick."

"Are all the apples round here poisonous?" said George, changing the subject.

"Nope. And these are fine as long as they're cooked properly. In fact, this one can go in the bucket for tonight's feast."

The boys' eyes lit up at the mention of food.

Maria chuckled. "This way!"

As they followed Maria through the trees they noticed a small dagger tucked into the back of her belt. Its blade was wavy like a snake and its pommel was the shape of a lion's head.

"Right, my little magpies," she said, leading them through the orchard, "you'll have to tell me what the blazes you're doing here. But first..." Maria strode into the clearing. "Welcome to Little Breedy."

Chapter Twenty-three

Creaky Nan and the Burrowers

It had taken Jamie a good half hour to batter her way through the valley's thick reeds. But she had done it.

Knee-deep in mud, swamp water, and the occasional pool of quicksand, she waded through the quaggy mire, grateful for the cool mud that soothed her reed-scratched wound. But the day was drawing to a close, the sun now hung low in the lavender sky, and she still hadn't found food or water.

Noticing an area of taller, flatter and hopefully firmer earth, Jamie squelched towards it. She stood on the platform and found it remarkably solid. But when she looked down, she saw her sandals hadn't followed.

"Oh for Goddess's sake!"

She looked into the sludge. It ate her sandals quickly and then looked innocently back.

Coming to terms with the loss of her sandals, Jamie allowed herself a moment's rest. She was pleased to discover that the marsh's mud had plugged her wound shut. Her thirst, however, gnawed. She scanned the creek.

She left dry land and waded back through the mud, heading for the fast-flowing brook running through the centre of the swamp. Its water was muddy but surprisingly fresh. She scooped some into her mouth, and then jumped in.

The river was shallow. Just under the surface she discovered a clump of water-worms and some meaty mushrooms she knew were safe. Dinner! Grabbing the food, she half-waded, half-swam back to her previous platform.

Her dip in the brook had washed the wound of mud and it was bleeding again, but she'd quenched her thirst and was excited at the prospect of food. She chewed the worms and mushrooms slowly, and was savouring their taste when everything was plunged into shadow.

Jamie looked up. The sun had been eclipsed by a strange cloud. A cloud which was coming straight for her. By the time she realized the cloud was in fact a *swarm*, it was too late to run.

A mass of insects descended into the marsh—thousands of moths with dusty pink wings. The air was so thick with them that Jamie was scared to breathe. They spiralled round her like a tornado and the vibration of their tiny wings made the swamp shudder. She fell to her knees.

The moths covered every inch of her, beating their powerful pink wings. A couple deposited something in her mouth and instinctively she swallowed.

And then, as suddenly as they'd appeared, the moths were gone.

Jamie got to her feet. There was a bitter taste in her mouth and her skin was tingling.

"Child?" creaked a voice.

Startled, Jamie looked round to see who'd spoken.

The reeds on her left parted and a long, toffee-coloured snout poked through. The horse gave Jamie a discerning stare and ambled towards her.

Straddling the horse was a thickset, squat old lady. She wore sand-coloured dungarees and a straw hat that was too small for her head. A lasso was slung over her shoulder. Her weathered skin was so thick and folded that she resembled a giant grub. A few pink moths hovered around her. They were getting in the horse's eyes.

"What's wrong, girl?" The woman's voice sounded like a creaky door.

Not knowing where to begin on the list of 'wrong,' a shaken Jamie pointed to her knee.

The shamun stared dispassionately at the wound.

Jamie looked down and gasped. Her knee was no longer bleeding. In fact, it had scabbed right over.

"Good," said the shamun. "They found you, I see."

"They?"

A long, maggoty thing poked through the fresh scab. Jamie grew dizzy, and her legs gave way.

The old woman jumped from the saddle and scooped the girl up with ease. "I'm Creaky Nan," she said. "That was a Burrower. And we're going to heal you."

Chapter Twenty-four

Little Breedy

When the boys entered Little Breedy, their senses were assaulted. The noise was loud and unexpected: Strip Limpets' close-knit trees had been protecting Little Breedy's beating heart. Singing, stamping and laughing came from houses built on stilts, with horn-shaped roofs and tree-bark walls.

As they followed Maria through the village, George realized that the widely-spaced stilt houses were built in concentric circles—and they were heading for the bullseye.

A few minutes later, his guess proved correct. The seventh ring of houses opened out onto a large circle of earth, seventy yards wide. A hollowed-out cube of rock stood in the centre and a charcoal fire blazed inside it.

"That's Fireforge," said Maria.

She ran to the smallest house in the central ring and made a peculiar yipping noise. A face appeared at the window.

"Jason!" Max yelled.

"Max!" Jason cried.

"Ha ha!" Max leapt in the air. "I knew you'd got away!"

The door opened. Jason wore a tanned leather robe which reached down to his knees. Though he looked magnificent, Max giggled.

"You're wearing a dress!"

"We do things differently here," said Jason, smiling his half-smile.

Like Maria, he was adorned with beaded necklaces and bracelets. But curled around his fingers was a particularly special accessory. A little hand.

"Mama!" shouted the girl.

"Who... is... *that?*" said Max.

Maria giggled. "Your niece, silly! Maya, meet Max."

"Ak!" Maya squeaked, throwing her little sausage body at her uncle.

"So she didn't..." said Max, wrangling the toddler, "you were able..."

"We could never come back because of the Establishment's rules," said Maria. "But we are well. And we are safe!"

Max's eyes welled.

Maya wriggled out of her uncle's arms and tottered about. She looked as if she were drunk on fermented Honeydew. The boys erupted with laughter.

Jason jumped down. "What in the blazes are they doing here?" he whispered in Maria's ear.

"Heaven knows. I'm sure Empu Salim will have them explain."

A drum roll reverberated from the large house opposite. It was covered in sea serpents and winged creatures, and painted in black, red and white.

"It's time," said Maria to the boys, "for you to meet the ones who got away."

Little Breedy's small, widely-spaced houses suggested a population of several hundred at the most. But generations of families poured down each ladder. Eventually over a thousand people were gathered in the clearing.

They all wore leather or suede in various different styles: short skirts, long tapered trousers, crop tops and fitted jackets. Those of juvenite age and older all wore daggers on their backs.

The weapons looked as individual as the people carrying them. Some were long and straight, others were short and wavy. Some were plain, some engraved, some bare, some highly decorated. Max and George looked longingly at the beautiful blades. And then they saw the food.

The villagers were laden with brightly coloured salads, skinned rabbits and seeded bread. They put their offerings around the walls of the hollowed-out cube of rock and then sat cross-legged in rings around the fire.

The last family to appear came from the painted house with the booming drum. There were four adults, two juvenites, three toddlers, and a baby. All their faces were painted with spirals and wings.

A small muscular man with plaited hair descended last, carrying a leather drum. He climbed down the ladder slowly, careful not to tread on his long robe. On his back was a raven-headed sword.

The boys were stunned. They'd no idea how long this man had been alive, but it looked like forever. He was tremendously creased. He wore leather bracelets, wooden beads and amber charms. The charms glinted in the firelight, illuminating milky patches on his dark arms. Memories of long-gone burns. The ancient man fixed the boys with a piercing glare, before the corners of his mouth met his ears in a great grin.

"Welcome to Little Breedy!" he said. "My name is Empu Salim. And you, our honoured guests, must be..."

Maria prodded Max.

"Max!"

"George. And this is—"

"Kai," the little boy said.

"Welcome to our nightly feast. But first," said the Empu, "must always come the Fire Story."

"Oh, that sounds great!" said Max.

"I'm sure it will be," said Empu Salim, "for you boys are to tell it." He laughed mercilessly.

Maria prodded Max again. "Do as Empu Salim asks."

The boys stood up.

"Transparents have been going missing!" said Max.

Empu Salim snorted. His nostrils flared on his long flat nose.

Max persisted. "It used to be that a juvenite was only Taken once every few months. But recently, more and more juvenites haven't been returning from Dancing Ledge. And rather than rotten souls being Taken—"

"For example, the Tombland Gang," said George.

"Transparent souls aren't coming back."

"For example, our friend Ella."

"And my sister Charlotte!"

The crowd looked sadly at Kai.

"So what brings you here?" said the Empu.

"I had a... visitation last night," said George.

"In your dreams?"

George couldn't bring himself to lie. "From my hawk-friend Seveny."

Max wondered at George's continued flight of fancy. But to his surprise Empu Salim didn't seem troubled in the least, and whispers of 'Halfhawk Mortal' rippled through the crowd.

"So George, what did your Halfhawk friend tell you?"

"That Max and I had to find his sister."

Empu Salim turned to Kai. "And how did you come to join us?"

Kai opened his mouth, but nothing came out for a while. "I am an orphan," he said at last. "And Funnella took—took me in, after my sister was Taken."

"Funnella Fitzgerald?"

"She's our Headmistress." George explained.

Something flitted over Empu Salim's face. "So, Kai, why are you with these boys?"

"I was being escorted to school by Snodgrass, and I ran away, and I chased George and Max, and we spoke to Askerwell, and the coins made pictures, and the Ledge was dancing, and the Doctor's moustache turned into a snake!"

Empu Salim nodded like he'd just been told that fish swim. "More children are being Taken... the Doctor... a snake... Dancing Ledge..."

He paused. "What is life like in No Place?"

"All right," said Max. "As long as you're not Overripe, sickly or an unfortunate juvenite. And it's not just the number of Takings that has grown—so have the fences. More and more areas are Contraland, and it remains that no one is allowed to get Fruitful out of Wedlock."

"And after they're Wedlocked, they're not allowed to separate," said George, staring at his feet.

Empu Salim rose. "The Establishment!" he said. "Their rules and their fences and their fears. They haven't changed a bit!"

He beat his leather drum and stamped his feet. Soon everyone, including Maria, Jason and even little Maya, was on their feet crying and raging and dancing.

"This is exactly the sort of behaviour the Establishment say is dangerous," George whispered to Max.

"Because they have everyone dancing to *their* tune. Well, I prefer dancing to this one!"

Max and Kai joined the villagers in dancing off their anger, and even George began hopping from foot to foot before the drumbeat faded.

"We have been gifted with your presence," said the Empu to the boys. "To what end, I am not sure. But you'll be in danger if you return to Pity Me. This is your home now. You are Breedies!"

The surrounding Breedies yipped in celebration and trilled their tongues on their teeth.

The Empu noticed that the boys looked peaky. "And you are hungry. Let us feast!"

Chapter Twenty-five

Silly Whim

Jamie woke to the smell of beef. As she came to her other senses, she discovered she was lying on a woven reed mat, in a small room built of peat and timber. It was night. Orange light danced through the window from a fire outside.

And then she felt them. *Things* wriggling inside her. Jamie looked at her arm in the firelight and shuddered in horror. Her skin was rippling! Hundreds of tiny worms were slowly working their way over her muscles and around her bones. She was about to cry for help, when the door creaked open.

A figure loomed in the entrance. Overripe and then some, he was tall even with his hunchback, and he leaned on a gnarly branch. His clothes were smeared with blood.

"Please don't kill me!"

The old man looked down at his apron. "Oh, what must I look like? You poor little mite! I just killed the bull you can smell cookin' outside."

Jamie believed him at once. The man seemed thoroughly gentle. "I'm Jamie Tuff." she said.

"And I'm Creaky's husband, Old Cott!" He squinted his

eyes. "Ah, the Burrowers are a-burrowin' and look to be workin' hard!"

Jamie looked down at her moving flesh."The Burrowers are disgusting. Please get them out of me!"

Old Cott approached. It looked like Creaky Nan had stolen layers of her husband's skin: whereas hers was thick and folded, his was paper-thin. His face was crooked and crinkly, and his smile nearly empty of tooth. "Now just because somethin's urgly, doesn' mean it's bad."

Jamie wasn't sure whether he meant himself, the maggots inside her, or both.

"What are they doing to me?"

"Your soul's been poisoned by the Gang's assault and the Perfects' words," said Old Cott. "The Burrowers are takin' out the poison. They are ingestin' the bad."

"So I'm being eaten?"

"And reformed. Yes."

Jamie felt like heaving. "And when they're finished... how do they leave?"

"You'll soon see."

Jamie wanted out of the room. "Where's Creaky?"

"Out front, cookin' us dinner."

Jamie sprang up and ran out of the room, out of the house, and into the night. When she glanced back, she saw that she'd come from a white farmhouse. The words 'Silly Whim' were carved into its front door.

"The house in the vision," she whispered.

"You have the Sight?" creaked a voice. Creaky Nan was stirring a clay cauldron which hung above a wood fire.

"I... suppose I do."

"As do I. As did your friend, Miss Mackadoo. Miss Mackadoo said I must ready you for battle."

"Miss Mackadoo's gone!"

"I know, deary," said Creaky, stirring her pot. "But she waited to meet you before she left. You're very special, I hear."

"If you mean I have a talent for making anyone I've ever loved disappear, then yes, I am."

The Burrowers in her wounded leg rippled ferociously and Jamie lost her footing. Old Cott caught her, righted her, and walked her to a hammock that was close, but not too close, to Creaky Nan's cauldron.

He sat down beside her. "Let it out, girl. That's the poison talkin'."

Jamie needed no further prompting. "Miss Mackadoo said I had to fight the Doctor," she began. "I have to save the Island by confronting him and the Ancient Spectre, and I have something called the Golden Light, only I don't know what it is, or when I'll have to fight, or what I'll have to do." She sniffed. "And I miss my friends, and I miss my dad, and... and..." The tears came. "I'm doomed—we all are. We're all doomed."

Apart from the crackle of the fire and her sobs, there was silence.

"Well now," said Creaky Nan. "I don't know about your sense of doom, but we might be able to help you on the other fronts."

Old Cott smiled his almost-toothless smile. "Empty brain, starvin' stomach."

Creaky Nan took a ladle from the cauldron and sipped. "Aha! The Slumgullion's ready!"

She gave Jamie a large helping of the bull-and-potato stew. After a fortnight of insects and mulled vine, Jamie finished the bowl in under a minute. She went back for seconds. Back in the hammock, she savoured the second bowl as she took in Silly Whim.

Silly Whim Farm was much bigger in real life than in Nesbitt's puddle or her dreams. It had two stables, both full of horses. The toffee horse was looking over a fence, giving her that same knowing look. Hens were in coops, pug-nosed pigs in pens, and in the distance, cows mooed.

The farmhouse itself was larger than the room she'd awoken in suggested, and was white with black window frames and a crumbling chimney. A shack leaned unsteadily against one of its walls. From the smell of blood wafting out of it, Jamie figured that was where Old Cott did his butchering.

A thought struck her. "Did you two live in Rhyme Intrinsica with Miss Mackadoo?"

Old Cott and Creaky Nan looked uneasily at each other.

"Yes, dear," said Creaky at last.

Jamie smiled. "So you survived too. And the Doctor doesn't know you're here, that's why you were never taken Underground. So in a way, you two and Miss Mackadoo, and my mum and me, all escaped the Dispensary!"

"That's right, pet!" said Creaky.

But Old Cott had lost both his smile and his appetite. He put down his stew and limped back to the farmhouse.

After supper, Creaky Nan put Jamie straight to bed. She quickly fell into a deep sleep and didn't stir when Old Cott entered the room. As the old man looked at the sleeping juvenite, a tear rolled down his crumpled cheek.

For in more than one way, Jamie had been taken in.

Chapter Twenty-six

And what of Tommy?

Two weeks later, Pity Me School was officially out for summer and preparations for tomorrow's Summer Sacrifice were in full swing. The Summer Sacrifice was one of four festivals the No Placers celebrated, the others being the Autumn Harvest, the Winter Wailing and the Spring Fury. Each festival welcomed in a new season, but the Summer Sacrifice was everyone's favourite. Not  that it was much of a contest: the Summer Sacrifice was the only festival that actually involved any kind of celebrating. Everyone looked forward to it, even No Place's hardest-working labourers, who were now out in the school field building a giant bonfire, laying out fireworks, and erecting stalls.

But celebrating was the last thing on Miss Humfreeze's mind. Though the students had broken up yesterday, she'd had to work an extra day. A teacher training day. Her Sunday had mainly consisted of walking in circles. Deputy Phosphor-Jones had been given the job of directing the training, under Funnella Fitzgerald's watch. The Deputy Head and the Head of English weren't exactly friends, and he'd singled out Miss Humfreeze for special attention. He'd made her do so many solo circles of the Grand Hall in her (very heavy) cape, barking all the while for more grace and solemnity, that she'd ended up feeling like an obese crow with balance issues. Caped circling over, she'd then had a lecture on sticking to the syllabus, being too fair with her marking, and not reporting students with an "excess of imagination" back to the Establishment. Wanting to shove the Deputy's crook down his own throat, Miss Humfreeze took the first opportunity she could to skulk back to her classroom and "reflect on the improvements she should make." By now she'd done her time and all the other teachers had left. But Miss Humfreeze was still pacing her classroom.

Five of her tutor group had disappeared in the last month. Five! Two were accounted for: Seveny had Tombstoned and Ella had been Taken. But Max, George and little Kai had been missing for two weeks, lost somewhere in Contraland if Snodgrass was to be believed. And the earth seemed to have swallowed Jamie.

She'd spent the last fortnight counselling distraught parents. Max's were near-hysterical, having now lost two children mysteriously, the Buttons blamed each other for losing George, and Moonshine had become Violet Last's best friend. Since the day Jamie disappeared, Geoffrey Tuff had been a human fountain. He was convinced that his daughter's position on *G and D* had landed her Underground.

To add insult to injury, Funnella had banned any search for the boys. She'd said that if they didn't make it back from Contraland, it would serve as an example to everyone about respecting Establishment boundaries.

Something had to be done. Unfortunately, Miss Humfreeze hadn't the slightest idea what.

"The Dispensary..."

The English teacher spun round. Funnella Fitzgerald was leaning against the door frame.

"...is a wonderful place!" The Headmistress stroked her poreless face. "Have you thought about making an appointment? You could do with it."

Miss Humfreeze didn't know how to react, though the Establishment's tight faces started to make sense.

"You know I'm not allowed down there. In any case, I have bigger concerns than whatever the Doctor does to you in private."

"Such as?"

"My ever-decreasing form group!"

"Oh, yes. You know the Establishment are watching you?"

"Watching *me*?" said Miss Humfreeze. "*You* Called Ella, you punished Seveny, you bullied Jamie, and as for not organizing a search party for Max, George, and Kai—the thought of those boys lost in the Great Forest!"

Funnella laughed. "Pot, kettle, black, my dear! Ever gone searching for Tommy Crackpot among his people? He'll be out of the Dispensary by now, surely. Have you checked on him like you promised? Or for that matter, what about your own children? The ones you abandoned so we wouldn't kick you out? Ever even thought of visiting them?"

"I can't," said Miss Humfreeze. "You know I can't."

"And what of Tommy?"

Miss Humfreeze's face crumbled.

"So there you have it," said Funnella. "You pretend to care, while doing absolutely nothing. But please don't let me interrupt."

Funnella Fitzgerald turned on her heels and clicked her way down the corridor.

"I don't pretend to care, I *do* care!" Miss Humfreeze yelled after her. "And I *shall* visit the Crackpots!"

Something fluttered through the hut's empty window and tapped Seveny on the head with its wing.

"What time do you call this?" she groaned through her pillow.

By the time she'd sat up, Tommy was back in human form and in his dressing-gown.

"Mid-afternoon," he said. "Time to continue your training. Are you ready?"

Seveny's brain was still bruised from yesterday's Mindmoving exercise, and her muscles ached from the night-flight practise Tommy had insisted on.

"Do we have to?"

"Yes. Mindmoving has the potential to save yourself and others. And getting it wrong—"

"—has the potential to kill. I know!"

Seveny couldn't really grumble (though she'd spent the last fortnight doing just that), for someday soon, though the Farseers hadn't told them when, the Doctor would complete his bargain with the Ancient Spectre. If Jamie was to fight the Doctor at Dancing Ledge, Seveny wanted to be fully prepared to help her.

Seveny jumped out of bed, washed herself in the cold stream, ate some fried fish, drank some green tea, and stretched in preparation.

"Today," said Tommy, "I don't want you just to Mindmove the latch and push the door open. That's too easy for you now. Today, I want you to do it from outside the hut."

"So I can't see the latch? That's impossible!"

"Impossible, eh?"

Tommy marched out of the hut and closed the door. Seveny watched him curiously through the window. He walked ten feet, stopped, and stared at the door.

The latch lifted smartly and the door opened.

Seveny felt a mixture of emotions. Part of her found his talents exciting, but she was annoyed at how easily he'd lifted the latch. And she didn't want to be beaten.

"Fine!" she said. "I'll do it!"

They swapped places. He shut the door and latched it, and she walked ten paces.

"All right. Here goes…"

"Hang on!"

Tommy changed into hawk-form and flew through the window to join her.

"Wouldn't want to be behind that door while you're fooling around with it," he hawkthought by way of explanation.

Seveny glared at him.

Tommy changed back to being human. "When you're ready, then."

Seveny stared at the door and extruded an invisible line of force between her eyes. She focused the tip until it was needle-thin and projected it forward. When it touched the door, it connected with, then reached *through* the wood.

Her brain throbbed.

"Good," said Tommy. "Now find the latch."

She searched around with the tip of the line until it brushed against something that felt like the latch, and she caught on. Her aim was good: the latch joggled. But it didn't lift.

She stamped her foot. The force snapped back with a *plink*, stinging her brain like a rubber band. She clenched her fists and tried again.

Bit by bit, the latch began to lift. In a couple of seconds it was clear of the catch. She pulled the line back, and the door smoothly opened.

"Damn I'm good!" Seveny clapped her hands and did a twirl.

"Yes, you're fully fledged!" said Tommy. "Now you have an enormous head!"

She went to slap him—but was stopped by a dark object hurtling out of the sky and landing on her feet.

It looked nothing like Tommy's grey falcon or her own brown and golden eagle-hawk. This bird of prey was pitch black except for a thin white line at the tip of its tail. It hopped off Seveny's toes, and its head became human.

He was about ten. His long silver hair hung in a ponytail, and he looked up at Seveny with glacial eyes.

"Who are you?" she said. He didn't look like a Crackpot, but he was Pity Me School age and she'd never seen him at school.

"Sebastian." The boy's voice was sweet as a flute.

"Sorry, Seb, I haven't got round to telling Seveny about the rest of us," said Tommy.

"The rest of who?"

"You didn't think we were the only Halfhawk Mortals, did you?"

"Well I—" Seveny paused. "Actually, I don't know what the hell to think, because you teach me lots and tell me nothing!"

"Right. Yes. Sorry. Halfhawk Mortals all have their own territories. And the Island is much bigger than the Establishment say."

"How much bigger?"

"Ten times bigger. Sebastian comes from a large country just past the so-called Uninhabited North."

"And you're a Halfhawk Mortal already? You're so much younger than us."

"Whereas some Halfhawks never discover their Gift, Sebastian discovered his Gift early."

"I was eight when it happened," said the boy.

An image from the boy's past flashed into Seveny's brain and it made her seethe. "Bullying drove you over the edge."

Sebastian nodded. "I'm much happier as a Halfhawk Mortal. Now I have a family."

"Yes, we haven't had a Halfhawk party in ages!" said Tommy. "But I take it that's not why you're here."

"No. The Farseers sent you a message and you haven't picked it up."

"We've been doing a lot of Mindmoving," said Tommy.

"Ah!" Sebastian looked at Seveny kindly. "It is the hardest skill to learn."

"And she's nailed it!" Tommy said quickly.

"What does Mindmoving have to do with anything?" Seveny asked.

"Mindmoving tends to drown out any Farseer transmissions in the area because of the power it requires," said Tommy. "That's why we missed the message."

Seveny raised an eyebrow. "How useful."

"They asked me to pass the message on as I was closest to you—"

"—and Seb's the swiftest flyer," said Tommy.

Sebastian smiled. "So here it is. Your Doctor has arranged another meeting with the Ancient Spectre, whatever that is. They're due to meet at sunset on Dancing Ledge."

"And the Farseers want me and Seveny to attend?"

"Yes."

"Well then, Seveny, it's time for your first Watch."

Seveny flushed with excitement. "Are you coming with us, Sebastian?"

"I can't. Our country has its own problems, even greater than yours. The Farseers have a lot to deal with at the moment."

"I wondered why they were being so elusive," said Tommy. "They've not even spoken to Seveny."

Seveny bridled.

"Don't worry," said Sebastian, "it means they're not worried about your progress. I'd better go."

The manshu's face disappeared inside his bird neck and an eagle's head replaced it. He was up in the sky as quick as a bullet.

"His country has problems *greater* than ours?" said Seveny in disbelief.

"Sebastian's prone to exaggerate, but you'd be surprised. The Island is much larger than you think."

"You're not going to tell me any more, are you?"

"Now's not the time. We have to leave at once if we're to reach Dancing Ledge by sunset."

Chapter Twenty-seven

Bog butter

The boys' heads poked out of Maria and Jason's living-room window. The object of their gaze was Empu Salim, along with whatever he was blacksmithing at Fireforge. The Empu had been hammering away at the forge between noon and sunset for two weeks now.

It had only been a fortnight and the boys already felt like Breedies. Maria and Jason had turned their living-room into a bedroom for them, and the villagers had provided them with mole fur cushions and blankets galore.

Max and George had settled in nicely and, since entering Little Breedy, Kai had re-found his voice. In fact, he'd become quite the orator. The only thing he wouldn't talk about was Funnella Fitzgerald.

Jason had shown them how to fish, and Maria had crafted them bows and arrows, made them hunting leathers, and taught them to hunt. "Phase out extraneous noise. And scan your field," she had drilled into their brains.

George was a good hunter in theory but rarely in practice. He could see exactly how to use a bow and what trajectory to arc the arrow, but he couldn't actually do it. Max was a good shot and had bucket-loads of confidence, but he was far too loud. Kai, on the other hand, was as quiet as a mouse from years of creeping past Mr Gribbin. And though he wasn't allowed a weapon, he had a keen eye for prey.

Two weeks later, Max had learned to be quiet when it was called for and was reliably bringing down game. And although George was still hopeless with a bow, another talent had revealed itself: he was an excellent trapper. Together the three boys had caught lots of small game for the village: pheasants, rabbits, even a baby deer. But yesterday, and with hardly any help, they'd taken down a wild boar. Kai spotted it, George snared it in a trap of his own design, and Max finished it off with arrows. Last night's Fire Story had been followed by a tremendous feast.

Today they hadn't needed anything for breakfast or lunch: they were still stuffed from the barbecued boar. But by late afternoon their tummies were starting to rumble.

"Bread and bog butter?" Jason called down to the boys below.

The boys dragged their eyes away from the window and Empu Salim. "Yes please!"

Jason climbed down the ladder and went into the kitchen. The room was just storage cupboards and a table, really, but it was all they needed: Fireforge did double-duty as the tribe's furnace and oven, and the cool bogs of Shwing Moor served for cellars.

Jason took some sunflower-seed bread out of a cupboard and slathered it with bog butter.

"Tea is served!"

The boys had discovered the bog butter on one of their fishing trips. It turned out that Shwing Moor had barrels of the stuff, churned by the Breedies' top cook and preserved in kegs beneath the peat. At first they'd been suspicious of the waxy substance made of goat fat and milk. Now they considered it delicious.

The boys chowed down, the noise of their chewing punctuated by the constant hammering from Fireforge. They'd just finished their snack when the hammering stopped. Jason looked out of the window.

"Kai!" Maria called from upstairs. "Maya's asking for you!"

Kai rolled his eyes, smiled, and scurried up the ladder.

Jason turned to the boys. "You must prepare yourselves."

"Prepare?" said George. "For what?"

"Empu Salim has something to discuss with you."

"What is it?" said Max.

"No questions. Clean yourselves up, get your hunting leathers on, and be at Fireforge an hour after sunset. You'll want to look your best."

The boys weren't sure whether to be excited or frightened. They gathered up their hunting leathers.

Chapter Twenty-eight

The Watch

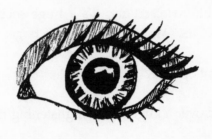

After Sebastian's swift departure, Seveny and Tommy immediately left for Pity Me.

The journey would take two hours but it was only an hour and a half until sunset. They would have to fly fast if they were to arrive at the Ledge in time for the Doctor's meeting with the Ancient Spectre—faster than Seveny had ever flown. But the night patrols and Tommy's flying lessons had paid dividends, and she proved more than capable of keeping up with her personal trainer. Wing to wing, they soared south across the Great Sea.

Seveny was buzzing with excitement. She was going on her first Watch. *This*, she thought, *was what I was born for!*

"Seveny!" Tommy hawkthought, interrupting her reverie. "You must be prepared for what we may encounter. A Halfhawk Mortal Watch can be extremely dangerous. I've heard of one Watch that went so wrong an entire squadron of Halfhawks perished."

Seveny's heart flew to her mouth. She glanced at Tommy.

"Before every Watch the Farseers give us a target," he continued. "Occasionally the target finds out they're being Watched. Often they are armed. And those the Farseers have us Watch are not afraid to kill."

"But the Doctor doesn't carry a gun like the Crackpots," Seveny hawkthought. "Or a blade like the Breedies."

"No," said Tommy. "But he's a master Dreamweaver. If he finds us spying he could possess us. And with the messages we're responsible for carrying, it's a huge security risk if he infiltrates one of us. And he has another, larger weapon in his arsenal…"

"The Ancient Spectre," said Seveny.

"Yes."

They glided over a huge shoal of glistening fish a thousand feet below.

"Have you ever seen the Spectre?" said Seveny.

"No," said Tommy. "I knew the Doctor was up to something after Watching a couple of Takings from inside the Ledge's postbox. But if the Farseers are speaking the truth, which they always do, then the Ancient Spectre's real."

"So the Spectre does Take juvenites at Dancing Ledge! And he lives in the Underworld?"

"To be honest, I don't know what the blazes is going on," said Tommy. "But the Spectre must be real if we're to spy on a meeting between Him and the Doctor. And He can't be living in the Underworld. He must live in the Great Sea."

"Do you think He'll be like that shrivelled snake hanging from the eagle in the Grand Hall?" Seveny hawklaughed nervously.

"Wouldn't that be nice!" Tommy hawklaughed back. "But I think it's more likely that He's every yard the giant Serpent of legend."

Seveny's mind whirred as she thought of the dangers the Watch might hold. She felt a little less excited and a little more scared. For the next half hour, as the dull sun sank in the sky, neither hawk hawkthought as they prepared themselves for the Watch.

At last they saw the coastline and Pity Me's identical houses and rows of fences. In the centre of the school field, labourers were raising a huge wooden steeple shaped like a serpent using a complicated web of hoists, pulleys and ropes. It would become the centrepiece of the already constructed bonfire, and the focus of tomorrow's Summer Sacrifice.

The two birds passed over the Orphanage.

"Do you know, the Summer Sacrifice used to be my favourite day of the year?" Seveny hawkthought. "It was nice seeing *everyone* surrounded by the school fences for once. And us orphans always got free titbits from the food-stalls. But I won't be sorry to miss it this year. The fireworks are always pretty good, but everything else is a pile of—"

"Quick!" Tommy hawkthought. "The sun has set. We have to get to Dancing Ledge."

As the sky darkened to a deep greyish-blue Seveny flapped her wings as hard and fast as she could. In a matter of minutes they'd reached the Ledge. But something was missing from their Watch. They had no one to look at.

"Oh Hellfires!" said Tommy. "We've missed the meeting. The Farseers are going to give us the biggest bollocking."

But Seveny wasn't listening. She was staring at the sea on the other side of Dancing Ledge. There was something wrong with the water. As well as the usual waves washing in and out, there was a second set moving diagonally across them. They seemed to be coming from the bay on the other side of the cliffs.

"Look," Seveny hawkthought. "There's something in the water."

Tommy looked at the waves peaking strangely against each other. "The Doctor and the Spectre must be round the corner," he said. "As soon as we pass the cliffs, they'll see us. We need to make ourselves small."

Seveny and Tommy shrank to the size of sparrows. As they flew over the Ledge, Seveny noticed that as a small bird it took a lot more effort to get a lot less far.

"It's not natural, flying at this size," she hawkthought. "The air feels like treacle."

"But you're doing it," Tommy replied, as they rounded the cliff.

And then they saw the tail. Its blue-black scales glinted as it undulated in the water, and its tip beat the air like an enormous metronome.

"I guess it's the giant option!" Seveny hawkthought, veering off course.

"Concentrate!" Tommy hawkshouted. "Stick close to the cliffs or they'll see us! And you don't want to get caught in the Spectre's tail-wind. Not the size we are. It could be fatal."

And there, in the water, the Ancient Spectre rested in its monstrous entirety. Standing before Him on the wet pebbly sand was a tiny figure dressed in crushed red velvet.

"Now!" Tommy hawkthought. "Quickly, before they notice us!"

The two tiny birds flapped their wings as fast as was Halfhawk-humanly possible and made for an outlying thicket of moonflowers growing on the beach.

Seveny and Tommy buried themselves amidst the tall-stemmed, spherical flowers. They were just twenty feet away from the Doctor and the beast.

"...and I'll be collecting her later, Master," they heard the Doctor say. His mouth was thick with Moonshine. "You have no need to worry, my Lord. She is right where I want her."

"GOOD, GOOD!" the Ancient Spectre hissed. "I KNEW YOU WOULD NOT FAIL ME. AND MY FEAST? WHAT OF MY FEAST?"

The Ancient Spectre's giant nostrils flared. It flicked out its forked red tongue as if ready to taste its banquet.

"It's fitting that you'll become a God on the night the Great Goddess is most celebrated. The last batch of souls will be sacrificed tomorrow."

"YES!" said the Spectre, in a smoky voice not unlike the Doctor's. "YOU HAVE HONOURED OUR BARGAIN. WHEN I BECOME THE ISLAND'S GOD, YOU SHALL BE MY PRINCE!"

The Doctor blushed, and twirled his moustache. "You may make me a Prince," he said. "But what is a Prince without a Palace?"

"INDEED." The Ancient Spectre's voice made the earth tremor. "WE HAVE BOTH BEEN NEGLECTED. YOUR GENIUS WAS STYMIED UNDERGROUND, WHILE I LANGUISHED IN THE UNDERWORLD. BUT WITH YOUR HELP I HAVE RECLAIMED THE GREAT SEA, AND TOMORROW I WILL RECLAIM THE LAND. YOU SHALL HAVE YOUR PALACE, BUILT FROM THE FINEST MARBLE. THE NO-PLACERS WILL MINE IT."

"The No-Placers are diseased, fat and weak!" spat the Doctor. "They will not make me a castle fit for a king. But I know who will!" He swayed with excitement. "Master, have you heard of a place called Little Breedy? It is north of Mount Venusius, deep in Contraland. The Fruitful were disappearing and I didn't know where. But a few years ago I made a Fruitful girl in my Dispensary squeal. Such a sweet child. I told Miss Amina to be gentle. She had a quick expiration once I'd got from her what I needed."

The Ancient Spectre's lips curled into a terrible smile.

"Hundreds of Fruitful women, and those who donated their seed to them, have been running into the woods. They have turned *wild*. In Little Breedy, so I'm told, they indulge in the most hideous practices." The Doctor wrinkled his nose and swallowed hard. "But apparently they're as fit as fiddles."

"HEATHENS!" cried the Spectre. "ONLY FIT TO BE YOUR SLAVES. YES, THEY SHALL BUILD YOUR PALACE!"

The Doctor rubbed his hands in anticipation. "They thought they could escape my clutches. I can't wait to see the looks on their faces after I hunt every last one of them down!"

"And if they don't come easily?"

"Then they shall be yours, Master. Body and soul."

The Ancient Spectre's eye-slits widened in pleasure and its colossal head sank beneath the sea. The waves resumed their usual movement, but the Doctor started shaking with excitement. Still shaking, he walked away from the water's edge, up the pebble beach, and disappeared from the Halfhawks' view.

"Right," Tommy hawkthought. "We must be on our way before—"

The earth crunched next to them. The Doctor's hand plunged into the thicket of moonflowers. One of his fingers brushed Seveny's wing.

"Oh Hellfires!" she hawkthought. "I'm a sparrow-sized seahawk and you're a falcon the size of a finch. He's sure to spot us. That's it, we're dead!"

But the broad leaves of the moonflowers protected them from the Doctor's sight. He grabbed one of the stems and severed it with a razor-sharp fingernail. His hand withdrew.

The Doctor examined his catch happily. "What a wonderful specimen you are!" he said to the moonflower. "You'll look perfect sweating out your life in my Laboratory!"

And the Doctor walked back towards Dancing Ledge and his Underground Dispensary.

"Tommy," Seveny hawkthought. "He didn't spot us, we're safe!"

Tommy wasn't moving.

"Tommy!" she hawkshouted. "Tommy?" Seveny crept towards him. "Tommy?" Her tiny hawk-eyes looked into his.

Tommy's eyes looked dead.

"TOMMY!"

"What?" Tommy hawkthought. "Why are you shouting?"

"Why am I shouting? The Doctor nearly found us. I thought you were—"

"Dead? No," Tommy hawklaughed, "I just got a transmission from the Farseers. They congratulated us on a successful Watch and gave us a message to deliver. I'll explain on the wing."

Tommy flew into the air, turning back into a falcon-sized falcon. Seveny followed suit.

"We've got to warn the Breedies!" she hawkthought.

"Yes," said Tommy. "Little Breedy's where we're going."

Chapter Twenty-nine

Evershotat

 The sun had set by the time Miss Humfreeze reached Giddyfoot County's jaunty signpost. It would be a while before she hit Evershotat, but she was already steeling herself: the sounds of Crackpot whack-shots weren't so distant anymore.

The Crackpots were named after the first family who made their home in the limestone caves riddling the Island's south coast. As their numbers had swollen they'd expanded into Giddyfoot County above. These days several thousand of them lived above-ground in the county's only town, Evershotat.

The town lived up to its name. At the hansum age of twenty, all Crackpots received a gun and a snuff tin. What they snorted from these tins was unknown. That it was mind-altering was common knowledge. Crackpots were a jolly, wonky lot: wonky-looking, wonky-walking, and blessedly, given they all carried guns and frequently used them, wonky-shooting. *If* they shot to kill, they never succeeded.

This didn't ease Miss Humfreeze's nerves. She decided that if she stayed as low to the ground as possible for as long as possible, the chance of her being hit would drastically lessen. So she crawled the last quarter-mile to Evershotat on her hands and knees. She'd just reached the town's bullet-punctured "Welcome to Evershotat" sign when the first whack-shot pinged past her ear.

Continuing at a slightly quicker crawl, she held her mettle as the rock-bullets flew around her. She soon noticed that whenever she stopped to take a breather so did the whack-shots, leading her to conclude that either the Crackpots were loath to waste their hand-crafted bullets on non-moving objects, or they weren't trying to harm her. Enough was enough! Her knees creaked, her hips had begun to stiffen, and she was sick of the gravel eating her palms. Miss Humfreeze rose to her feet.

Walking as casually as she could while being shot at, she passed through the small, damp alleyways of Evershotat, past its many soup kitchens and underfed cats. Soon she reached Giddyfoot Market.

Crackpots were craftsmen, fishermen, clothes-makers, railway workers, farmers, musicians and pest controllers. But mainly they were traders. Without them, life in the poorer parts of Pity Me would have been unbearable.

Giddyfoot Market heaved with cheaply-priced goodies and overpriced tat. The stalls overflowed with strange teas, snake extracts, disposable fashions and 'imperishable' herbs.

Hungry after her long walk and crawl, Miss Humfreeze bought a pound of green grapes from a beetle-faced woman with dirty fingernails. She wolfed them down as she passed through the Market. As she ate she reflected on the Crackpot pastime of shooting to miss. She decided that as a sport, it held some merit.

She reached the coast without further incident and spotted the uneven row of limestone tunnels. A narrow stream flowed out of the smallest one.

She followed the stream into the tunnel and arrived in a small white cave honeycombed with stalagmites and stalactites and entrances and exits. The little stream came from a large, shallow pool in the middle of the cave, which in turn was filled by a broad, slow-moving underground river that inched its way out of the cave's largest tunnel. That tunnel would lead Miss Humfreeze to Catacomb City.

Catacomb City was the Crackpot capital, a place where Crackpots lived, worked and played. *Hard*. That's where she'd find Evelyn Crackpot, Chief of the Crackpot Clan, also known as Tommy's mother.

Miss Humfreeze had heard that a ferry worked the narrow river, conveying Giddyfoot Crackpots (and the occasional thrill-seeking No-Placer) to Catacomb City from sundown, and back again from dawn. She scanned the cave for a boat, but could hardly see a thing. Little light remained in the sky outside, and even less filtered into the cave. It took her a while to realize she was alone, and a few seconds more to understand she'd missed the sunset boat.

Miss Humfreeze weighed her options. She could wait for the next ferry of the evening, but who knew when—or if—it would come. She could travel to the city by foot, but the Catacombs were labyrinthine. And then she wondered if the whole venture wasn't a giant wrong turn and this was the dead end. Yes, she wanted to find out what had happened to Tommy, but what about the missing juvenites? Why wasn't she looking for them?

A moment later, day finally lost its fight with night.

"I promised *him* I'd never go Underground," she muttered in the blackness, rooted to the spot like a mushroom. "Yet here I am! And as for talking to Tommy's mum, I don't know what's happened to her son. If it's... the worst, wouldn't she blame the school? Confronted with me, wouldn't *I* be a target? She'd want to kill me. And it's not like she'd be unarmed..."

As she scolded herself, her eyes adjusted to the dark. The cave appeared to have turned into a crypt full of daggers. Frightened out of her paralysis, she swerved round the spikes and headed for the exit.

And then the lights turned on.

A dozen silk threads dangled from the cave's ceiling. They looked like strung water droplets or chains of tiny pearls. The beads faintly pulsed, and more importantly, they *glowed*.

Entranced by the light bearers, Miss Humfreeze touched one of the threads. The sticky string switched its light off and retracted to the ceiling. She laughed in amazement. Then her thumb began to throb.

"The blighter's given me a shock!"

Thankful for the other lights (which she carefully avoided), Miss Humfreeze jumped and jiggled her way past the stalagmites and stalactites, now perfectly innocent again in the light, and over to the cave's large pool.

"What should I do?" she sighed, dunking her sore, warm thumb into the cold water. "I so wanted to be brave."

She wasn't expecting an answer, but she got one all the same.

The pool grabbed her, pulled her, dragged and took her down, down, down...

* * *

Chapter Thirty

Little Sea

Once Miss Humfreeze had got over her surprise at being swallowed by the pool, she noticed the suggestion of a door floating before her. It quivered like a vision in smoke. Or water...

So that's what sort of pool you are.

Miss Humfreeze had never spirit-travelled by water.

Indeed, it had been a long time since she'd spirit-travelled at all. But just like riding a horse, the essentials came back quickly. Sharpening her subconscious, she stabilized the vision.

What do you want to show me?

There was something written on the door. The letters protested, as in a dream, at being asked to reveal themselves. With effort, she got them in focus:

RE-EDUCATION CLINIC
FOR JUVENITE DELINQUENTS

Miss Humfreeze concentrated hard—and floated through the solid door.

Pale juvenites lay on rock beds, bathed in cold sweat and hardly breathing. Some had open eyes from which tears softly trailed.

Gently, Miss Humfreeze moved her Sight to look upon those nearest her.

Billy.

Charlotte.

Ella.

The surprise unbalanced Miss Humfreeze and disturbed her vision. But she managed to refocus her mind in time before she was pulled back to her body. She moved carefully down the room, examining and recognizing every face. The faces of the Taken.

"He-he-helloooo?!" A voice ripped through the vision.

No, not now! thought Miss Humfreeze.

"He-hello! Are you OK?! H-H-H-H-Helloooooooooo, can you h-hear meeeeeeeeee?"

The ceiling parted and Miss Humfreeze was dragged upwards.

* * *

She returned to consciousness to find herself sitting in the shallow pool. A young man hovered over her.

Nesbitt's little longboat floated on the water. The hansum was at the helm, a long pole in his hand, his violin strapped to his back.

"Wowsers!" he said. "Just you stay there. I'll get some he-help."

The idea of being helped by Crackpots made Miss Humfreeze nervous. She tried to stand up, but didn't succeed.

Seconds later, she woke with a splutter. The hansum was holding a rusty tin under her nose. Its contents smelled pungent.

"I didn't know what else to do," said the hansum, removing the tin and putting it in a pouch on his belt. "But I've heard the effects are temporary!"

"I'm fine," said Miss Humfreeze, starting to sway. "Or I would be, if it weren't for what I've just Seen..."

"Seen?" Nesbitt looked stunned. Had this lady travelled without intending to, like that girl Jamie?

Miss Humfreeze nodded—and kept on nodding. "I was wondering what I should do, and then I travelled."

"That's Little Sea for you," said Nesbitt. "You've been shown the path you should follow."

"The pool—I mean Little Sea—showed me the Dispensary."

Nesbitt gulped. "And?"

"There were Pity Me schoolchildren. Their souls had been sucked. I know the signs. Their bodies are waiting to expire."

Nesbitt squeaked.

"But Jamie wasn't there," Miss Humfreeze said, her head still nodding. "The juvenite I thought I'd find."

"Jamie?" Nesbitt's eyes grew rounder and, curiously, his hair more floppy. "Is your Jamie a boy or a girl?"

"A girl," said Miss Humfreeze, continuing to nod. She giggled. "Though the case is arguable. She's got boy-hair and climbs trees."

Wonky, she thought. *I feel really very wonky.*

"Does she h-have reddish brown hair and impish ears?"

"Why, yes! Her earlobes are so pointed they could cut cheese!" Miss Humfreeze chuckled at her creativeness. She felt remarkably jolly.

"But... But... Oh Jamie!" Nesbitt whimpered. "What ha-ha-have I done?"

"What *have* you done?" said Miss Humfreeze, crashing quickly back to Earth.

"I saved h-her from the Gang. But she was injured. The blood wouldn't stop flowing. I h-had to deliver h-her to the Dispensary."

The last vestiges of jolliness left Miss Humfreeze. She now felt very sober. *Funnella*, she thought, *has got her wish.*

"When was she delivered?"

"Nearly a month ago," said Nesbitt, his puddle-eyes filling with tears. "I'll show you where I left h-her."

He helped Miss Humfreeze out of the pool, and led the way down Come Down Passage. A soaked Miss Humfreeze squelched behind.

Chapter Thirty-one

Fireforge

When the boys arrived at Fireforge, Empu Salim was silhouetted against the dark purple sky by the furnace's orange glow. He'd been joined by two others.

To his left was a beautiful woman with impossibly high cheekbones, wearing feathers in her ears and holding bellows. It was the Empu's great-niece Fira. To his right, holding a sledgehammer, was Striker: a fearsome-looking man of very few words. The Empu was even more decorated than usual. Strands of silver birch were woven through his hair. A golden eagle was painted on one side of his face and an emerald snake on the other. He was heating something in the furnace, and did not look up as the boys drew near.

"Oh Goddess," said George. "What do you think he wants?"

Empu Salim gestured for the boys to look into the forge. Shielding their eyes from the heat, they could just make out a piece of steel lying in the forge. It was long and thin and glowing red.

Empu Salim threw some sunflower seeds in the furnace. They popped like miniature firecrackers as they came in contact with the coals and the metal.

The Empu's niece worked the bellows, fanning the flames until the steel glowed an orange-yellow. Grabbing a pair of wolf-jaw tongs, Empu Salim whipped the metal from the fire and laid it on a perfectly smooth rock which did duty as the village's anvil. Striker swung the sledge-hammer and delivered blow after blow. Sparks flew everywhere.

"Shouldn't we be wearing goggles?" George whispered.

Empu Salim's hand went to an embroidered bag on his belt from which he withdrew a small file and a chisel. As the boys watched, he sharpened, filed and polished what was becoming the blade of a sword. While he worked, he snatched the odd look at Max and sang something unintelligible under his breath.

At last he beckoned Max over and showed him the still-hot blade.

"I give you this weapon as a sign of maturity. May it give you strength."

Max was quite overcome. The sword's blade was wavy like a snake. He counted its curves: there were nine of them. "Well, they do call me Nine Lives!" he said.

Empu Salim opened a large silk bag and told him to pick something out of it. Max quickly selected one of the objects inside. It was the hilt of a sword. Crafted from silver birch, it was pale, light, and smooth to the touch. It was the shape of a snake's head.

"As I thought!" said the Empu.

He picked up the scorching blade in his tongs and dipped its shaft in a jar of something black and tarry which bubbled from the heat. "There's nothing stronger than birch-bark glue," he said, as he slid the tarred shaft into the pale wooden hilt. He offered the weapon to Max.

"This sword is alive and aggressive, Nine Lives," he said. "When you are in danger it will rattle like a snake. And as long as you carry it, you will live up to your name."

Max held the snake-head hilt, careful not to touch the hot blade, and grinned. His dimples grew impossibly deep.

The Empu put a second piece of steel in the flames.

"George."

George was on the opposite side of Fireforge, keeping a sensible distance from the sparks and flames. Nervously, he rounded the furnace.

This time, Empu Salim dropped in peppermint leaves as his niece fanned the flames. Then he picked up the glue-bucket and flicked some of the tarry substance over the steel. The fire swelled and the metal went from blood-red, to orange, to a warm golden-yellow. Quick as a flash the Empu whipped it out of the furnace and laid it on the rock. Striker's task was different now. His hammer wasn't used to bend but rather to lengthen, to fold, and finally to snap.

George got hit by an iron splinter.

"Quick!" said Empu Salim. "You must offer the gift!" He grabbed George's head and held it over the glowing blade.

A drop of blood fell from George's brow and sizzled on the hot steel. Empu Salim released him, then set about filing and polishing while he sang his strange song, snatching looks at George who was fussing over his graze.

Finally, the Empu gripped the blade in his tongs and raised it to the sky.

"It is done!"

George couldn't hide his disappointment. Like Max's blade, his was flat, asymmetric, and wide at the base. But it was straight as a pin, and half the length.

Empu Salim saw his expression. "We do not choose our weapons, George. This dagger will lie dormant until it scents the blood of an enemy, and then... Well. Its name is 'Executioner.'"

George did not find this comforting.

The Empu smiled. "I am glad it is in your hands."

He offered George the same silk bag, laden with possibilities. "Choose your hilt."

George fished around for a considerable time. At last he pulled out a painted, bejewelled eagle's head. Empu Salim didn't look surprised.

"Your weapon will See," he said to George. "While yours," he said to Max, "will Feel."

Empu Salim dipped the second blade in the birch-bark glue and pushed it into the decorated eagle's head. He handed the dagger to George and pointed to a tall jug standing next to Striker.

The boys dipped the hot blades in the jug. This made a great deal of smoke and steam, which smelt of apples.

"The apples, when uncooked, are toxic," said the Empu.

Max coughed. "Aware of that!"

"The juice draws out the steel's heat, and its acidity brings out the differences between the nickel and the iron."

Max fidgeted, fearing a science lesson, but George's curiosity was piqued.

"The iron comes from the mountain," said the Empu. "It is born of Venusius, a legacy of the lava she birthed when she last erupted. The nickel we collect from Blister Sands, where the last meteorite hit."

Both boys were impressed.

"So you see, there is stardust within your weapons, as there is within you. Like you, they now possess a soul. Take a look."

The boys removed their blades. Before, they'd been a uniform dull grey. Now they pulsed with life.

"The acid darkens the iron and lightens the nickel," said the Empu. "And you are left with—"

"Rainbows," said Max.

George, struggling to see through the smoke, raised his blade to take a closer look. "And tears."

"Careful where you point that blade!" Empu Salim warned. "If it targets a person, you mark them out for death!"

The apple-smoke cleared. Max looked taller, George broader. Both seemed to have gained in years.

"Welcome to our family!" said a thousand voices behind them.

The boys spun round. All the Breedies were gathered in the clearing, with Jason, Maria, Kai and little Maya at the front. The Breedies trilled their tongues in celebration.

Fira put down her bellows and someone handed her a yellow corn-snake. Striker put down his sledgehammer and was handed a long, curved sword. Empu Salim put down his tongs and took up his leather drum.

Fira danced to the beat of the Empu's drum, and the yellow snake danced with her, writhing in time with her moves and the beat of her heart.

The boys looked on in awe. They still found snakes terrifying, despite the Breedies' assurances that, like all of Earth's creatures, snakes should be respected, not feared. But as Fira danced, at one with the snake, the scales of their fear began to fall.

Then Striker balanced his long sword on his head. Circling his wrists and rolling his hips, he spiralled to the ground. He lifted the sword off his head with his bare feet and balanced it on his toes. The Breedies yipped their approval and they too started to dance, fluttering their tummies, snaking their arms, clanging finger-cymbals, clapping, and trilling their teeth.

The clapping, trilling, yipping and clanging was halted by a fluttering of wings.

A hawk glided over the clearing and landed on Striker's sword. Its head snapped back and was replaced by a girl's face. Her golden hair spilled out into shimmering pools. Striker's legs shook.

Seveny hopped off her metal perch. "Can I have two blankets, please?"

"Seveny!" Kai, not scared at all by the curious sight, ran over to the girl-hawk and buried himself in her hair.

"Didn't I tell you?" said George to Max, whose head was shaking and whose eyes were blinking.

But Max didn't respond. For once, he was lost for words.

Maria ran inside her house and came back with rabbit-skin blankets. A grey falcon joined Seveny and they both became human and wrapped themselves in the furs.

Seveny addressed Empu Salim. "Sorry to interrupt. We are—"

"Halfhawk Mortals!" said the Empu. "You are our friends."

"Yes!" she said, surprised at his knowledge of her kind. "I take it you know we're messengers?"

Empu Salim nodded. "And what is your message?"

"Just now, Tommy and I saw the Ancient Spectre speaking to the Doctor on Dancing Ledge."

A murmur of disbelief swept through the crowd.

"Impossible!" said the Empu. "The Ancient Spectre's not real. The Establishment invented the idea!"

"You're right," said Tommy. "They invented the idea of the Ancient Spectre and fanned the fear of it to help them rule. But the Doctor has taken that fear, focused it, and put it in the Underworld. He thinks he's resurrected the Spectre, but he has in fact brought Him to life for the very first time. Now the Spectre is not only real, He is strong enough to leave the Underworld and live in the Great Sea."

"How?" Kai asked. His big eyes searched Seveny's.

Seveny couldn't bring herself to look at him. "Because the Doctor has been feeding the Spectre. On the souls of juvenites."

"Charlotte!" Kai cried.

"The Takings at Dancing Ledge," George gasped.

Seveny nodded. "The Doctor only needs to sacrifice one more group of souls before the Ancient Spectre will be strong enough to leave the Great Sea and live on land, where He will continue to feast. In return, the Spectre will make the Doctor his Prince and he will rule the Island."

Empu Salim looked grim. "If the Doctor succeeds with this sacrifice, there will be no freedom. There will be no escape.

There will be nothing but darkness, and the Doctor's will, and the Spectre's jaws. We must break his spell!"

"But how?" said Seveny.

"We open the No-Placers' eyes."

"You mean we show ourselves to them?" said Fira.

"Yes."

"But we have freedom here!"

"No!" For one brief moment the Empu raised his voice. "We live a good life here, Fira, but so long as the Establishment reigns, it is not free."

"But our children!" said a villager. "The Establishment call them Children of the Underworld. Mutants! The No-Placers will take them to the Dispensary and have them killed!"

The crowd erupted with shouts of agreement.

"Not if we wake them up!" said George. "Show them that children born out of Wedlock are not Children of the Underworld. That they've been lied to all these years."

"My sister's dead!" shouted Kai.

"And our other friends are dying," said Max. "And unless something happens, the deaths will continue!"

The crowd hushed.

"There's something else," said Tommy. "Under torture, a Fruitful girl told the Doctor of her fears and her plans to escape. Needless to say, she never made it here. But the Doctor knows about Little Breedy and he wants you back. And once he is Prince, he'll either enslave you... or kill you."

The Breedies were mute with horror.

"We have no choice," said the Empu. "It falls to us to save the Island. However, tomorrow's full moon marks The Summer Sacrifice. There will be no Taking until next month. We have some time to prepare."

"No," said Seveny. "The Doctor doesn't need a Taking: he already has his prisoners. He'll feed the Ancient Spectre at the next full moon. At midnight. Tomorrow."

"Then we must act quickly," said the Empu. He addressed his people. "We will leave for No Place at dawn. Gather your things. Sleep well. You will need your strength for the battle ahead."

The Empu solemnly raised his raven-headed sword to the heavens. One by one, the Breedies' blades joined his in silent support, until every weapon was pointed to the sky.

"And remember," said Empu Salim. "Our blades are not weapons. They are shields. We may not use them to attack, but we have every right to defend. For, tomorrow night, this Island shall be free! We will be counted! We will be seen!"

Chapter Thirty-two

Practical Magic

Night had fallen. The only
thing illuminating Jamie's
room was the fire outside,
burning below Creaky's
cauldron.

Jamie examined her knee in
the dim light. When she found
the place where the wound had
been, she stared in disbelief.
The open cut had vanished,
leaving not even a scar as a
reminder.

The first week the Burrowers had worked inside her, her flesh
had continuously rippled. Old Cott said it was because they
had such a lot of work to do. In the last few days their activity
had decreased. Yesterday, she'd only felt one flurry. And today,
nothing at all. Those ugly grubs had healed her, just as Creaky
Nan had promised. She was free of poison. Her blood felt clean.

Jamie felt much healthier in general. Though she missed
Miss Mackadoo and the Brainticklers terribly, she didn't miss
waking up exhausted from her dreams, or being woken in the
middle of the night to experience some hideous Dreamweave.

But her days at Silly Whim were as taxing as her nights were
restful. Creaky Nan didn't so much teach her to fight as give her
shields—impenetrable shields of Spirit. "If you always protect

yourself," she said, "you won't *need* to attack."

Creaky Nan's technique was imagination-based, and Jamie had lost count of how long she'd spent imagining her soul glowing big, bright and shiny. She'd questioned the wisdom of this at first. "Imagining my soul shrinking let me hide from the Doctor," she'd said.

"Disappearing has its uses," Creaky Nan had replied. "But no fight is won by an absent warrior. Disappearing never wins."

Jamie didn't relish the idea of confronting the Doctor, or the monster he'd created. But if she was destined to go into battle as Miss Mackadoo had prophesied, she intended to be fully prepared. So she listened carefully to Creaky Nan, and even did extra homework in the evenings. This evening was no different.

As always, she began by imagining a sun in front of her. Not the increasingly pale sun that lit and fed the Island, but a giant golden sun hovering just in front of her chest. She brought the orb closer and closer until it was inside her, melting any darkness away. And now, her soul *was* the golden sun…

Her skin tingled. Jamie looked down in astonishment.

Rays of light were bursting out of her and illuminating the dark! For the first time since she'd started doing the work, Jamie saw her Golden Light.

She was about to run and tell Creaky Nan the news, when a snatch of conversation was carried through the window on the evening breeze.

"…tell her what happened to her mum," said Old Cott.

"And destroy everything she's achieved?"

"Revenge is strong."

"And anger's cloudy."

Jamie's mind raced back to when she'd last seen her mother, and her Golden Light faded. She felt her mother's breath on her cheek. Only this time it was followed by a piercing scream.

In a few seconds, Jamie was out of the front door.

Over the fire boiled a cauldron of something truly noxious. Creaky Nan was sweeping the yard, and Old Cott was swinging in his hammock.

He waved Jamie over. "Join us!"

Jamie didn't move. "What happened to my mum?"

"Well, girl—"

"You should know deary, you were there!" said Creaky Nan rather harshly, continuing to sweep.

Jamie gritted her teeth. "I said, what happened?"

"Just you go and sit with Old Cott."

Though Jamie felt like spitting feathers, she sat down on the hammock.

A deep, low hum filled the air. After a few moments, Jamie realized that the sound came from the depths of Creaky Nan's belly. The shamun dipped her broom in the foul-smelling cauldron and held it to the flames. The bristles caught fire with a whomp, and gave off a cloud of smoke even darker than the night around her. Raising the flaming broom above her, she spun in a strange, hypnotic dance, making smoke rings in the cool night air.

When the acrid smoke reached Jamie she felt very queasy. From nowhere the notion flew into her head that the Burrowers were ready to leave.

She felt a sharp prickling all over. When she looked down, she saw pink moths crawling their way out of the white cloth pyjamas Old Cott had given her.

As they broke free they flew towards the spinning Creaky Nan. A thousand more dived out of the sky, and thousands more came from the nearby trees. They flew in spirals around the flaming torch, alighting on every inch of Creaky Nan and her broom, apart from its burning bristles. Creaky Nan was so cloaked in the pink insects that she looked like one herself.

Jamie stared, amazed. "Old Cott, the moths at the marsh! Nan called them?"

"Yes," he said. "She knew you were at Swire Valley and she called on the Great Goddess's energies."

Jamie was mesmerized. "Nice trick!"

Old Cott looked serious. "This is no trick. It's magic. Learn, child."

He pointed at the flaming bristles.

"See how close the moths sit to that torch, but never touch it?" he said. "The fire's *real*. They can land anywhere but on it."

"I... I see."

Creaky Nan smiled. Her grin looked eerie in the firelight. She shook the moths from her arms and levelled her broom at the hammock. The insects flew straight at Old Cott and Jamie and then off into the night. Stubbing the blazing bristles out, Creaky Nan headed off in the direction of the stables.

Old Cott's face grew heavy. He eased himself out of the hammock and pointed behind Jamie with his cane.

The sky was dark and swirling. The moths dispersed, the smoke cleared, and a fast-moving shape shone out of the blackness. A tall white horse was galloping towards them.

And as it neared, Jamie's blood ran cold.

For she recognized its rider.

Chapter Thirty-three

Dead End

A couple of hours after heading down Come Down Passage, Miss Humfreeze and Nesbitt reached a dead end. The teacher looked mortified.

"Don't worry," said Nesbitt. He pushed a small stone in the rock-face and a section of wall flipped down like a drawbridge to reveal the Dispensary's marble corridor. "H-h-here we are! This corridor circles the Dispensary. If you follow the path round—" the hansum looked left "—this way, you'll come to the Main Entrance. It's the one door they don't lock. You search for Jamie, and I'll distract them."

"Distract who?"

"The two creatures I gave her to. And the Doctor if need be."

Miss Humfreeze tensed. "What do these creatures look like?"

"The man's big and sad, and the woman looks hu-hu-hungry."

The schoolteacher's hands went to her stomach. "Those juvenites had their souls sucked," she said. "And now I'm pretty sure I know by whom."

"Yes. Me too."

"Then why are you doing this?"

"Guilt," said Nesbitt, simply. "I brought h-h-her here."

"But they'll take take your soul as well! Don't you know what that means?"

"Yes," said Nesbitt. "It means you'll come and find me."

The schoolteacher was unnerved by the hansum's intuition, but she couldn't deny he was correct. She *would* go looking for his soul. And she had a fair idea where she would find it.

She headed for the Main Entrance.

Once Miss Humfreeze was out of sight, Nesbitt walked to the Ward of Extraction. From behind the polished oak door came a sound like a baby snake learning to purr. Nesbitt was just building up the courage to knock when the locks withdrew and the door opened.

"Delighted to see you!" said Miss Amina.

She dragged him inside, slammed the door shut, and opened her moist red mouth, revealing rows of pointy little teeth. She gave him a coquettish wink.

Nesbitt hoped she would continue her charm offensive: toy with him for a bit, then suck his soul out in a while. That would give Miss Humfreeze longer to find Jamie. And though Nesbitt would never admit it, he wanted to enjoy the sweet before the sour. The closest he'd ever come to embracing a curved object was his fiddle.

Alas, she was only after one thing.

Miss Amina violently embraced him. Her lips grazed his. "I should introduce myself," she said. "My name is Miss Amina. I am the Doctor's daughter. And I'll be your personal escort down to the Golden Orb."

The Golden Orb?

She clutched his head and whispered loudly in his ear.

"Did you think martyring yourself would absolve you of your sins? You brought the girl here. You knew what would happen to her. And so you are still... *GUILTY!*"

Miss Amina kissed him. Nesbitt experienced reptilian writhing, sharp teeth, forked tongue, lips sucking...

And then, Miss Amina took his breath away.

Chapter Thirty-four

Old Cott and the Doctor

"We've kept our word," said Old Cott, backing away from Jamie. "She is to remain alive."

"For now," said the Doctor, on his white horse. "Jamie, I made a mistake. I was scared of your power and I tried to destroy you. But I've had a change of heart. What's the use of killing you? That powerful soul of yours would go all to waste."

Jamie and Old Cott both understood the implication of the Doctor's words.

"Now, son. That's not what we agreed."

Son?

"No, Pa. Indeed it isn't."

Pa?!

"But you're a sentimental fool!" said the Doctor. "You'd never have given her to me if I'd been honest with you. Why should she stay intact when she'll only seek to ruin me?"

"You'll make her one of those zombie children?"

"Yes. And like the others, she'll be sacrificed. Tomorrow."

Old Cott was rigid with anger. "I won't let you take her!"

"How can you stop me, father?" The Doctor jumped from his horse and kicked away Old Cott's cane. The old man stumbled.

"Is *this* my thanks for letting you stay Up Above? For keeping you hidden from the Establishment? Without me, you'd be Underground!"

"You made that rule!"

"And perhaps I should have had the courage to follow it."

The Doctor lunged at Old Cott. Something glinted in the darkness between them. The old man's tongue fell from his mouth. He thumped to the ground.

"Snake poison!" The Doctor withdrew the needle from his father's heart and laughed. "It's a wonderful thing."

"Naaaaaaaaaaaaaaan!" Jamie screamed.

The measured tread of hooves came from the stable. Creaky Nan held Toffee's reins in one hand, and in the other her lasso. When she saw her stricken husband she ran to him and put her hands over his mouth.

And choked out the last gasps of Old Cott's life.

"You're a good girl, Jamie," she said. "A girl of many talents. But I'm afraid, like my late husband, you are far too trusting."

The content of Creaky Nan's lessons suddenly made sense to Jamie. *That's why she never taught me to fight! She's been fattening my soul up, ready for the slaughter!*

Jamie ran for her life. Hooves pounded the ground behind her. If she could just reach the steep steps down to Swire Valley she had a chance of escape: the horses couldn't gallop down them. She'd just got to the first of the stone steps when something flew over her head. The wind was knocked out of her. Her tailbone met stone.

Pain rippled through her spine as she levered herself up from the ground. With the lasso biting at her waist, Jamie walked back to her captors before Creaky Nan (who was now in Toffee's saddle) could reel her in.

Jamie faced the Doctor, her chin held high. She knew she'd be taken back to the Dispensary. And the time had come to fight.

Chapter Thirty-five

The Dispensary

 Miss Humfreeze was making for the Main Entrance when a sound like milkshake being sucked through a straw echoed loudly down the corridor. Nesbitt was providing the distraction he'd promised.

But the mother in Miss Humfreeze couldn't bear to leave the hansum while he had his soul sucked out. Besides, she reasoned, if she could grab his body once they were done with him, she'd have only his soul left to retrieve. And she didn't need to be at the Dispensary to do that.

She walked back past the eerily silent Infirmary, its door thick with fire-beetle web, towards the noise. As she drew closer, Nesbitt's dregs appeared drained and the sucking sound was replaced by muffled voices.

One was slimy and female, the other a husky baritone. They came from behind a door marked "Extraction." She put her ear to it to hear them better.

"I'm tooooo good!" said the slimy voice.

"I wouldn't say so," said the husky one. "Anaesthesiology is the hardest part of any operation. And the most necessary."

"Ugh! Will you let that gooooo?"

"It would only have taken a minute to give him some, and you would have saved him much pain."

"Well, what does it matter? They all end up in the same place. And as Daddy says, it isn't the journey that counts, it's the final destination. Daddy says I am the best Psychopomp around! Anyone can guide souls up to the Blanket of Stars *after* they're dead. But only *I* can send them down to the Golden Orb while their bodies are alive!"

"Don't you sometimes think that what we're doing might be wrong?" asked the husky voice. "Don't you ever wonder what it might feel like to live Up Above?"

"No, you ungrateful plank!" said the slimy voice. "Daddy says the people Up Above are uncivilized. He's protecting us. Maybe I should tell Daddy what you've been saying. He often says he's glad he spent more time in the Surgery working on me, because I'm more use to him than you. Daddy says he regrets not working harder on you. He says you could do with a little more re-ordering!"

The husky voice didn't reply.

"I shall wait for Daddy to get back," said the slimy voice, "and then I shall tell him what you said!"

There was a flurry of footsteps, a door slammed, and then there was silence.

Miss Humfreeze decided that this was her chance to get Nesbitt. She looked through the keyhole to check the coast was clear. But her eye's view was blocked.

By another eyeball.

Fright propelled her down the corridor as fast as her squat legs could carry her. The eyeball's owner gave chase. When Miss Humfreeze chanced a look back, she was relieved to find that the curve of the corridor concealed her from sight. But her pursuer was gaining on her and she needed to hide. She decided to seek refuge in the next room she passed.

Its door bore the unpleasant title "Sanatorium of the Weird and Wicked." When she tried its handle, she remembered why she'd been going to the Main Entrance in the first place: all the other doors were locked.

The footsteps drew closer. Knowing her chance to run had passed, Miss Humfreeze threw her entire weight at the door. It made a horrendous noise—and didn't budge an inch.

Strong hands grabbed her shoulders.

Miss Humfreeze was prepared for a soul-sucking, so it came as rather a surprise when the grab became an embrace.

"Mother?" the husky voice whispered. "It's me!"

Miss Humfreeze turned in her captor's arms and stared at him. The man had a beautiful, if sad face. But it wasn't her son's.

And then she saw his amethyst eyes, and she didn't want to stop looking, not ever. For a precious few minutes many years ago, she'd gazed into them and known a happiness she'd never thought possible.

"Magnus?"

He nodded.

And then she was hugging back as tightly as she could. Hugging this man. This soul-snatcher.

Her son.

"Wait." Magnus gently pushed his mother from his arms. He produced a large set of keys, selected one and unlocked the door of the Sanatorium. "In here."

They went inside.

"Let me out!" cried a young voice in the darkness.

"You're hurting me!" cried another. "Make it stop!"

"My schoolchildren?" said Miss Humfreeze.

"No, Mother. Not the ones you're looking for."

Magnus struck a match.

The room was full of beds. All of them were empty. Judging from the dust and the cobwebs, they'd been empty for a long time.

"I haven't been in this room for over twenty years," said Magnus, lighting a candle on a nearby table. "Not since I was nine."

"Please, no more!" wailed an old woman's voice.

"Father brought me in here," Magnus said, "and introduced me to a young man." He pointed to one of the cobwebbed mattresses. "That was his bed. He was a bitter man, made angry by the world, by the Establishment, and by the fact that he couldn't feed his family. He could hear the room's voices and begged Father to make them stop. I could hear them too, and scared as I was, I told him so. Father cuffed me, apologized for my insensitivity, then told the man that he was physically strong but mentally defective. He took us to the Surgery for the Disordered and put us both to sleep."

Miss Humfreeze's breath caught in her throat.

"When I woke up, I felt tender. Different. To my side was a table with a sheet over it. There was something bulky underneath. I peeked under and discovered..." Magnus struggled to keep his voice steady. "Leftovers. Parts from me, and parts from the man who'd come to the Doctor for help. He was dead. I had been—" his jaw clenched "—re-ordered. But compared to my sister I was lucky. Miss Amina's had much more work done than me."

Miss Humfreeze tried to swallow and found she couldn't. She grabbed her son's hands. "Why did I ever leave you?"

"You had no choice. But you must know the extent of Father's insanity."

Magnus opened the Sanatorium's inner door.

"Please don't go!" said a sad voice.

"The voices are as real as you or I," said Magnus. "Except they've been separated from their bodies." He checked the coast was clear. "Come. I must show you the Surgery."

Miss Humfreeze followed him down the corridor. There were so many questions she wanted to ask.

"Do you and your sister both have the Sight?" she whispered as they walked.

"I have the Sight. My sister has more potent talents, which she uses blindly and for harm. Despite everything he's done to her, she trusts 'Daddy' completely."

They reached the Surgery's door. Magnus paused.

"Father doesn't do surgery these days. Miss Amina and I were his only successful re-orderings, and it took a lot of experimentation before he was willing to try the technique on us. Now the Surgery is merely the store-room for his early work."

He swung the door open. Inside the dark room were large glass vats. Not all of their contents were still.

Miss Humfreeze's olive skin turned ashen.

"I'm sorry, Mother," said Magnus. "I had to show you. You had to see what he's capable of... Mother?"

Miss Humfreeze's eyes were glassy.

"Mother, you have to listen. The children you're searching for. Their bodies are here at the Dispensary, but their souls are not. Father has them locked in a cage at the bottom of the Spirit Realm. They're the last batch he needs. Mother, he's going to kill them all! At midnight tonight he's going to offer them up to the Ancient Spectre, and in exchange the Spectre will make him Prince of the Island!"

"Where is your father?" Miss Humfreeze managed to croak.

"Out. Recapturing a girl who escaped. Mother... Mother?"

Miss Humfreeze had gone to a far-off place.

"Mother!"

Magnus tried to shake her out of her paralysis.

"You can't stay here!" he urged. "If Miss Amina found you... and with Father due back!"

Miss Humfreeze was completely unresponsive. Magnus grabbed hold of his mother's head. He stared into her eyes, and his pupils dilated until his eyes turned entirely black.

Miss Humfreeze slipped from his grip.

Magnus didn't catch her. Nor did the cold stone floor. But her fall was caught.

Jamie was being pushed down the Dispensary's circular corridor, one of Miss Amina's talons lodged in her backbone. Behind them, Creaky Nan and the Doctor congratulated each other.

"Great work, Ma!" said the Doctor. "You fattened her soul up nicely. The Ancient Spectre shall feast!"

They reached the Ward of Extraction. Miss Amina paused to unlock the heavy door.

"Anything for my son," said Creaky Nan. "Such a shame your father never saw your genius."

"Ah, yes," said the Doctor. "But we showed him."

Miss Amina pushed the door open and shoved Jamie inside. Something lay crumpled in a corner of the room. The hansum was grey, and his breathing was light and laboured.

"Nesbitt!" cried Jamie. "What have you done to him?"

Miss Amina smirked. "A simple operation. One you'll become very familiar with." She scooped the girl up and dropped her on the operating table. Her forked tongue licked her lips. "Your soul practically radiates! Such a large extraction is going to hurt..."

A figure crashed into the room, gripping a large and painful-looking hypodermic needle.

"Good morning Father, Grandma. Miss Amina, I insist on anaesthetic!"

Miss Amina gave her brother a withering look. She positioned her mouth over Jamie's, ready for the removal.

The Doctor whispered in Jamie's ear. "Do you remember how your mother *screamed*?"

Magnus plunged the loaded needle into Jamie's arm, and she fell asleep quickly.

But not quickly enough.

Chapter Thirty-six

Falling Angel

Seveny felt her heart explode.

The shock toppled her off the branch where she'd been keeping watch over a thousand breakfasting Breedies. As she fell, she lost all shape. She hit the ground not as an eagle, but as a girl with golden wings.

Kai got to her first. He wound her hair round his fingers and wouldn't let go. Behind him came Maria, a blinking Max and a solemn George.

Empu Salim knelt beside Seveny and began to sing one of his unfathomable tunes. The stunned folk of Little Breedy gathered round the sorry exhibit. They paused in silent vigil, hoping for the girl to breathe.

Moments later, Seveny coughed into consciousness.

"Wriggle your toes," said the Empu.

Seveny managed this little task and the crowd cheered. Some of the Breedies danced in celebration. No one dared ask the Halfhawk Mortal why she'd lost her balance.

Seveny looked up at the tree from which she'd fallen. "Sorry, Tommy."

The falcon was hopping from foot to foot on his branch. He glided off it and landed neatly beside her.

"You could have been killed!" he hawkthought. "If you die as a hawk, you die. End of."

"You think I fell on purpose?" Seveny hawkthought back. "It felt like part of my soul was being ripped away!"

Tommy looked at her quizzically, and made the change.

Max and George stopped wondering where to look and went to find the Halfhawks some breakfast. Empu Salim brought blankets for them both and they gratefully received them.

"Thank you for guiding us!" said the Empu, sitting down beside the Halfhawks. "I didn't believe we'd reach Rammed Earth Coven so quickly. But then, I hadn't counted on you two leading the way."

On the Empu's orders, the Breedies had set out while it was still dark. Empu Salim wanted to make sure that with such a large group they'd reach Pity Me in good time. Except for the smaller manshu and those needed to care for them, all the Breedies had embarked on the journey. They'd passed through large fields of hemp, acres of sunflowers and dark woods full of peppermint and fennel, and reached Rammed Earth Coven at dawn.

"Happy to oblige," said Tommy.

Seveny smiled at the Empu's compliment, though she could have completed the trip eight times over in the time it had taken the Breedies to reach this point. But the sky was void of obstacles, and the earth here definitely wasn't: it was filled with deep arteries of red clay and covered in tall, conical Pyre Ant nests. The nests resembled giant tusks or a collection of enormous witches' hats, and they'd obscured the thousand-strong group from each other as they passed through them. Seveny had often had to circle round and guide lost stragglers back to the group. It was slow going—the Breedies had to carefully skirt round the nests so as not to anger their fearsome occupants.

Tommy finished his breakfast and went back up into the sky on lookout. But he wouldn't let Seveny join him. He said she still looked shaken from the fall. So she sat and picked at the hemp-seed bread and rabbit kidneys her friends had brought her to eat, and took in her surroundings.

The sky-scraping trees that walled Rammed Earth Coven were silhouetted in the dim dawn light. They were a menacing presence with dark bark and crooked limbs. For a moment Seveny thought she could hear the distant cry of a screaming baby. And then she remembered the creatures she'd spotted in the woods. It was the howl of a wolf. The wind picked up and the leaves of the nearby trees began to whisper. "Seveny," they seemed to say. "Seveny, Seveny, Sevenyyyyyy!"

Seveny was sick of these earthly disturbances. She stared at the horizon, longing to be back in the sky.

Which was when she spotted the building.

The trees almost concealed it, but she could just make out the dull red clay of its walls.

Rammed Earth Coven got its name from the hat-like nests of its Pyre Ants—that's what most people said. But some told a darker tale. The legend went that hundreds of years ago, witches had lived here in a large house with red clay walls. In that house they flayed the skins of those unfortunate souls who, lost in the wilderness, entered the building for shelter.

"The Coven," Seveny whispered.

"What?" said George, sat beside her, nibbling some bread.

Pointing out the building won't help anyone, thought Seveny. *Let alone George.*

"Rammed Earth Coven. It's an interesting name for a place, that's all."

George smiled and offered her the rest of the loaf.

Seveny shook her head. "I'm full."

And yet, she thought, remembering her tumble and the pain in her heart, *I've never felt so empty.*

Chapter Thirty-seven

Tickler therapy

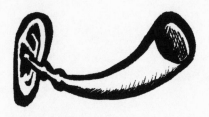

Miss Humfreeze woke to find her eyes strapped shut.

"The anaesthetic hasn't worked!" she said. "Please stop, I'm awake!"

"Decamp!" said a small voice.

The pressure on her eyelids lifted. She tentatively opened them.

Light shone through the limestone cave's entrance and bounced off dripping stalactites. She was out of the Dispensary and back at Little Sea. Night had become day.

As relief swelled, guilt crashed. Though she'd escaped the hospital, the same could not be said for Nesbitt. And the horrors she'd witnessed were still vivid in her memory.

Her mind sprang back to the present. Who had saved her?

"Down here!" said that same small voice.

Miss Humfreeze looked down. She was in a pool of Ticklers.

"The shock knocked you out, but we was there to catch you!" said Sam O'Brady. His tiny chest swelled with pride. "If we wasn't so pushed for time we'd have taken you to Tickler quarters. But as you was opposite Come Down Passage, we brought you here. All in all, yours was a simple evacuation, not dissimilar to Jamie's."

Miss Humfreeze stroked her head. "Jamie?"

"Tuff, so to speak!"

"Jamie Tuff? I went to the Dispensary to find her!"

"You'd have been a long time looking, missus! She wasn't there when you was, but she's back now and will be getting soul-sucked any minute."

The news sickened Miss Humfreeze. But the presence of Brainticklers didn't concern her: when she was still 'practising,' the Farseers had told her of their kind.

"How did you find me? Through Little Sea?"

The Ticklers laughed raucously.

"No, through Magnus's eyes! Your son, so to speak, has a special kind of Sight. When he has something to tell us, he sends old O'Leery there a vision."

Sam pointed to an ancient Tickler who was resting in a rocking chair. Perched on his crow nose was the thickest pair of spectacles Miss Humfreeze had ever seen. He waved cheerily in her general direction.

"We is grateful for Magnus's Gift," said Sam. "Without your son, we couldn't have saved the few shamuns we did from the Dispensary. And it is nice for old O'Leery—" Sam whispered the next part "—as he is not seeing much of anything these days."

Miss Humfreeze smiled at crow-nosed, crow-faced O'Leery. "Thank you," she said.

"What did she say?" asked O'Leery, holding up an enormous tiny ear trumpet.

"He's deaf, too. Begging your pardon, missus," said Sam, "when we arrived, Magnus kept calling you 'Mother!' And we was wondering, how come him and Miss Meany is your children? Why is they Underground, when from the looks of you, you is more of an Overgrounder?"

Miss Humfreeze sighed. "I have not spoken of this in nearly thirty years."

The Brainticklers looked at her expectantly, a peculiar mix of concern and anticipation on their birdlike faces.

The little critters did save me, she thought.

"Very well. Thirty years ago, I met the Doctor for the first time. I'd just begun to teach, and he'd just become the Establishment's chief Doctor. It didn't take long for us to discover that we both had Gifts we were concealing from the world. He was a Dreamweaver, and I a spirit-traveller and close-contact mind-reader. Nothing works like shared secrets to make you want to share... other things. It wasn't long before we were lovers."

The Ticklers were spellbound.

"He couldn't marry me without the Establishment's permission, which for their own fickle reasons they wouldn't give us. But he wanted to be with me nonetheless. He lavished me with attention and lauded my skills."

Sam O'Brady nodded. "So to speak, continue."

"A time came when the Doctor's dreams were plagued with nightmares. We discovered that a demon, a succubus, was feeding on him as he slept. I taught him how to trap her in the Spirit Realm. And from that day onwards he had sweet dreams. But when I found out I was Fruitful the rot set in."

Now that Miss Humfreeze had started, her tongue ran away with the tale.

"The Establishment had just passed the law proclaiming that children born out of Wedlock had rotten souls. That they were Children of the Underworld and had to be aborted. The Doctor told me it would ruin his career if the Establishment found out the baby was his. He said that if I didn't name him as the father, he'd beg them not to punish me. He'd persuade them to let me keep my place at the school. He'd even ask them to let our 'rotten' child survive, so he could keep it in the Dispensary for observation.

"I was relieved when the Establishment agreed to his terms. I thought he was doing me a favour out of love. I was deceived."

The Ticklers were biting their tiny nails.

Sam O'Brady furrowed his unruly brows. "How did you not see the darkness in him? Why could you not read his twisticky mind?"

Miss Humfreeze shrugged. "Everyone has a blind spot. Mine was him."

"So then what happened, so to speak?"

"I went to the Dispensary to give birth. The Doctor himself would deliver the baby. When the day arrived, he came to my bed and made me swear that I'd never seek out my child. If I refused... Well. There *would* be an abortion. And moreover, 'something would go wrong on the operating table.'"

The Ticklers gasped in horror.

"I gave birth to not one, but two of the most beautiful creatures I'd ever seen. The Doctor named them Amina and Magnus. A few minutes later, I was slung out of the Dispensary.

"After that day, I wanted to close the door on my past. I swore never to use my Gift again. And I haven't. Not until last night."

Miss Humfreeze's face suddenly twisted. "My babies were *not* Children of the Underworld! They did *not* have rotten souls. Nor were they 'mutants' as the Doctor made the Establishment believe. Twins are not mutants! *He* mutated them. He destroyed..."

Thirty years of grief overtook her.

Eventually the waves stopped crashing, and the rocking schoolteacher came to a still.

There wasn't a dry eye in the house. Sam O'Brady delved into his jacket pocket and took out a spider-silk hanky. He blew his hidden owl-nose and wrung out his ginger beard.

"That Doctor is a very wicked man," he said. "But we shan't ever let him or anybody hurt you. As long as you is with us, you is safe!"

BANG!

A whack-shot skimmed Miss Humfreeze's head. It bounced off the wall, ricocheted round the cave and hit a stalagmite, which smashed to smithereens.

One of the cave's entrances was smoking. The smoke cleared to reveal a small woman wearing frayed trousers, a flat cap, and a no-nonsense frown. In her hands was a huge, cocked rifle.

Miss Humfreeze recognized her at once.

"Where's my son?" said Evelyn Crackpot.

Miss Humfreeze got to her feet and faced Tommy's mother.

"I haven't seen Tommy in over two years. After he was put on the Gifted and Dangerous Register, he didn't return to school. It's the reason I'm here, actually. How is he?"

"Dead."

Miss Humfreeze froze.

"When he heard the news he was to be re-educated, Tommy jumped off a cliff," said Evelyn. "So I want nothing more to do with your terrible school, but thanks for your interest. I'm searching for my *other* son."

Evelyn Crackpot looked at the cave's banked boat.

"Nesbitt!" she yelled. "My Nesbitt's tall, lanky, with goofy teeth and a surgically attached violin. He works a boat between here and Catacomb City, and last night he didn't come home for dinner. Seeing as you're here, have you seen him?"

Miss Humfreeze's eyes darted between the barrel of the rifle and the nearest exit, wondering if she could count on whack-shots rather than accurate ones if she ran.

"Yes," she said at last. "He's in the Dispensary."

"The Dispensary! He's gone looking for that girl. Jamie!"

Evelyn started pacing the honeycomb cave.

"He said he'd delivered a girl there a few weeks ago and wished he hadn't. He's been going on and on about it. Oh Nesbitt, you stupid boy! What have you done?"

"He escorted me to the Dispensary to look for Jamie," said Miss Humfreeze. "I'd no idea he'd be so brave."

"What do you mean, brave?" Evelyn's eyes bored into Miss Humfreeze, sharp as glass.

"He offered himself up for soul-sucking," the schoolteacher confessed. "He wanted to provide a distraction while I searched for Jamie."

"Pahhhhhh!" Evelyn doubled over with the giggles. "That's the funniest thing I've ever heard! My Nesbitt? My floppy-haired, stammering, 'baccy-shy Nesbitt?"

"Yes."

The Crackpot convulsed with laughter. "My cowardly, no-gun-slinging, fiddle-wielding boy?"

Miss Humfreeze nodded.

"Nesbitt? *My* Nesbitt? My Nesbitt's *gone?*" Evelyn's voice cracked.

"I'm so sorry."

"I DON'T WANT YOUR APOLOGIES! I WANT MY NESBITT!"

Evelyn crumpled to the ground. Miss Humfreeze, expecting to end up with a bruising or worse, put her bulky arms round her.

"I know where to find him," the schoolteacher said. "And we *will* bring him back."

Evelyn shrugged off Miss Humfreeze's arms and hoicked herself up off the floor. "Well, what's your plan?"

Miss Humfreeze looked at the central pool.

"Little Sea is potent... Evelyn, if you are anything to go by, the Crackpots are broad-minded... Braินticklers are strong..."

"And we is pleased to meet you, Missus Crackpot!"

Evelyn's eyes flew to the floor. *"WHAT THE BLAZING BOILS?"*

"Well now, you don't have to be like that!" Sam O'Brady puffed himself out. "We is not Blazing Boils, we is Brainticklers. And we is going to help you get your Nesbitt back!"

Evelyn's hand went to her holster. "How?"

"We'll need two groups of Crackpots and Brainticklers," said Miss Humfreeze. "One group will retrieve Nesbitt's soul, while the other rescues his body. And then—" she clapped her hands together. "We reunite them."

"You make it sound so simple!" said Evelyn hysterically.

"It would be, if it weren't for one thing," the schoolteacher replied. "Nesbitt's soul isn't the only one we have to rescue."

Evelyn's eyes narrowed. "There are others in the Dispensary?"

"Juvenites, yes. Their bodies are there. Their souls are... somewhere else. Evelyn, we have until midnight to rescue them, body and soul, before the Doctor feeds them to the Ancient Spectre on Dancing Ledge."

"That's right, Miss Evelyn!" said Sam. "The Doctor's Turning juvenite souls and feeding them to his giant snake!"

"Turning?" said Evelyn.

"He's managing to make them travel down to the Spectre when they die, instead of up to the Blanket of Stars," Miss Humfreeze explained. "Sam, if that's true, its worse than I feared. Evelyn, could you introduce me to your Clan?"

"What about us, ma'am?" said Sam O'Brady grandly. "If we is all in this together, shouldn't us Ticklers meet the Crackpots?"

"Yes!" said Miss Humfreeze.

The other Brainticklers flibbertigibbeted and their vertical forehead lines became increasingly furrowed. But moments later, Evelyn and the Ticklers were aboard both the project and Nesbitt's flat-bottomed boat.

Chapter Thirty-eight

The Golden Orb

Nesbitt had been falling through nothingness and discord for what seemed an eternity. Down, down, down...

But now he spotted a speck of gold-dust in the black. As he fell towards it, the speck became a sphere and the sphere became a cage. When he was sure he'd crash into the golden curiosity, two of its bars bent open and a force dragged him through the gap. The bars snapped back into place.

Nesbitt looked at his fellow prisoners.

Thirteen juvenites floated in the golden cell. Some were wailing, others were shouting, and a few were biting, scratching and hitting themselves. But one juvenite was staring at him: a plump girl in a white dress with a pink rose in her hair.

"What are you doing here?" she said. "You're not a Child of the Underworld!"

"I delivered someone into the jaws of evil," Nesbitt admitted. And then, remembering his own experience, he added: "Literally."

"Who was this someone?"

"A girl called Jamie Tuff."

"Jamie?" the blonde girl looked surprised, saddened, and then relieved. "Well she's not here. Which has to be a good sign. Who are you?"

"Nesbitt Crackpot. And you are?"

"*CHILD OF THE UNDERWORLD!*" she screamed. "I'm Ella," she then said pleasantly.

Something suddenly distracted Ella, something behind Nesbitt. The cage bars opened and Jamie shot through them. The hansum and the juvenite faced the latest arrival.

"Guilty!" Nesbitt shouted.

"You don't think I had anything to do with this, do you?" said Jamie.

Ella's face darkened. "*CHILD OF THE UNDERWORLD!*"

"Ella, whatever you think I've done, I haven't, I promise!"

"I'm sorry I delivered you to the—Guilty!" Nesbitt bleated.

Jamie, realizing she wasn't the object of their accusations, held Nesbitt's hand. "You weren't to know what danger I was in," she said. "And even if you *had* known, I'm sure you had no choice." She linked arms with Ella. "And you, Ella, are the sweetest person ever to exist!"

"*STUPID!*"

Jamie spun round.

The boy who'd shouted was now smiling sweetly.

Jamie's legs turned to jelly. "Billy? You're still alive!"

Billy moved slowly towards her, stopped, and punched himself in the head.

A girl with candyfloss hair approached the group.

"Charlotte!" Jamie spoke softly, hoping the girl wouldn't harm herself like Billy. "I thought I'd never see you again!"

Charlotte was sobbing uncontrollably. "*NOBODY'S FRIEND.*"

Jamie tightened her grip on Nesbitt and Ella. "I think we should keep hold of each other. And try not to listen to the voices in your heads."

Chapter 38. The Golden Orb

The two of them nodded. But Jamie didn't notice. She was distracted by the soft breath on her cheek.

And her mother's tortured scream.

Chapter Thirty-nine

Catacomb City

Miss Humfreeze and the Ticklers were sailing through the Catacombs. Hand steady on the punt, Evelyn Crackpot guided Nesbitt's boat through Glowfly Grotto.

"The pearl chains are baby gnats," said Evelyn. "The twinkling lights are giant maggots."

Miss Humfreeze could have managed without the constant commentary, but she could see it provided the Crackpot with a welcome distraction.

"And to the left, you can see our famous albino ants!"

After sailing smoothly through the wide waterways of the Grotto, the Catacombs began to twist and turn.

"Breathe in!" yelled Evelyn, as she punted them through a particularly tight passage.

A minute later the tunnel opened out into a vast cavern.

Evelyn glowed with pride. "Welcome to Catacomb City!"

The boat sailed into the City, and the river widened. They were deep inside the mountain, and the cavern's limestone walls scaled great heights. Its honeycomb had been divided into ten-storey flats. The dwellings were plentiful and compact, and each apartment was abuzz with activity.

They carried on upstream and soon passed a small playground. Mini manshu were sliding down a propped-up railway sleeper, arguing over whose turn it was to go next. The sight of the young children playing made Miss Humfreeze smile.

And then she smelled the food.

The schoolteacher had missed dinner and, as they glided past the City's many kitchens, her mouth watered at the prospect of breakfast. Each kitchen had a shutter out of which cooks dispensed bowls brimming with tasty-smelling gloop. The boat veered towards a particularly scrumptious-smelling cook-house, but Evelyn had no intention of stopping. Her punting gathered pace.

As they sailed past it, Miss Humfreeze eyeballed a grubby little man in a large overcoat. "That man didn't pay!"

"Us ground rats look after each other," Evelyn explained.

As the soup kitchens thinned, they turned off the main river and punted down a tiny crawlway. Its walls were covered in glowworms. Most were green with red heads, though some of them glowed blue. Miss Humfreeze found them mesmerizing.

"Railroad beetles," said Evelyn.

"They are much like our *Nocturluminous Lampi Gigantae!*" added Sam O'Brady, not to be outdone.

Soon the lights became sporadic. The river began to tremble and the limestone walls vibrated. Low thuddings and rumblings filled the air. They made a sharp right turn into a long, narrow tunnel which was filled with empty boats queued up nose-to-tail.

"We're here!" said Evelyn.

She joined the chain of boats and slipped a mooring rope over a hook on the next boat's stern. She held Miss Humfreeze's hand and they made their way up the tunnel, using the boats as stepping stones. The Brainticklers followed them, nervously twittering as the thuddings and rumblings got louder.

They traced the thuddings and rumblings to a dented metal door set deep inside the tunnel's wall. On the door was painted:

The Dirt and Flirt
Bar, wrestling, dancing,
≥ MUSIC ≤
Just try and leave without getting your feet wet!

"I'll call you when we're ready," Miss Humfreeze told the Brainticklers. "Until then, stay put."

Sam O'Brady looked deflated, but the other Ticklers' forehead lines became noticeably less depressed.

"You ready?" said Evelyn.

Miss Humfreeze nodded. She took a deep breath, and turned the handle.

Their reception was explosive.

Chapter Forty

A United Front

"Duck!" cried Evelyn.

A whack-shot struck the wall behind them.

"Do as I do!" Evelyn said, taking the schoolteacher's hand. "We're heading for the stage."

The Dirt and Flirt was a vast, dimly lit cave-cum-stadium. Most of the light came from luminous plants housed in large, water-filled glass pillars. Giant glowworms on the ceiling pulsed blue, white and red. A drinks bar ran round the perimeter, propping up Crackpots in various stages of intoxication. It had been a messy night. It continued to be a messy morning.

Miss Humfreeze held on tightly as Evelyn led her through the stadium, ducking when she ducked and swerving when she swerved.

At the centre of the cave was a raised wrestling ring, lit by bright quicklime spotlights. A match was in progress, cheered on by dancing boys and girls dressed in dazzling sequins.

They were accompanied by the strangest, loudest band Miss Humfreeze had ever heard.

The fifty-strong band was housed in a ditch-cum-orchestra-pit. Crackpot fashions were legendary for being bizarre, and these musicians took style to the extreme. They were particularly pierced and spectacularly inked.

The orchestra was a collection of strings, drums, spoons, jugs, saws, buckets and many other instruments Miss Humfreeze could hardly describe, let alone classify. The musicians improvised with vigour and sensitivity, producing a wild, rousing tune that was both melodious and moving.

"Ah! They're having a Skiffle!" Evelyn shouted.

The two women dodged and swerved as they worked their way closer to the wrestling ring.

"Can't we make it stop?" said Miss Humfreeze. A rock-bullet whizzed past.

"No, they don't do requests, it'd wound the musicians' feelings!"

"I mean the shooting! Can't we make the shooting stop?"

Evelyn's eyebrows raised. "Oh no! You'd risk your life if you asked for a gun-break!""

They finally made it to the centre of the stadium. They ducked under the wrestling ring's rope and hauled themselves onto the stage. Their presence in the ring stopped neither the fighting nor the music. In a final attempt to garner the Clan's attention, Evelyn shot a bullet to the ceiling. It pinged off the roof and hit one of the luminous plant houses. The glass pillar smashed, releasing its water. The plant stopped glowing and slumped to the ground.

"My Nesbitt's dying!"

The stadium grew quieter.

"The Doctor's got him, this woman can save him, and we need your help!"

By the end of the sentence, the rocks had stopped flying, the fighters fighting, the dancers dancing, and the musicians playing.

"Did the Doctor get Nesbitt c-c-c-cause he's so weak?" said a hansum boy from the auditorium.

"No!" said Evelyn. "He did something braver than any of you ever would. He sacrificed his soul to help find a girl."

"Have a crush did he?"

The stadium filled with laughter.

"That's right, laugh at my Nesbitt!" Evelyn yelled. "He may only pretend to sniff the 'baccy and roll his eyes. But different can be bloody wonderful! My boy delivered an injured No Place girl to the Dispensary. And when he heard that something bad had happened to her there, he did something about it."

The crowd murmured.

"We've all heard the rumours," said Evelyn. "Tales of No-Placers tortured in the Dispensary. But do we speak of it? No. We drown out our fears with Skiffle and Blues! We shoot, we fight, we drink, we dance, but we don't confront it, do we?"

An embarrassed hush fell over the room.

"But Nesbitt made a stand. And I, for one, am ready to stand with him. It's time we did something about the Doctor and his experiments! Who's with me?"

Not one Crackpot moved a hair.

Finally, a man at the bar put down his giant carafe of liquor and got to his feet. "I'm wiv yer."

"Thank you," said Evelyn, rather sadly. "Now who's with Ray?"

At once, the whole Clan rose from their seats and popped their fists in the air.

"Great!" said Evelyn. "I shall now pass you over to Miss Humfreeze." She patted the schoolteacher on the back. "They're all yours."

"Who the hell are you?" shouted a toothless man.

"I am a teacher at Pity Me school. And I am here because Nesbitt and I travelled to the Dispensary together to find—"

"You got 'im caught!" Ray shouted.

"No, Ray, just listen!" said Evelyn.

"She's 'ere out of guilt!"

"Guilt," said Evelyn, "is as good a reason as any! It's why our Nesbitt sacrificed himself in the first place!"

Ray's jaw dropped.

"So did you find, um... er...?" the toothless man asked.

"Jamie," said Miss Humfreeze. "No. But I found many others. Children without souls."

"Children of the Underworld?" said an adolescent.

"Juvenites, like you. Only they've had their souls sucked out."

"By the two that look like vampires!" said a hansum girl.

Miss Humfreeze knew where those vampires had come from. "Yes."

"And Nesbitt?" said Ray.

Miss Humfreeze nodded. "His soul's been taken too."

Ray sobbed. "I can't 'ave another child of mine go missing! I can't. I just can't!"

"Ray, Tommy's not missing." Evelyn said this as though they'd discussed this many times. "No one survives a plummet off a cliff."

Miss Humfreeze's eyes boggled. "Ray's your—"

"Husband, yes," said Evelyn. "Though we separated after Tommy died. Ray saw Tommy fall and spent days in the water searching for his body. He never found it. To this day, he's convinced Tommy's alive."

"How are you goin' to get Nesbitt back?" Ray shouted.

"He's being held in the Dispensary with about ten juvenites," said the schoolteacher. "Their bodies will be easy to recover; it's their souls that pose the problem. But I think I know where their souls are—and how they've been imprisoned."

"How do you know?"

"Because I *created* the prison."

The stadium exploded with anger.

"It was never meant to be used for soul-catching! It was a demon trap!"

The Crackpots booed.

"I taught the Doctor a lot of tricks because I trusted him!"

"Who was the Doctor to you?" said a sequin-clad dancing girl with numerous facial piercings. Her hair was molded into five roof-pointing spikes.

Miss Humfreeze looked at her feet. "The Doctor was my lover."

The Crackpots groaned.

"So those devil children...?" the same girl asked.

"I'm their mother."

The groans became gasps.

"But," Miss Humfreeze said quickly, "they've lived with the Doctor since they were babies. And he has done unspeakable things to them."

"You abandoned your own kids?" said Ray.

Miss Humfreeze spoke plainly. "I turned my back on them for the same reason you Crackpots have done nothing about your suspicions. Because I was scared, and I wanted to survive."

Miss Humfreeze had the Clan's attention.

"Now. I have the knowledge and skills necessary to retrieve their trapped souls, but I'll need help to do it. I need three volunteers and a small group of musicians. The volunteers will travel with me to the very depths of the Spirit Realm. The musicians will play to keep us under.

"If we fail to free the children, then at midnight tonight the Doctor will sacrifice them to the Ancient Spectre. In exchange, the Spectre has promised him absolute power. The fate of the whole Island, including your City, rests in your hands. Who'd like to volunteer?"

A bitter calm enveloped the stadium as the meaning of her words soaked in. Not one Crackpot raised their hand.

"It'll be an adventure!" said Miss Humfreeze, going for the hard sell. "And when we return, what a tale you'll have to tell!"

A murmur came from the crowd, predominantly from the hansums. The noise encouraged the schoolteacher.

"Our three volunteers must be intuitive, brave, and—" Miss Humfreeze coughed "—clear of head."

"So you don't want us filled from crown to toe with direst Cracky-baccy!" said the hansum girl with the facial jewellery and the sky-high spikes.

Perhaps they're not as wonky as they're painted, thought Miss Humfreeze. "Would you like to give it a go? Uh—"

"Suzy. Yeah, sure. Why not?"

"Get in!" said Evelyn, excited.

"Thank you, dear brave Suzy. Now if anyone else thinks they have what it takes, please make your way to the stage."

The air filled with the sounds of Crackpots discussing obvious choices and jollying people along. But no one came forward.

Finally, Frank, a hunky wrestler with greased black hair and a dimpled chin, swung himself onto the stage. He winked at the crowd, and the Crackpots swooned.

The final volunteer was a booze-soaked Ray. The Crackpots murmured. Ray had their respect, or at least their sympathy. He also divided them.

"Ray shouldn't go!" someone hollered from the bar.

Shading her eyes from the quicklime spotlights pointing at the stage, Miss Humfreeze identified who'd spoken. The man wore his beard in a plait and was all elbows.

"Ray," the man said, "I love yer, but you're not clear of 'ead!"

A whack-shot was fired.

Blood trickled down the neck of the man who'd spoken. "Ow! Ray, that was my ear!" he said.

Evelyn did what she had to. That is, she kneed her husband in the groin, twisted his gun arm behind his back, and wrenched the weapon from his hand.

"This isn't about you!" she said. "This is about our Nesbitt, those kids and, from the sounds of it, the future of the Island."

Ray wept.

Evelyn kissed his forehead. "Would someone sort out Clive and get Ray a drink?"

First aid was swiftly administered to Clive's ear, and Ray was helped off the stage.

Miss Humfreeze addressed the crowd. "I'm afraid we just don't have the numbers. It'll be a stretch even getting to the Spirit Realm with three of us. Let alone springing the soul-trap."

"That's not a problem," said Evelyn. "Because there's four of us. I'm coming too."

"But Nesbitt's your son, and..." Miss Humfreeze looked at Ray, crying into his liquor. "Emotion can cloud the judgement."

"I'm not strong like Frank," said Evelyn. "Or intelligent like Suzy. But I'm a fighter. I'm coming with you."

Miss Humfreeze took her hand. The stadium cheered.

"Warrubout us?" slurred a woman from the orchestra pit. She had hurly-burly curls and a great deal of cheek.

"Oh my goodness," said Miss Humfreeze. "I'd forgotten about the musicians!"

"Good luck," said Evelyn. "You thought choosing the volunteers was hard."

"We don't have time for dithering!"

"Alright. Will the musicians' lives be at risk?"

"No, their souls will remain here."

"So you just want the best musicians?"

"Yes."

"TIMOTHY!" Evelyn yelled. "They're a little deaf," she whispered to Miss Humfreeze.

"Spoons at your service!" said a scruffy-looking juvenite. He tapped out a rhythm of incredible complexity.

"Oh, he's good!" said Miss Humfreeze.

"The best!" Evelyn sniffed. "My Nesbitt and Tim used to play beautifully together. *NEXT!"* She pointed to a hansum girl with pigtails and spectacles.

"My name is Georgie Skittlesworth, and I play the glass harp or the ghost-fiddle, or the ghost harp or the glass fiddle, or more simply, glasses."

Evelyn scowled. "Just play them please!"

Georgie ran her moistened fingers round the rims of her twenty-six glasses and improvised a haunting tune.

"Bob Thwack at your service ma'am!" came a twangy voice from behind a white moustache.

"I didn't introduce you," said Evelyn, exasperated.

"No hard feelings. My instrument, ma'am, is the cigar box guitar."

Bob thwacked away and twanged his strings and deftly thumped his box.

"Remarkable!" said Miss Humfreeze. "He doesn't look capable."

"Oh, Bob's capable of many things," said Evelyn, as Bob twinkled in her direction.

"Who's next?"

Evelyn sniggered, like she knew something the schoolteacher didn't. "Minnie, it's your turn, pet!"

Snore.

"MINNIE PET, YOO-HOO, YOU'RE NEXT!" Evelyn screamed.

She was answered with another snore.

The woman who'd asked about the musicians in the first place was now fast asleep. Her arms were curled around what appeared to be half a tree trunk, from which issued a mad assembly of strings, keys, reeds, whistles and horns.

"Are you sure there isn't someone else? Someone a bit less—"

"Nope. Someone give her a thump!"

The girl next to Minnie gave her a thorough wallop.

"Wos going on?" Minnie hiccuped.

"You've been selected!" the girl barked. "Tell 'em who you are!"

"I am Mrs Minnie Gligalot."

"And what is the name of your..." Miss Humfreeze paused. "Instrument?"

"Fred."

After Fred's first bowel-worrying bass notes, Miss Humfreeze had to concede that he would provide just the added oomph required. Though it mystified her how tiny Minnie found the strength to lift him.

The quartet was formed.

"I think it's time," said Miss Humfreeze.

"I think you're right," agreed Evelyn. She faced the crowd. "We have some friends to help us. Please welcome... *THE BRAINTICKLERS!*"

"Bra'nticklers? You mean like head-lice, right?" said Frank.

"Evelyn's gone crazy!" said Suzy. "I int never heard of no Braintickler!"

"That's because you haven't been looking for them," said Miss Humfreeze.

"Please clear a gangway," said Evelyn. "And open the door."

The Crackpots made an aisle, and four thousand Brainticklers processed in, Sam O'Brady proudly at the helm. They marched to the stage, heads cocked in the air.

One Crackpot bent down to get a closer look at the little creatures. He picked up a hansum Tickler and rolled her between his fingers.

"Cute!" he said.

"Yuck!" she squeaked.

"PUT HER DOWN!" Evelyn Crackpot yelled.

A woman at the front of the gangway shifted from foot to foot. "Ooh, they *do* look squishable!" she said, a bit too loudly. Miss Humfreeze noticed at once, alerted by her super teacher hearing. This time, just a look sufficed.

Once the Brainticklers reached the stage, some formed a ladder and the rest somersaulted, pirouetted and crab-walked vertically up it. Sam O'Brady reached the top first and hopped onto the stage, followed by a thousand others. The Crackpots cheered the Ticklers' acrobatics.

Sam O'Brady eyed up Frank the wrestler's muscles. *"BUILT!"* he shouted.

Frank flexed.

Sam's appreciation resulted in all the wrestlers and dancers flaunting themselves at the Ticklers.

"Enough!" bellowed Miss Humfreeze. With all the focus on the exotic and hardly any on the *feet*, she was worried that some of the most admired, and admiring Ticklers could get squished. "If this is going to work, we need quiet, calm, and *space*. Apart from Frank and Suzy, could all the wrestlers and dancers please leave the stage?"

The wrestlers and dancers sighed, but they did as they were told and swung themselves down.

"How are the Brainticklers going to help us?" said Suzy.

"That's a good question," said Miss Humfreeze. "The Ticklers' best Tickling Team will Braintickle us as we travel down to the Spirit Realm, to the Sea of Life and Death."

Frank lost some of his swagger. "The Sea of *huh?*"

"The rest of the Ticklers will enter the Dispensary by the main entrance and storm every clinic, rescuing anyone they find. Sam, you must lead the army."

Sam O'Brady puffed out his chest.

"And that is where the rest of you Crackpots come in. The Brainticklers can evacuate the Doctor's victims speedily, but they're no fighters. We need a group who *are*, and who are prepared to fight, not just for Nesbitt, but for the very future of No Place."

The crowd weren't convinced.

"Given your numbers and your guns, it shouldn't take much for you to overpower the Doctor and... whomever else you have to."

The stadium erupted in lively discussion.

"Could you organize them into teams?" Miss Humfreeze asked Evelyn. "Make sure those joining the Crackpot army want to be there. And keep Ray away!"

As Evelyn gathered the troops, Miss Humfreeze asked Suzy if the army could be well fed for the battle ahead. Besides, it had to be nearly lunchtime and she'd missed both dinner and breakfast.

Much to her delight, gut-buckets of chitterlings rapidly appeared.

Around half an hour later, Miss Humfreeze wiped the pig juice from her mouth and looked over at Evelyn who, lacking the stomach for intestines, was nibbling extra-salted anchovies.

"Ready to release some souls?" the schoolteacher said.

Evelyn grinned.

Shortly after breakfast the Breedies passed out of the southern end of Rammed Earth Coven. As they came down from the highlands, the land flattened and grew green.

One hour later, the Northern Mountains had become hills with copse-softened outlines. The copses marked the start of the Great Forest, which stretched southeast like a long green finger all the way to Rhyme Intrinsica.

By noon, the Breedies had got much further than expected. George and Max could even make out the hemp fields of No

Place's farthest-flung hamlets.

But up in the sky, Seveny could see further than her friends, and she was beginning to suspect a serious flaw in their plan.

The Breedies were out in open grassland, and as they walked south they were getting closer and closer to tilled fields. If the fieldworkers saw them, their arrival in Pity Me would not be the surprise that Empu Salim said he needed.

Seveny was about to swoop down and warn the Empu when, as if he'd read her mind, the line of Breedies halted. After some confused minutes the party started north for the hills, making for the cover of the Great Forest.

With the treeline between them and the fieldworkers, the Breedies resumed their march for Pity Me—though at a much slower pace.

It's just as well, Seveny thought, *that we've been making good time.*

Chapter Forty-one

The Sea of Life and Death

Once Miss Humfreeze had gathered her Crackpot and Tickling teams for the expedition to the Spirit Realm, they sailed back to Little Sea in Nesbitt's boat.

Once there, Sam O'Brady's second-in-command, Barry, organized the Brainticklers into four teams. Miss Humfreeze, Evelyn, Suzy and Frank all lay down, and each team gave one of the travellers a swift, thorough Tickle.

"It feels like my brain is being grated!" moaned Frank.

"It's as abrasive as ant-acid," squawked Suzy.

"Do not be alarmed," said Miss Humfreeze, as the Ticklers tickled. "This will be the least uncomfortable thing you experience for the next few hours.

"In a moment, we'll take Nesbitt's boat down to the very bottom of the Spirit Realm using Little Sea as our point of entry. Before we set sail I'd better go through the rules.

"There will be rather a lot of ghoulies in the Spirit Realm. We'll encounter most of them as we pass through the Sea of Life and Death. Creatures like spiders, snakes, scorpions and lions. You mustn't make the slightest move to avoid them. But oh! Do avoid the fanged sort."

"The fanged sort?" said Evelyn. "The *fanged* sort?"

"Yes. Those are formed of our fears. Confronting your own is fine, agreeable even, but confronting someone else's is fatal. And on a group trip there's no telling whose fear is whose. So it's better not to face them at all, as you'd probably lose."

"Lose what?" said Frank, trembling.

"Your lives."

Frank shook.

"So what do we do when we see the fanged sort?" asked Suzy.

"Move briskly and purposefully away."

"Anything else?" said Evelyn.

"Yes. They only bare their fangs at the last second, so reaction time is all-important. As a beginner I had some close scrapes, I can tell you... But I didn't have Brainticklers on board to keep me snappy. They ought to make it much safer. And the music will make it far easier to stay down in the Spirit Realm. Even when it gets scary."

"Oh Goddess," said Evelyn. "I'm too old for this. I'm having a flush. I just need a moment... Aaaaah! What if I have a moment—a senior moment—down in the Spirit Realm? Ticklers! More tickling please!"

"Evelyn, set an example! Now, when I say 'leave the boat,' leave the boat. Always remain in sight of one another, and if you see someone fading don't let them go! Grab them and tell them to concentrate. When the mission is complete, I'll shout 'all aboard' and then we'll all get back in the boat immediately. If one of us dies in the Spirit Realm, we *all* die. If one of us gets trapped, we *all* get trapped. If one of us, due to panic or lack of concentration, is dragged back to Little Sea, we *all* get dragged back. Understand?"

The Crackpots nodded.

Miss Humfreeze turned her attention to the slack-jawed quartet.

"It usually takes years of training to navigate the Spirit Realm. Your music will allow these brave volunteers to stay under and stay together. One duff note from you and the mission could unravel. They'll feel discord as pain, which could drag us back up. That would spell disaster. If you get out of sync, it will manifest in the Spirit Realm as differences in space. The smallest discrepancy in your music could separate us by thousands of feet. To be truly lost in the Spirit Realm is impossible, but they would *feel* lost, and that would inspire fear, and that—"

"—would spell disaster," said Minnie, hugging Fred for comfort.

"Exactly," said Miss Humfreeze. "In conclusion, even one of you stopping would direly affect them. Their panic would then spread to the waters around them. And believe me, you don't want them sailing the Spirit Realm on a choppy sea."

Once Miss Humfreeze was sure each of them understood their part, she and Evelyn pushed Nesbitt's banked boat out onto Little Sea.

"The pole for punting?" asked Evelyn.

"We won't be needing it."

Miss Humfreeze assumed a position at the helm of the boat. Evelyn, Frank and Suzy sat behind her, accessorized with moving Tickler hats.

The musicians set up on dry land as close to the boat and each other as possible. Minnie set the pace with Fred, Timothy followed on his spoons, Georgie rubbed her glasses, and Bob thwacked his guitar. The Brainticklers began to chant.

Miss Humfreeze held her breath and plunged into the Spirit Realm, pulling her Crackpot compadres down with her.

* * *

Moments later, the group were sailing in a boat without a paddle on the surface of a deep blue sea. They were surrounded by lavender sky.

And thousands of eyes.

"Oh-h-h-h!" Evelyn shuddered. "I've never seen so many crawlies!"

The sky was full of birds, bats and… spiders. The arachnids hovered in the air without anything holding them up. To Evelyn's relief they were large but gummy.

"Keep calm. Keep cool. And concentrate!" said Miss Humfreeze.

Splash!

A giant eel rocked the boat, throwing the two younger Crackpots overboard. Frank and Suzy gasped for help as they sank beneath the water.

Miss Humfreeze didn't give them so much as a backward glance. "Air does not exist here, so you can't be suffering from the lack of it. Water does not exist here, so it would be impossible to drown."

Suzy's and Frank's heads popped back up from under the 'water.'

The eel swam nonchalantly off.

"Anyway, it's time to leave the boat."

Miss Humfreeze joined the two already in the sea.

"But I can't swim!" said Evelyn.

"Nonsense!" Miss Humfreeze offered her hand. "Onwards and downwards!"

"What about the boat?"

"It'll come when we need it."

Evelyn grasped the schoolteacher's arm and jumped into the water.

As the four sank through the sea, the Crackpots were surprised to discover that no matter how deep they went, the birds and bats kept flying just as they had on the surface. And land animals walked on invisible ground.

"It's all one and the same!" said Evelyn.

"Yes," said Miss Humfreeze. "What we are floating in is a matter of life and death."

Evelyn frowned. "You're so comforting."

Miss Humfreeze was pleased with the Clan leader's progress. She wondered how the others were faring. Frank's tight shorts and oiled body made him very streamlined, and he was swimming through the darkening sea with ease. Suzy was so relaxed she'd started to play. And her technique could not be faulted: she sliced down through the sea in a straight line, swimming backwards and at speed. Miss Humfreeze was greatly encouraged by the smooth ride they were enjoying.

Suddenly a large mass of orange interrupted the indigo water. A striped creature the size of a house stalked towards the group, licking its whiskers and extending its claws. Its jaws separated to reveal a set of needle-like fangs.

Crackpot arms and legs flailed.

"We shall swim around it briskly and peacefully," said the schoolteacher. "And as Suzy has discovered, relaxing makes you go faster!"

Miss Humfreeze, Evelyn and Suzy swerved round the tiger easily, but Frank was in trouble. He slowed to a crawl, then stopped completely. The fanged beast came straight for him.

"I don't want to get eaten!" he cried.

"If you cling on to crises, you will sink!" said Miss Humfreeze.

But Frank had gone into free fall. He was turning translucent.

"Suzy!" Miss Humfreeze shouted. "Frank's starting to go!"

Suzy was with him in under a second.

"Please let me go!" Frank begged. "I'm nearly back at Little Sea!"

"And you'll drag us wiv you! Just to remind you what that means, Nesbitt and the other juvenites will not never be reconnected wiv their souls, there will be a mass Taking tonight, and the Island will be doomed!"

Frank stopped splashing and once more became opaque. The tiger was now only a yard away. But Frank still didn't move.

"Swerve!" screamed Suzy, grabbing his arm.

"No," said Frank. "It's my fear, and I shall own it."

He wriggled from her grip and swam straight for the cat. Flexing his muscles, he entered its jaws.

Miss Humfreeze couldn't watch. Frank's fear hadn't necessarily created that monster. And if one of them died...

"It's all right!" said Evelyn.

Miss Humfreeze unscrunched her eyes. And discovered three smiling Crackpots, and not a tiger in sight.

"Very well played, Frank," she said. "Don't do it again."

After that, things continued in a much smoother vein. The group encountered a cloud of bats, a rash of rats, and some lizards lounging overhead. They ignored all these non-fanged obstacles beautifully.

As they dived, the sea darkened nearly to black, and their path became strewn with luminescent fish and not much else. Then even the fish disappeared, leaving them in total darkness.

The air was thick and heavy.

"Aha!" said Miss Humfreeze. "We have left the natural behind and are now entering the supernatural."

"I'm not sure much was natural about the last section," Evelyn muttered.

"Soon we'll reach the Valley of Souls." Miss Humfreeze avoided its more frightening moniker, The Dark Crypt of Silent Screams. "And now we have just one more hurdle to face."

"We'll be fine," said Frank. "I just exploded a demon!"

Miss Humfreeze wondered how long Frank's cool would last. Turned out not very: something knocked him sideways.

"What the—what was that?" said Frank. "Suzy? I might have almost landed you in the jaws of death, but you didn't have to slap me!"

"I never slapped nobody," said Suzy indignantly. "I'll have you know-oh-oh-*owwwww!*" She began to jerk about. "Stop pulling my hair!"

"Let go!" shrieked Evelyn, as she whooshed past Miss Humfreeze, led by the nose.

"Welcome to the Pit of Pinches," said the schoolteacher. "We must release this group of spirits before proceeding further. These poor invisible things have forgotten, for some reason or other, where they were supposed to go."

Evelyn careered back past the schoolteacher. "What are these things?"

"Oh, they're very simple beings. Hardly more than misplaced thoughts, really. If they lose their way, they've no way to get back on track, and when that happens they end up here."

Evelyn nosedived a hundred feet.

"And until someone reminds them, they remain trapped in a perpetual state of confusion. Confused spirits are fierce."

"I'm getting that!" shouted Evelyn, who was now circling the group at breakneck speed.

Suzy found the sight hysterical, even though her spiky hair continued to be yanked. She then felt something down below: one of the invisible spirits was methodically crossing and uncrossing her toes. Suzy's eyes crossed in sympathy.

Frank howled with laughter, before stopping abruptly. "Oh, pickle my plums!" he yelped, in a strangely high voice.

As Miss Humfreeze monitored the situation, her ear became the axle about which she rotated.

"Do you want to leave this place?" the human wheel asked the spirits. "I can return you to your homes, but you must let go of us at once!"

The Crackpots were relieved to feel an immediate loosening around their parts—Frank particularly so, having been grabbed by his nethers.

"Good!" the twirling teacher said as she slowed.

Evelyn's nose was released and she came to a halt. "Great crowd control!"

"That's thirty years of teaching. Thank you for releasing us," she said to the invisible spirits. "I shall return the favour, but first I must beg your help. Some souls have been trapped in the Dark Crypt below. I believe they're encased in a web-like sphere as strong as steel and as lustrous as gold. If such a prison exists and any of you know the way, please grab my little finger—gently! And kindly lead us to it."

Moments later, her finger descended, followed by the rest of her, followed by the group, and they left the Pit of Pinches. But the air around them stayed heavy as the spirits travelled with them.

They dived for what seemed like hours before the sea changed to a colour none of the Crackpots had ever seen. Miss Humfreeze explained to the astonished group that it was the colour on the *other side* of black. After that came great banks of mist which rolled over them forever. Finally they arrived at their destination.

"You have guided us well," Miss Humfreeze said to the invisible spirits surrounding them. "Allow me to help you home."

Miss Humfreeze concentrated for a few seconds. The air that had been heavy with sorrow was suddenly light and clear.

"Have they gone?" said Evelyn, expecting a pinch for an answer.

"Yes."

"But you didn't do nothing!" said Suzy.

"You're right, I did a lot! They had forgotten where they were going, and I jogged their memory."

"I wish I could forget where *we* were going," said Frank. He gazed at the giant golden sphere flickering in the distance.

Miss Humfreeze's eyes narrowed. "The Doctor has been renovating," she said. "When I created that trap, it was no larger than a Brainball. Welcome to the Golden Orb."

Chapter Forty-two

Black Village, Blue Wood

 It was an arduous trip through the Great Forest. Its trees were thorny and its trails intended more for badgers than Breedies. And though the villagers were loath to blunt their blades, they were forced to hack a way through.

By the time they reached the southernmost tip of the forest the tired sun had set, and when the Breedies left the cover of the trees they found themselves in blackened streets.

"Rhyme Intrinsica!" said George.

Empu Salim gazed at the ruins. The charred houses were terrible in the darkening light. The village hall was an oblong of ash, and the scattered debris around them spoke of a village's life cut short.

"No more," said the Empu in a low growl. "No one will suffer such a fate again."

The road out of the burned village took the Breedies straight to Blue Wood. Its clearing, bisected by the fallen oak, was just large enough to fit everyone inside.

George and Max looked at each other, remembering the last time they'd been here—and who had been with them.

"We'll get them back," said Max.

George nodded. "We have to."

Standing on the clearing's sundial for height, Empu Salim addressed the group.

"The Summer Sacrifice begins in two hours. For those of you not born here, this means the whole population of No Place will be gathering on the school field, inside its barbed wire fence.

"We'll find the No-Placers circling a huge bonfire, hurling some of the most precious objects they possess into its flames. The Establishment have told them that the Great Goddess demands they do this to atone for their sins. The more valuable their sacrifice, the greater their atonement."

The crowd rumbled.

"Between us and their bonfire stands Pity Me town, which will be deserted. We shall march down the main street and enter the school grounds by the only gate. If we can take the No-Placers by surprise and make them listen to us, I am certain that together we can put a stop to the Doctor's plans."

"Why not go straight to Dancing Ledge?" said Fira. "If the Doctor's there—"

"The Ledge is visible from the school field. If the No-Placers see an army marching onto it during their Sacrifice, who knows what they would think? I wouldn't be surprised if, having stopped the Doctor, we found ourselves driven into the Great Sea by a terrified mob. No, we have to get them on our side first. And I am confident we will."

Seveny, flying above the clearing with Tommy, hoped the Empu's optimism wasn't misplaced. The Breedies were a thousand strong, but there would be ten times that number of No-Placers crammed inside the school grounds. The No-Placers wouldn't be armed, but they would be scared, and scared in a confined space...

"Those who left No Place most recently will enter first with me," said the Empu. "The crowd will recognize them easily, which will make us seem less of a threat. The rest of you will follow behind with your blades on your backs as usual.

Remember, we are not there to fight—or even to intimidate. We are there to gain an *understanding*."

Empu Salim glanced up at the moon.

"Soon, we'll make our way to Pity Me School. If the No-Placers are gathered as they should be, they won't see us approach. For now, rest, drink, and eat for dinner the food you missed at lunch. You'll need your strength."

Chapter Forty-three

Spider Prison

"The Golden Orb's beautiful!" said Suzy. "Twenty four carat!"

"Yes," agreed Miss Humfreeze. "It's one shiny web."

As they neared the golden prison, the schoolteacher saw the enormity of their task. They had no bewitching demon to contend with: the succubus she'd helped the Doctor capture years ago was nowhere to be seen. But over a dozen juvenites were caught in the soul-trap, and releasing them was going to take time. Time they didn't have.

"How come these souls have got bodies?" Evelyn asked.

"The invisible spirits in the Pit of Pinches were little more than stray thoughts. They never had any sort of form on any plane of existence. But the souls in the Golden Orb have living bodies and they know it. Knowing you have, or once had, a body creates a version of it in the Spirit Realm—and, indeed, most places."

"So all this is just a mirage?"

"Unfortunately not. No. That would make soul-retrievals easy, and our job will be anything but."

As the Crackpots neared the Orb they heard the occupants talking.

"Nobody likes a know-it-all!"

"Sissy!"

"Fat!"

"Waste of space!"

Frank gulped. "What's happened to them?"

"Their souls are being Turned. The Doctor knows each student well enough to know their worst fear. And I suspect that before sending each soul down to the Golden Orb, he's been planting a poisonous thought inside them. A personal demon, if you will. This demon will attack them until they believe they're not worthy of existence. That's why the juvenites he's already disposed of have been seeking a home in the Spectre's jaws—and why their souls have gone to the Underworld instead of travelling up to the Blanket of Stars."

"So how do we get them out?" said Suzy.

"Through manipulation. Or failing that, brute force."

Evelyn raised her eyebrows—and there they froze. Now they were just yards from the Orb, they could see its captured contents clearly.

"Nesbitt!"

"Mum!" Nesbitt released Jamie's hand and grabbed Evelyn through the bars.

"Miss Humfreeze!" Jamie floated over, still linking arms with Ella. "How come you're here?"

"We're putting a stop to the Doctor's plans. I'll tell you more once we've got you out."

Jamie looked at the cage around her. "There is no way out that I can see."

"Jamie Tuff, as your English teacher I have faith in your imagination."

Jamie's mouth suddenly dropped open and she screamed.

Nesbitt tore his hand away from his mother and he began to whimper. "Guilty!"

"Hellfires!" said Evelyn. "They've been got too!"

A few seconds later, Nesbitt and Jamie shook off their horror.

"It feels like a memory's haunting me," said Jamie. "One I can't quite grasp. But Nesbitt, Ella and I have held on to each other—and our sanity."

Ella, who had been entirely vacant until now, saw Miss Humfreeze for the first time and tears of joy prickled her eyes. Her lips then curled into a snarl. "*CHILD OF THE UNDER-WORLD!*" she howled.

Miss Humfreeze sighed. "I'm afraid Ella will soon be like the others."

The other juvenites were wailing, screaming and shouting. Billy was thumping himself after every second "*STUPID!*" and Charlotte was constantly crying "Nobody's friend."

"It's taken two months for the Doctor to Turn Charlotte and Billy," the schoolteacher continued. "Their souls must have been very strong. We'll free them first. Nesbitt, Jamie—would you please bring them to the bars of the Golden Orb?"

"Can I help?" said Ella. She now looked the essence of calm.

"You deserve a rest," said Miss Humfreeze. "Being in here must be quite exhausting."

Ella's features clouded over. "I don't deserve anything! I'm a *CHILD OF THE UNDERWORLD!*"

The girl's behaviour confirmed the schoolteacher's fears: Ella's soul was on its way to Turning. Miss Humfreeze clapped her hands. "Right," she said. "Let's get going!"

Nesbitt beckoned Billy over. But he wouldn't budge.

"*STUPID!*"

"Charlotte?" said Jamie, gently.

"Nobody's friend."

"Well, that makes life simpler," said Miss Humfreeze. "Brute force it is!"

Nesbitt gulped, but he didn't move.

"Nesbitt Crackpot!" yelled his mother. "You do as you are told!"

The next time Billy tried to strike himself, Nesbitt intercepted the move. He yanked the boy's arm behind his back and wrestled him to the cage walls.

"He learned that move from me," said Evelyn, proudly.

Jamie dragged Charlotte over to the bars with relative ease—she was too weak to put up much of a fight.

"The Doctor's done a thorough job of Turning them," said Miss Humfreeze. "There isn't time to un-Turn them down here. The best we can do is put them back in their bodies."

"But look at the state of them," said Evelyn. "When they go back, they'll want to kill themselves!"

Miss Humfreeze eyes lit up. "Evelyn, you're right! And we can use that to our advantage... Charlotte! Billy! The bars of the Golden Orb are all that keep you in this tortured state. If you want to die, *will* them to disappear. Then you can return to your bodies and kill yourselves, and the world will no longer have to suffer you being in it."

Evelyn looked aghast. "What an awful thing to say!"

"Disgusting," said Miss Humfreeze. "It should do the trick."

Suddenly part of the cage snapped out. Charlotte and Billy shot through the gap and whooshed up into the darkness. The bars regrew as the juvenites vanished.

"Brilliant," said Miss Humfreeze. "Two souls successfully retrieved."

"Where did they go?" said Nesbitt.

Suzy sniggered. "Back to their bodies, silly!"

Jamie frowned. "Aren't our bodies still in the Dispensary?"

"Not for long," said Miss Humfreeze. "The Crackpots and Brainticklers have organized an army. Even as we speak, they're storming the Dispensary."

The unassuming door of the Dispensary's main entrance swung open. Led by Ray, the Crackpot army spilled into an anteroom, empty except for two tall levers rising out of the floor. The room broadened into a large stone chamber with fire-beetle lanterns welded to the steelwork adorning its walls. And above...

A huge steel sculpture of a spider filled the hall's domed roof. Two huge cogs protruded from its abdomen, and heavy chains ran down its long legs and disappeared into eight giant claws.

In the centre of the room stood a stone plinth. The Crackpots and Ticklers gathered round it and discovered a circular steel map bolted to the top, its details obscured by dust. Ray blew the dust away and read out the words:

Dispensary For The Disenchanted
(Kindly Funded by statutory donations)

According to the map, the Dispensary was shaped pretty much like the spider above them. The domed chamber was the body, and the eight corridors leading off it formed the legs. In the dim light, they made out the names of the Dispensary's strange departments:

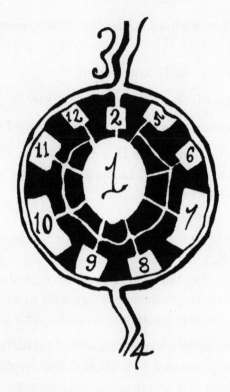

1. Central Chamber
2. Antechamber
3. Main Entrance
4. Come Down Passage
5. Defruiting Room
6. Laboratory and Doctor's Quarters
7. Re-education Clinic for Juvenite Delinquents
8. Surgery for the Disordered
9. Ward of Extraction
10. Infirmary for the Overripe
11. Sanatorium of the Weird and Wicked
12. Furnace

"We're in the Central Chamber," said Ray, tracing the dusty map with his fingers. "Get in yer teams and I'll give you yer rooms."

The Crackpots were getting in their groups when Sam O'Brady, perched on the brim of Ray's cap, spotted something which concerned him. Dangling over the map, a few inches in front of Ray's face, was a scarcely visible wire thread. Sam traced the thread up through the darkness, up through the gently-expanding dust-cloud, until it disappeared inside the belly of the spider.

Sam was about to say something when the displaced dust went right up Ray's nose. His powerful sneeze threw his head forward—and the stiff brim of his flat cap hit the wire.

It quivered.

The cogs of the great spider began to turn and the chains binding its legs suddenly slackened. Its giant claws hit the floor with mighty clangs, sealing off all eight corridors. The Crackpots ran for the anteroom but a portcullis slammed down between them and the exit.

They were trapped in a prison of steel and stone.

Chapter Forty-four

The Summer Sacrifice

The 'greeting party,' as George christened them, were crouched outside Pity Me School's barbed-wire fence, hidden from view by a dark, dense bush. The party comprised Empu Salim, George, Max, Maria, Kai, and those who'd most recently left No Place.

As they watched, Fira and Striker crept along the fence to the lone nightwatchman guarding the school gate. The ravishing Fira blew a kiss in his direction, quite stunning him—at which point Striker's fist finished the job. They tied the watchman to a nearby tree.

"Nicely done," said George, as the pair crept back.

"Striker, send the rest down," said Empu Salim. "The moment we're through, I want them streaming in behind us. Looking—"

"—calm and smiling and friendly." Striker's fearsome face vanished into the darkness.

The Empu's eyes twinkled. "Let's take a look at our neighbours."

Peering over the bush and through the spiralling wire, the greeting party surveyed the scene. The Halfhawks hovered high above the school field, also watching.

It seemed that all the Island, save the Crackpots, had come to pay their respects to the Great Goddess. Thousands bustled about on the school's enormous field. Hundreds of grey orbs arced through the sky, accompanied by delighted manshu squeals.

"I've never seen so many Brainballs in all my life!" said Max, forgetting to whisper.

Empu Salim's eyes narrowed at the sight of the coral.

Food stands lined the perimeter. Sweet Cheeks was coining it with their Sugarbomb Mountains, and enticing smells wafted over from Paul's Popcorn and Frankie's Fish.

As usual, the back of the field was cordoned off. Behind the barricade was a giant spiked wheel decorated with rags. The cardboard shells of fireworks covered the grass, waiting for their midnight sendoff. And past the fireworks, the barbed wire and the bay beyond, the full moon shone over Dancing Ledge.

The school field was lit by a huge central bonfire: a giant, spiralling wooden steeple; an enormous serpent reaching to the sky. A second spiral of No-Placers wove around it, casting their valuables to the flames: months-worth of food, the clothes off their backs, valued coins, babies' cots.

"The celebration's old," said Empu Salim. "The serpent's new."

"It's pretty much the same thing every year," George explained. "A symbol of the Ancient Spectre being destroyed by fire."

"What a dangerous idea!" the Empu said. His eyes alighted on a long raised platform in front of the snake steeple.

Funnella Fitzgerald was centre stage. Her makeup was even more trowelled-on than usual and her red quiff was impossibly high. Beside her sat Deputy Phosphor-Jones, and seated on either side of them were the rest of the Establishment. They reclined in elaborately carved thrones and wore magnificent purple satin robes in honour of the occasion.

"How do they move?" said Empu Salim.

"In a pack!" said Max.

George's brow furrowed.

The Empu opened his mouth to ask the same question in a different way when nine hundred and fifty Breedies rustled into position behind them. "I think it's time we reintroduced ourselves," he said.

Something was niggling at George. "The gate!" he said. "If it closes on us, it'll lock."

"Then someone had better keep it open," said Empu Salim. "Maria? Kai?"

Kai was excited to be given such an important task. Maria was pleased, too. If there was going to be trouble, she wanted Kai as far away from it as possible.

Moments later, Empu Salim strode into the field with Max and George at his side. The thousand other Breedies followed behind them.

The Brainballs soon stopped flying.

"Children of the Underworld!" somebody shouted.

"They're going to kill us!" someone else screamed.

Max and George realized that they must look strange with their painted faces and leather clothes, not to mention the blades at their backs. But the Empu's strategy soon paid off. In seconds, one of the most recent runaways was recognized.

"Max!"

Max's father pushed through the crowd and hugged his son tightly. "You made it back!"

Max grinned. "Better than that, Dad. I brought Maria with me. She's by the gate."

Max had never seen his dad run so fast.

Word soon spread of the missing's return. A stream of tearful No-Placers pushed through the crowd to meet long-lost relatives and friends. Many discovered grandchildren they never knew existed.

"George! Did the savages do anything to you?" George's mother gave Empu Salim the evil eye.

"No mum. Please don't worry."

"Please let us through," said the Empu as the crowd jostled around them. "We have an announcement to make."

The No-Placers were too stunned by the Empu's looks and age to do anything but fall back and clear a path to the stage.

The Establishment were adjusting their glasses and scratching their heads. The Empu walked towards them, flanked by Max and George. All three stepped onto the stage.

Funnella smirked at the boys. "You don't know how delighted I am to see you—but I see Kai didn't make it back? What a *shame*."

"He did. He's over there," said Max.

Funnella clapped her hands and sniggered.

"Well, Funnella, aren't you going to introduce me to your friends?" Empu Salim gestured to the Establishment around her. They were doing their damnedest to ignore his presence—and the thousand smiling savages behind him.

"I'm afraid I don't know you."

"Oh, we go way back." He looked carefully at Funnella. "Or at least, some of us do..."

The Establishment started to fidget. Spectacles were taken off and hurriedly replaced and handkerchiefs mopped across sopping brows.

"No idea!" grunted Phosphor-Jones, fiddling with his thick hair.

"Then let me remind you," said the Empu. *"RHYME INTRINSICA!"*

The Establishment sat bolt upright in their seats. They gripped their crooks so hard their knuckles turned white. Not one of them spoke.

Empu Salim faced the shocked crowd.

"Allow me to introduce myself. My name is Empu Salim."

"You are way Overripe!" Blake Scarpel's voice snarled from out of the crowd. "Why aren't you Underground?"

"These limbs have seen better days," said the Empu, "but some fruits rot early, while others grow old and stay sweet."

He pointed towards the cordoned-off rag wheel where the oldest Breedies were stationed. They were more wizened and ancient than anyone the No-Placers had ever seen, but they looked as fit as fleas. Fitter than many in the gawping crowd.

"Ghosts!" cried Phosphor-Jones, clutching at his arm and neck. "Ghosts of the artists who burned themselves to death!"

"No," said Empu Salim. "Not ghosts. Not suicides. Survivors!"

He raised his scarred arms.

"Some of us, with the scars to prove it, made it out of Rhyme Intrinsica when the Establishment turned our village to ash, though their fire murdered the majority." Empu Salim paused. "Including my only love, Empu Miss Mackadoo. My glorious Brigid."

Phosphor-Jones turned a hot pink and began to pant.

"But against all odds," the Empu said, "a few of us survived and made a new home for ourselves to the north. And as bees pollinate flowers, word of that home spread. Little Breedy became a sanctuary for the Overripe and the Fruitful, for those terrified that they or their children would be sent Underground to die."

The No-Placers stared at the Breedies, and the Breedies stared back. And then, quite unexpectedly, complete strangers found themselves in each other's arms.

Empu Salim faced the Establishment.

"See? Some things are not in your control. No matter how many fences you build or laws you pass. Things like hope, love, and dreams!"

Phosphor-Jones slammed his iron crook down on the platform.

"Do you have *any* idea who you're speaking to? Do you know who I *am*?"

The crowd pulled away from their embraces.

"Yes," said the Empu. "You're Phosphor-Jones. Though your looks are somewhat changed, you're still the same bully I locked horns with *fifty years ago!*"

Thousands of eyes bored into the Deputy Head as their owners tried to make sense of what the Empu had said.

"But I *am* fifty," Phosphor-Jones said to the crowd. "I'd have been ruling No Place from my cot!" He waggled his crook at the Empu. "You can see he's Overripe! He's a raving loony!"

But he'd lost his audience. Their attention had shifted to a much more interesting exhibit.

Funnella Fitzgerald was unpinning her wig, revealing a scalp covered in scar tissue and stitches.

"I have had quite some work done," she said, fingering the ugly scars. "Stretching back the face will hide the wrinkles for a time. But ultimately, snake venom injections are a shamun's best friend."

The rest of the Establishment were nervously stroking their poreless faces.

"Wouldn't you agree, *Deputy Head?*"

Funnella seized Phosphor-Jones' thicket of hair and yanked it off his head. A member of the Establishment coughed in shock at the undignified sight and lost a set of false teeth in the process. They shot out over the open-mouthed crowd.

"I reckon they're older than my dad, and they said *he* was Overripe!" yelled a man.

"And my gran!" wailed a child.

"Yeah!" said Dino Scarpel. "Why aren't *they* Underground?"

"Because the Doctor's treatments have let them stop the clock!" said Empu Salim. "And in return, they haven't bothered to look too closely at what else he's been doing in his Dispensary. Unknown to them, the Doctor has created something that could destroy the whole Island."

Phosphor-Jones rose from his seat. "Poppycock! The Doctor's a pillar of this community. I won't hear of it!"

"Let the man speak!" said Funnella.

"No offence, but you've clearly lost your marbles."

"No offence, but you're my Deputy, and you'll do as I say!"

Empu Salim's hand went to his sword. The Deputy Head sat back down.

"Perhaps you've noticed I've a snake painted on one cheek and an eagle on the other?" the Empu asked the crowd. "Hundreds of years ago, the survivors of the Great Storm adopted these symbols when, like a phoenix, No Place rose from the ashes and, like a serpent, it grew itself a new skin. The Eagle and the Serpent were symbols of rebirth. Symbols of hope.

"But soon another school of thought developed. What if the Great Storm was sent by a Mighty Power who was angered at all the evil in the world? What if She found out that some evil had survived, and sent a greater storm to finish the job?

"Recognizing the power of this idea, the Establishment perverted the meaning of the Eagle and the Serpent. The Eagle came to stand for everything great and divine—"

"The Great Goddess!" Sylvia Scythe-Crawley piped up from the crowd.

"That's right. And the Snake came to represent an evil force seeping up from the Underworld."

"The Ancient Spectre!" Edward Illustrious-Banks chimed in.

"Yes. The Establishment wanted obedience from the beginning. And they knew that terror had more power than love to compel it. So they invented a vengeful Great Goddess for you to worship, and an evil Ancient Spectre for you to fear."

The Establishment coughed and spluttered, but the crowd was still. Silent.

"The Doctor has taken your fear of the Spectre and fed it on juvenite souls snatched from Dancing Ledge. Now the Lord of the Underworld is no longer an Establishment fantasy. He is very real. And at midnight, when the moon reaches its height, the Doctor will sacrifice his last batch of juvenites, and the Ancient Spectre will be truly brought to life!"

The crowd were struck dumb.

"What a load of guff!" came a deep voice from the silence.

"Really? What is in your hands?" said Empu Salim.

Rosacea looked down at her grey, grooved Brainball.

"It seems more and more Brainballs are being coughed up by the Great Sea," said the Empu.

"And?"

"What do they need to survive?"

Rosacea shrugged.

"The sun, obviously!" said Crawley and Banks.

"And nutrients," added Herbert Snodgrass thoughtfully.

"Correct. They need a certain level of sunlight, they're living closer to the surface to get it, and they're dying prematurely. What does that suggest?"

"We get to play more Brainball?" Dino Scarpel laughed at his own genius.

George realized what the Empu meant. "It's getting darker."

Empu Salim nodded. "The world sits at the very centre of two opposed forces: the light, full Blanket of Stars, and the dark, empty Underworld. These forces are no longer in balance. The Doctor doesn't realize it, but by filling the empty Underworld with souls, he's destroying everything. For without light there can be no dark, and without dark there can be no light. And without light or dark comes complete *expiration.*"

The Islanders froze in fear.

Blake Scarpel screeched. "The Doctor's going to kill us all!"

"Not if we stop him." said Empu Salim. "The Ancient Spectre still needs one more meal of souls. If we stop the Doctor's final sacrifice, the Spectre will die and the Island will survive."

"Well what are we waiting for?!" the Tombland Gang shouted.

The Empu looked at the Establishment. Apart from Funnella, who was smiling creepily, they all looked defeated. Not even Phosphor-Jones dared meet his eye.

"Nothing!" the Empu said, jumping lithely off the stage. "To Dancing Ledge!"

But suddenly Empu Salim was gasping for breath. Phosphor-Jones' crook was hooked round his throat.

"This," said the Deputy, rising to his feet, "is what happens to people who disrespect the Establishment."

Phosphor-Jones clambered off the stage. For a moment, the pressure on the Empu's neck lifted, giving him a chance to draw his serpentine sword. But as soon as he had done so, something smacked into his back.

The wings of Phosphor-Jones' crook had hooked Empu Salim's belt, and what the Deputy lacked in agility, he more than made up for in strength. He shoved the Empu forward, relentlessly pushing his catch towards the serpent bonfire.

Towards the flames.

The boys looked on in horror from the stage.

"You act not out of power, but because you fear you are weak," said the Empu calmly.

"Says a man who makes snake-shaped swords! You're not a warrior. You're still only a dreamer. And you *know* where dreaming gets you."

Flames licked the Empu's face. One more push of the shepherd's crook, and he would burn.

George tried to think logically. The Empu had told him never to point his blade at someone because it would mark them out for death. So he drew his dagger... and pointed it straight at Phosphor-Jones.

Max thought George's death-curse was a fine idea, but there was no guarantee it would strike quickly enough to save the Empu. So he snatched George's blade and hurled it at the Deputy.

Executioner flew through the air and buried itself deep in the Deputy's shoulder.

Phosphor-Jones screamed and dropped his crook. In a flash, Empu Salim tore the winged hook from his belt. He spun to face the Deputy and brandished his sword.

"Sorry!" the Deputy said, backing away from the Empu's blade. "Please don't kill me! This is all a horrible mistake. I... I..."

And then, pulling George's dagger from his shoulder with a terrible shriek, Phosphor-Jones *charged.*

As the Deputy came for him, Empu Salim held his ground and raised his sword in self-defense. He had prepared himself for battle when, just inches from him, Phosphour-Jones stopped.

The dagger fell from the Deputy's hand. His hand clutched at his breast. His face turned a ghastly red... and then he toppled forward.

Empu Salim tried to catch him but his huge bulk was unstoppable: Phosphor-Jones careered straight past him and was swallowed by the fire-serpent's flames.

The Deputy screamed in the roaring blaze.

The Empu grabbed the shepherd's crook and tried to drag him out, but he struggled to gain purchase. When he finally succeeded, all that was left was charred, dead flesh.

And silence.

The Empu faced the stunned, scared crowd. "Are you still with me?"

Everyone cheered. Except the Establishment, of course. Apart from a strangely serene Funnella, they were cowering behind their thrones, scared to show their faces lest they end up like the Deputy.

The next few minutes passed quite smoothly. Possessions, food, drink and Brainballs were all downed, and the stands round the edge of the field were broken up for torch wood. Torches lit, the No-Placers and Breedies made for Dancing Ledge.

They were accompanied by an unexpected guest.

Ever since the great wig unveiling, Funnella Fitzgerald's behaviour had been very strange indeed. After the Deputy's demise, she'd begged to come with them to Dancing Ledge, insisting that they would need her help to defeat the Doctor.

Though the Headmistress's motives were far from clear, there was no denying that she'd helped to dethrone her own Establishment—who were now tied to their thrones thanks to a fast-working Fira and some of her friends. So the Empu granted Funnella's request to accompany them. But he kept her right where he could see her. By his side.

Chapter Forty-five

A Fine Kettle of Fish

Inside the Golden Orb, Nesbitt and Jamie were still wrangling juvenites towards Miss Humfreeze and the rescue team.

It was difficult just wrestling them into position, but it required all their energy to keep them in place while the English teacher worked her magic. Some hung on to the prison's bars even after they'd opened a gap to escape through. But on those occasions Frank's muscles came into play: he tore them from the golden bars and lovingly booted them to the surface. The process was interrupted whenever Nesbitt and Jamie had to deal with their own demons, but eventually, only three prisoners remained.

Nesbitt and Jamie seized Ella and dragged her to the cage wall.

"*CHILD OF THE UNDERWORLD!*" said Ella, snapping like a rabid dog.

Miss Humfreeze looked stern. "Yes, Ella Rose Last, you *are* a Child of the Underworld! And for that reason, you should not exist!"

"No," said Ella, tearfully. "I'm not. I'm not!"

"Oh dear," said the schoolteacher. "Her soul hasn't quite Turned."

"Isn't that a good thing?" Evelyn asked.

"No. Unlike the others, she doesn't want to die. She knows that as long as she's in here, she's still alive."

"So what do we do?" said Jamie.

"You and Nesbitt should reunite with your bodies. We'll give Ella some more time."

"We can't leave her," said Jamie. "She'll be alone. She'll be terrif—"

Jamie's eyes rolled back into her head, her mouth hung open and she screamed.

"Guilty!" choked Nesbitt, sinking to his knees.

This time, the two of them recovered painfully and slowly.

"Ella will be with us, and she'll be fine," said Miss Humfreeze. "But you and Nesbitt will be no use to anyone if you Turn!"

Jamie threw herself against the cage wall. "Then how do we get out?"

"Believe hard enough," said Miss Humfreeze, "and the Spirit Realm will bend."

Jamie and Nesbitt looked at each other, and then back at the cage wall. A gap opened.

Nesbitt jumped first, and shot up into the black void. Jamie looked at Ella one last time before she too made the leap of faith.

Ella had retreated to the middle of the Golden Orb. Her face was contorted with rage.

"She's caught between wanting to live and wanting to die," said Miss Humfreeze.

"So what do we do?" said Evelyn.

"Frank's going again!" Suzy shouted.

Frank's nostrils were flaring. He was beginning to fade.

"I've got an itch!"

"Where?" said Evelyn.

"How am I to know?" he said, fading fast. "I think it's on another plane!"

"Shall I scratch him?" said Suzy.

"No," said Miss Humfreeze. "Nothing can be done from this side. We have to hope the Brainticklers notice before Frank is dragged back."

"Bringing us wiv him!" said Suzy.

"And leaving Ella behind," said Evelyn. "Oh Ella. Ella, you are *not* a Child of the Underworld! The Golden Orb does not exist!"

The cage began to disintegrate.

"That's it, Ella!" said Miss Humfreeze. "You've got the right idea. Children of the Underworld *do not exist!*"

Ella moved towards Evelyn and Miss Humfreeze. The cage crumbled like brittle sugar, one golden bar at a time.

As they concentrated on the girl, Suzy focused on Frank.

"Stay here, do you hear me? Else I'll not never forgive you!"

"But—" Frank pleaded. "An itch is an itch!"

"You're a wrestler, Frank," said Suzy. "Your days consist of tight shorts and pain!"

As she bawled him out, Frank regained his opaqueness.

"I'm back!"

With Frank whole again, they joined Evelyn and Miss Humfreeze in telling Ella the truth. They explained why she was imprisoned and what the Doctor had in store for her. The cage fell away in bigger and bigger chunks, and Ella floated towards the group.

"Right!" said Miss Humfreeze. "All aboard!"

A high-pitched whine filled the darkness above, gradually dropping in pitch. The group looked up. They could just make out a tiny dot of brown in the black. The brown dot lengthened, then thickened—and Nesbitt's longboat shot down out of the gloom, stopping an inch above their heads.

The Crackpots jumped in and Miss Humfreeze took the helm. Ella was less than a foot away—on the wrong side of the prison's few remaining bars.

"Ella!" said Miss Humfreeze. "Come with us!"

"Manipulation?" Evelyn whispered.

"No. As long as we're in the Spirit Realm she can travel with us. When our souls fly back to our bodies, so will hers."

Miss Humfreeze held out her hand. Ella went to take it.

And then the rug was pulled.

"Aaaaaaaahhgghhh!" the Crackpots yelled, as Ella and the Golden Orb were torn from sight.

The boat careered backwards through the Valley of Souls, out of the Dark Crypt, and up through the now Pinch-less Pit. Seconds later they surfaced on the Sea of Life and Death. But this time the sea was choppy. Giant waves threatened to overturn the boat.

"Though the water isn't real," Miss Humfreeze shouted, "you must hold onto the ship's sides!"

The terrified Crackpots heeded her words.

And Miss Humfreeze capsized the boat.

* * *

The Crackpots reinhabited their bodies and blasted out a hail of expletives.

"What the blazes did you do that for?" spluttered Evelyn.

"Yeah!" said Frank. "What happened to communication?"

"What the Spectre were you thinking?" said Suzy . "I've never experienced nothing like that not *never* before!"

"I had to get us here together, and fast," said Miss Humfreeze. "Didn't the terror send us hurtling back?"

"Well yes," said Evelyn, "but—*urrrrgggggh!*"

The Brainticklers were flibbertigibbeting, the musicians looked sober, and glass covered the cave floor.

"I am not angry," said Miss Humfreeze to the Ticklers. "But what in the Hellfires happened?"

Sam O'Brady's second-in-command answered.

"Well, you see, ah..." said Barry. "We started well. Us Ticklers were tickling you as needed and the music was exquisite! We had a slight worry when you'd been under for a while. What with the light fading outside, the cave got dark. But then these here lights came on!" Barry pointed to a dozen strings of glowing pearls hanging from the cave roof. "One of them came on, most helpfully, above the musicians' heads."

"Right..." said Miss Humfreeze. "So what went wrong?"

"Frank started sweating. We knew the signs. We're good at detecting itches. I directed every Braintickler to jump on him and give him a bit of a scratch. You know, enough to make him comfortable, but not so much as to bring him back. And we did marvellously! Frank's breathing returned to normal and his face was restored to its usual shade. So we somersaulted off him, as you know is our way. Except... one of our newer Ticklers ended up in the musicians' overhead light."

He pointed to a hansum girl. She was one of the more exotic Ticklers. She didn't have a beak-shaped nose and a human mouth, she had a beak-shaped nose-mouth—a beak, in fact. Her once flat hair now looked like a dandelion head.

"The sticky thread caught me, and it gave me the biggest shock! The shock jolted me off it, and the light switched off!"

Miss Humfreeze recalled her poor thumb's experience with the retracting threads.

"I should have warned you," said Evelyn. "Glowgnat babies are sensitive creatures and easily disturbed."

"Not to worry," said the Tickler. "I mean, I survived...but the shock confused my landing and my dismount was a mess!"

Georgie winced. "She fell in one of my glasses, at which point I missed a beat."

"But I hauled myself out of the water and onto the rim. Only my weight tipped the glass over, and—"

Bob Thwack interrupted. "—that glass went into another, and another, and another!"

"And because the light went out, I couldn't see my spoons," said Timothy.

"And with all that glass smashing, I couldn't hear Fred. It was all a bit distracting," chipped in a hiccuping Minnie.

Miss Humfreeze sighed. "Well, that explains the choppy sea, and how we came to be separated from Ella and the Golden Orb."

Barry's hands flew to his hawk-nosed owl face. "The mission wasn't a success?"

"Every other soul has been released, and likely Ella's too. But I can't be sure."

"Back on their heads, team!" said Barry.

The Brainticklers began to board.

"No!" said Miss Humfreeze. "We don't have time to go back. Once the Crackpots have got everyone out of the Dispensary, we can—"

"The spider's got 'em, so to speak!"

Sam O'Brady entered the cave, followed by a few thousand other Ticklers.

"What spider's got whom?" said Miss Humfreeze calmly.

"Ray and the others! They is trapped in the Dispensary!"

Evelyn groaned. "Why on Earth was Ray with you?"

"He said something about getting his son back and proving his worth, missus. Anyways, he burst through the main entrance with the others behind him, and before I could warns them, a metal spider *this big*—" Sam illustrated the point with his one inch arm-span, "—dropped from the ceiling!"

Evelyn's lip trembled.

"The spider's legs came down and they blocked off all the exits. Us Ticklers managed to escape because we is small, but the Crackpot army is big, and they is well and truly trapped!"

Evelyn jumped off the boat and paced around the cave. "Are you saying that my Nesbitt and those frightened kids have now got their souls back, and no one is around to retrieve their bodies? They'll still end up at Dancing Ledge!"

"Well, this is a fine kettle of fish," said Miss Humfreeze. "Barry, could you and a thousand Ticklers go back to Catacomb City and tell them we need backup?"

Minnie picked up her musical tree trunk. "Fred and I will go with Barry. We'll be hard to ignore and more easily spotted."

"Sam," said Miss Humfreeze, "we need levitating, so to speak."

Moments later Miss Humfreeze and the remaining Crackpots were horizontal, as teams of Brainticklers sped them through Come Down Passage and towards the Dispensary.

Chapter Forty-six

Re-inspiration

Nesbitt opened his eyes. He was back in the Dispensary lying on a rock-bed, and his violin and gun were on a table beside him. The juvenites he'd met in the Golden Orb were also stirring. The ones who'd hurt themselves in the Spirit Realm carried on hurting. Billy and Charlotte, along with some other juvenites, started climbing the stone walls.

Nesbitt looked to his left. "Jamie!" he whispered. "Are you all right?"

"Yes, but what about Ella?"

Nesbitt looked to his right. Ella's eyes were still closed. She was grey and barely breathing.

"Ella will be fine," he said. "Miss H- Hu- Humfreeze and my mum will see to that. And my Clan will be h-h-h-h-here any second, don't you worry!"

The door of the Re-education Clinic opened and the Doctor and his family entered. Miss Amina quickly locked the door to keep in the juvenites climbing the walls.

Other juvenites were crying; some were gnawing at their arms. Only three of them were still. Ella and Jamie were lying down, their eyes closed and their breathing shallow. And in between their beds Nesbitt was sitting bolt upright, petrified.

The Doctor chuckled. "You've been re-inspired, Crackpot! And I know who you have to thank for that." He glanced at Ella and Jamie's lifeless bodies. "But Humfreeze still has work to do."

He looked round the room, devouring the sight of the distraught.

"And her actions are futile, for their souls remain Turned. When they're released on Dancing Ledge, they'll still know where to go. Straight into the Spectre's jaws!"

Through the locked door came the sound of distant gunfire.

Nesbitt's eyes shone. "Not if my Clan rescue them first!"

"I'm afraid they'll find rescuing you hard," said the Doctor. "They're caught in my spider-trap. Thank you for providing the bait. Your Clan consistently live up to their reputation: dim-witted, and easily led."

He walked over to Nesbitt. "Your soul hasn't Turned, so I'm afraid you can't be sacrificed. But you can still be part of the show! Tonight's special, unannounced and *final* Taking, the *real* Summer Sacrifice, should have a fitting accompaniment, don't you think? A swansong."

The Doctor handed Nesbitt his violin. "Play."

Nesbitt's nose twitched as he tucked his beloved fiddle under his chin. He positioned the horsehair bow on the catgut strings and his trembling fingers started crying vibratos.

The Doctor leaned over Jamie's bed and opened her eyes. Jamie tried not to react but it was no use: she felt the rash spread up her neck.

"*So* Transparent," said the Doctor. "But your soul hasn't Turned, either—which is very disappointing. Well, my fellow Dreamweaver, you may have cheated my Master of his choicest morsel for now. But you will make a fine spectator!"

He snapped his fingers.

"Magnus, would you ensure that Miss Tuff is completely relaxed for tonight? Paralysed, in fact. But awake!"

His son thought for a moment. "I've just the potion," he said. "The right quantity of moonflower juice and snake venom will keep her awake but freeze her muscles. Only her eyes will be able to move."

"I've taught you well," the Doctor said. "And I anticipate your swift return from the Laboratory."

"Daddy," said Miss Amina, "Magnus could get lonely. Perhaps I ought to—"

"—shush?" the Doctor sneered. "Yes, perhaps you ought."

Chapter Forty-seven

A Crackpot Always Plays The Odds

The Crackpots were careering down Come Down Passage at breakneck speed. Sam O'Brady, perched on Miss Humfreeze's ear, claimed that he could tell the time by the glow of the fire-beetle lanterns: the brighter the green, the later it was. By his reckoning, it was a quarter to midnight when they arrived at the Dispensary's Main Entrance.

Miss Humfreeze entered the anteroom first, and was met by a hail of rock-bullets. She dived for the floor.

The rock-bullets eventually stopped.

"Sorry," a voice called out sheepishly.

The schoolteacher got to her feet, glared in the direction of the voice, and then examined the two levers set in the anteroom's floor.

Suzy, Frank, Timothy, Bob, Georgie and Evelyn peered round the door. As Evelyn saw the bravest members of her Clan all locked up, she struggled to keep it together. When she saw Ray she wanted to give him a rollicking, but her heart melted first. She raced over to the portcullis and clutched her estranged husband's hand through one of the gaps.

"Don't worry. We're going to get you out of here!"

"I'd say we have one chance in two," said Miss Humfreeze, staring at the two levers.

"Pretty good odds!" said Suzy. "If the first choice is wrong, the second oughta sort it out!"

"Those in favour of this possibly foolhardy approach, raise your hands... Well!" the teacher shrugged. "I suppose majority rules."

"I'll take one lever," said Evelyn.

"And I the other," said Miss Humfreeze. "You go first, and I'll second you if needed."

The two women stood in front of the levers.

"I love you all!" yelled Evelyn, plunging hers down.

Something whirred above the Crackpots.

"Oh Hellfires," said Evelyn. "That doesn't sound good."

"Maybe it's gettin' ready to raise its legs?" said Ray.

The spider's belly opened, and out dropped two fangs.

"That's not anatomically correct," Sam O'Brady whispered in Miss Humfreeze's ear.

A Crackpot tried shooting one of the fangs. The bullet glanced off it and ricocheted round the chamber, narrowly missing a hundred heads.

"Put your guns down!" shouted Miss Humfreeze. "You're already in danger of death, and your gunfire's not helping!"

Once the Crackpots had disarmed, Miss Humfreeze pushed her lever down, hoping the fangs would retract. Instead they started to wander, jabbing here and there and crisscrossing each other.

"*HELL BOTTOM FIRE BLAZES!*" yelled Evelyn, pulling her lever back to its original position.

"*PHEW!*" the Crackpots yelled back, as the fangs ground to a halt.

Something clunked down from the spider's belly to join the fangs: a circle of rotating teeth. The fangs resumed their wandering.

Miss Humfreeze hoicked her lever up, hoping for the best.

The fangs and teeth began to descend.

Evelyn went to move her lever again.

"FOR THE LOVE OF THE GODDESS!" screamed Ray, gripping the bars of the portcullis. *"DON'T!"*

Evelyn took her hand off the lever and stepped away.

Miss Humfreeze took stock of the situation. This whole debacle had cost them time. And not only were the Crackpots still trapped, they were now on the verge of being executed. But if the Doctor completed his plan...

"We have to save those children's souls," she told the caged Crackpots. "We must leave you here and continue on our own."

"But we're goin' to die!" said Ray.

"At the rate the blades are descending, you should have a good quarter of an hour. But it can't be more than a few minutes to midnight, which is when the Doctor will begin his sacrifice."

Evelyn kissed Ray's hand and tore herself away from the cage. "What's the plan?"

"We'll circle round the outer corridor to the back of the Re-education Clinic and enter there."

"That door's always locked!"

"I know. We'll have to break it down."

"Just us?" said Suzy. "That don't sound like no plan!"

"You're right, it isn't," said Miss Humfreeze. "But right now it's all we've got."

Sam O'Brady was the first to feel the floor vibrate.

"So to speak... Maybe it's not!"

The vibration became a rumble, the rumble a thunder, the thunder a stampede, and in the nick of time the cavalry arrived— or, rather, the hastily formed auxiliary wing of the Crackpot army. They burst into the anteroom with a tremendous shout, led by a man with a plaited beard and a bandaged ear.

"Someone said you needed backup," he said.

"Clive!" Ray yelled.

Clive eyed the jabbing fangs and revolving teeth. "Oh, Goddess. How can we help?"

"By leavin' us here and accompanyin' Miss Humfreeze!" said Ray. "If the Doctor isn't stopped now, there'll be no stopping 'im at all!"

"Ray is right," said Miss Humfreeze. "We have to go *now*, circle round the outer corridor, and break down the door of the Re-education Clinic."

"But that door's solid oak, lady," said Clive. "And we ain't got no battering-ram."

A small woman with a large accessory pushed through the heaving crowd.

"Then it's just as well," said Minnie Gligalot, "that we've got Fred."

Chapter Forty-eight

Instrumental

Miss Amina's eyes narrowed. "What took you so long?" She had to speak loudly to be heard over the noise of suicidal juvenites.

"I had to make it from scratch." Magnus drew a fierce-looking needle from the gently-bulging pouch at his waist. "Hold her down."

The Doctor held Jamie's shoulders to the bed and Miss Amina held her feet. Jamie struggled but couldn't break free. Then she felt the hot sting of the needle, her blood turned to ice, and she struggled no more.

Ella lay, hardly breathing, on her rock bed.

"What shall we do with this one, Daddy?" said Miss Amina.

"Nothing. Humfreeze will release her for me. And when she does, she'll be just like the others."

He sat on Jamie's bed and stroked her cheek.

"My son is a master of his craft. You cannot move, yet you see. And as Nesbitt plays such fine music, I can't wait to see how you fare as my audience!"

"I was actually wondering whether I could *stop* playing now?" said Nesbitt, shaking with nerves and effort.

"You will continue to play until your fingers drop off. Ma, pick up his gun and aim it at his head."

Creaky Nan picked up the hansum's gun. She fumbled with the unfamiliar object and took aim. "Crackpot! Play or you're dead!"

BANG!

The noise of a bullet on stone rang through the room.

"What in the Spectre's name!" yelled the Doctor.

"It wasn't me," said Creaky Nan.

"Open up!"

"Let us in!"

"Open the door!"

The muffled voices of a hundred angry Crackpots filtered through the bolted oak door. Something heavy crashed into it, and one of its hinges flew off.

The Doctor's family sprang into action. Miss Amina picked up Jamie, Magnus picked up Ella, and Creaky Nan held the gun to Nesbitt's head. The Doctor dragged the juvenites off the walls and pulled the remaining ones out of their beds.

There was another crash. The door began to splinter.

"Children of the Underworld," said the Doctor, raising his voice against the juvenites' wails, the battering ram, and the mob outside. "Stupid children, lonely children, unfit children, unloved children. Tonight, I promise that you will go to the place you deserve!"

The juvenites were relieved to hear this and formed an orderly queue to accept their fate.

CRUNCH!

A chunk of door broke off. For a second, a thoroughly pummelled horn and a glimpse of tree trunk filled the gap.

"One last push and we'll have it off its hinges!" Minnie Gligalot's voice hiccuped from behind the door.

"Daddy, quick!" said Miss Amina.

The Doctor pressed a rock in the wall that was slightly more polished than those surrounding it.

Stomachs hit feet as the floor jolted up. The Re-education Clinic had become a giant lift.

The door disintegrated as Fred crashed through it. Minnie let go just in time, narrowly escaping Fred's fate. Poor Fred fell into writhing darkness—into a pit of snakes.

Miss Humfreeze and the Crackpots stared open-mouthed down after him—and then open-mouthed up, as the floor of the Clinic rose out of sight.

"Oh Great Spectre Bottoms!" Evelyn wailed. "We're too late!"

"We're not," said the schoolteacher. "We'll just have to retrieve them from the Ledge."

"But as soon as they reach the Ledge, they'll want to jump off it! And any minute now, Ray and the others will be dead!"

"You're right, Evelyn. Our only hope is to get to the surface at once, capture the Doctor, and force him to disarm the spider-trap."

Sam O'Brady somersaulted off Miss Humfreeze's ear.

"Missus! There's old tunnels near here that goes straight up, and us Ticklers is super fast. So if you doesn't mind, could you all drop down and we'll transport you."

Miss Humfreeze nodded. "Let's do as Sam says."

Within seconds, Miss Humfreeze and the Crackpots were racing up through potholes, caves and rabbit warrens. They left quite a trail in their wake, along with some very alarmed-looking rabbits.

As the Crackpots and Ticklers travelled up through the earth, the Breedies and No-Placers stormed down the path to Dancing Ledge. To ensure the crowd moved quickly, Maria, Fira, Striker and the boys were bringing up the rear.

The earth suddenly exploded in front of Max and George, and a very familiar head appeared from an abruptly-widened rabbit hole.

Max goggled. "Miss Humfreeze! What *in* earth are you doing?"

The schoolteacher was overjoyed to see Max, George and Kai alive, even if they were flanked by three leather-clad warriors. "Please help!" she wheezed.

The Breedies quickly unearthed her. Having uncorked the bottle, a fountain of Crackpots poured forth.

"I don't know who you are," said Miss Humfreeze to the Breedies, "but the Doctor's on Dancing Ledge, and there are a hundred Crackpots trapped in the Dispensary. They'll die in minutes if we don't disarm the trap!"

"George!" said Maria. "You're the best trapper I've ever trained. You're their only hope."

George looked nervously at the rabbit hole.

"I'll give it a try," he said. "Only how will I know where to go or what to—"

Before he could finish, a sea of tiny chattery things flooded out of the hole, grabbed him, and pulled him Underground.

As a terrified George whizzed through the earth, one of the chattery things caught hold of his nose, swung itself up to eyeball height, and waved. George gawped.

"Mister!" it yelled. "I is Sam O'Brady. We is the Brainticklers. And unless you likes the taste of rabbit droppings, I'd close your mouth!"

Chapter Forty-nine

Smoke and Mirrors

A door in the cliff-face opened, and the Doctor strode out onto Dancing Ledge. His family followed behind, herding the docile, suicidal juvenites.

Miss Amina laid the paralysed Jamie flat on her back on a rock near the sea. "Enjoy the show," she said, before sashaying back to her father.

Magnus placed Ella close to Jamie and stood guard over them.

Jamie's paralysed body had been set, quite purposefully, so that she could see the entire Ledge. The Doctor wanted her to have a clear view of the sacrifice.

The full moon was now directly above the rock stage. It cast a harsh light over the scene.

The Doctor had lined the juvenites up against the cliff as though they were about to begin a race. Billy got the go-ahead first: the Doctor whispered in his ear and pressed his nail into his spine. The boy began a slow tread towards the water.

The Doctor repeated the process on the next child in line, and the next. Miss Amina did the same from the other end, until all twelve juvenites had joined the promenade to death.

Nesbitt's violin accompanied their solemn march. Even with the gun Creaky Nan held to his head, his music was sweet and graceful. And accompanying him was the song of the Great Sea. The sound of the waves sank into Jamie's skin, buoying her heart despite the situation.

Her soaring heart was joined by a whirling head as moonbeams reflected off the silvery ocean and threw up crystalline shards of light.

And then, over the cliffs, oh, the most beautiful sight! A ghostly waterfall poured slowly down onto the Ledge. The spherical white moonflowers were opening in their thousands and trumpeting to the stars.

Jamie felt like a heavenly body herself.

"The magic of the moonflowers!" said Magnus softly in her ear. "When the moon is full and at its height, the blooms open for just a few seconds and release their scent. That is Dancing Ledge's real secret. The moonflowers intoxicate the juvenites at each Taking, and occasionally one of them dances into the water and drowns."

The scent was already fading, but its effects lingered: Jamie was as high as a kite. Nesbitt's tune had become otherworldly, and he swayed wildly as he played. If Jamie weren't paralysed she could have danced for joy. But Creaky Nan and the others seemed quite unstirred.

Why, Jamie wondered through her delirium, *aren't the Doctor and his family affected?*

"The moonflowers' perfume is a powerful drug," Magnus whispered. "Breathe it in and every ounce of worry disappears. But its effects can be counteracted with the right antidote."

He drew a small syringe from his pouch, filled with a glittering orange syrup. Unnoticed by the Doctor and Miss Amina, who were watching the juvenites shuffling towards the sea, he plunged the needle into Jamie's cold, numb arm.

Is he killing me or helping me? Jamie wondered, though she was still too full of joy to be much troubled by either possibility.

But as the syrup flowed through her, her ecstasy faded, and warmth flooded back into her bones.

"Choose your moment wisely," said Magnus. "You will only have one chance."

George gulped. Sam O'Brady usually needed no excuse to speak, but he too was lost for words.

The Crackpots were crouched low against the walls of the Central Chamber. The spider's wandering fangs threatened to scalp them.

George grasped one of the anteroom's levers experimentally.

"NO!" the Crackpots yelled.

George stopped in his tracks and remembered Maria's rules of hunting. *Phase out extraneous noise. And scan your field.*

He channelled out the Crackpots' cries and shouts, the slicing of the scissor-fangs and the whirr of the teeth, and analysed the trap—its every wheel, chain and blade. He traced each part back to its origin, and his hands dropped sharply from the lever. He knew that if he moved it, the Crackpots would be dead. And then George grew suspicious—and that suspicion grew with every passing second. Was the trap's complexity somehow an illusion?

"He int doing nothing!" said a cowering man. "He's gonna stand there and watch us get killed!"

"He's just a boy," said Ray, peering at George through the grille of the portcullis. "We must accept our fate."

But George wasn't listening to them. He was looking past the Crackpots and through the whirling blades. His eyes had landed on something in the very centre of the spider-trap.

"Head for the map!" he yelled.

"What, so we can find a way out?" Ray laughed bitterly.

"Please, do as I say! If you do nothing, you're all dead!"

Ray shook his head, but began to crawl nonetheless. A few seconds later he reached the stone plinth.

"Now," said George. "Touch that steel thread."

"*NOOOOOOO!*" the Crackpots screamed.

"Why?" George asked.

"That's what got us into this mess!"

"It was Ray what pronged it in the first place!"

"He hit that wire and got us trapped!"

"Good," George said. "That's exactly what I hoped."

The boy's beaming face did nothing for the Crackpots' nerves. Neither did the wandering fangs and teeth, which were still descending...

...until they sliced into Ray's scalp.

As the Crackpots screamed, George looked into Ray's eyes. Life was swiftly leaving them.

"Please!" George begged.

Ray tripped the wire.

Chapter Fifty

Shooting Stars

Jamie was watching the juvenites' slow march towards the water when suddenly she heard the pounding of thousands of feet and the roar of raging voices.

The sky above Dancing Ledge was burning orange. The glow poured over the cliff-face and rolled down its slopes. Thousands of people carrying flaming torches were running down the path and spilling onto the Ledge.

We're being saved!

Relief bubbled up inside Jamie like carbonated Honeydew.

Until she saw the trailblazer.

"Funnella, you're a doll!" the Doctor crowed. "This is beyond my wildest dreams! Their fear and anger will make the Spectre even more powerful!"

Has Funnella invited the No-Placers to see the final Taking? Jamie wondered. As the Headmistress strutted across the Ledge to join her lover, Jamie decided she wouldn't put it past her.

And then she saw the No-Placers were not alone. They had a hundred-odd Crackpots with them, and a thousand leather-clad... others.

"Ah!" said the Doctor. "Even the escaped have returned for a look-see. Let's give them a show!"

Taking centre stage, the Doctor held Funnella's hand and bowed.

"Welcome, one and all, to a very special Taking. Tonight I will give new meaning to the hitherto symbolic Summer Sacrifice!" He gestured at the dozen juvenites shuffling sadly towards the water, and looked out to the Great Sea.

"I call forth the Ancient Spectre!"

Funnella suddenly dropped the Doctor's hand and punched him in the mouth. Staring at her in disbelief, he raised a hand to strike back, when the ground shook beneath their feet.

There was a ripple on the horizon. Something vast and dark was weaving through the water, swimming towards the Ledge at speed. It flew out of the sea and dark scaled coils soared past the terrified crowd. It spiralled up into the night sky and roared.

The Serpent had to be miles long. Its head alone was the size of the Ledge. It twisted and coiled through the air, seawater drenching the crowd below. It lowered its head to meet them, and invitingly opened its jaws.

"Behold!" screamed the Doctor. "The Ancient Spectre!"

The No-Placers ran back in fear, but the Breedies stood their ground, blades drawn, and the Crackpots blasted a thousand whack-shots at the beast. The rock-bullets bounced off its thick scales and flew back towards the Ledge. The Crackpots stopped firing.

"O Great and Generous Spectre," cried the Doctor, "receive my sacrifice and grant me power!"

The juvenites walked calmly towards the Spectre's wide jaws. Its hellish breath steamed out, and the crowd smelled the burning sulphur of the Abyss.

"Where is your Goddess now?" asked the Doctor. "Do you really think she'll protect you? You, who desecrate my Master's form?"

He pointed across the bay. In front of Pity Me School, the fire-serpent was still burning. The Islanders stared at their bonfire. Apart from the flames, the real Spectre looked exactly like the fire-serpent they'd just left—only impossibly vaster.

Apart from the flames...

Suddenly the Ancient Spectre was ablaze! Its blue-black coils turned to blood-red flames.

The Doctor guffawed. "Your Master thanks you for your fear! See how He appears in the form you most understand. Worship, mortals! Worship your new God!"

The juvenites halted: the first of them had reached the water's edge. Billy looked inside the Spectre's fiery jaws and humbly bent his legs.

Nesbitt's violin jarred to a stop.

Jamie couldn't bear to watch.

Then there was a sudden crack of thunder, and across the cliff blew a gale of such force that it threw Jamie from her rock. Her paralysis stripped by the antidote, she raised her head and faced the eye of the storm. Her heart raced. This gale was no Island wind.

It was the beating of millions of tiny wings.

Great clouds of moths were pouring out of the night sky and swarming towards the Ledge. The twelve juvenites vanished under a crawling mass of insects.

And then, the moths began to *lift*.

Each juvenite became the eye of a pink tornado. The moths whirled them into the air, away from the Spectre and high above the crowds, inland and out of sight.

Jamie didn't doubt who'd sent them. Even now, she heard Creaky Nan change her call.

But why would she send them? Jamie wondered. *She's working with the Doctor. She wanted us dead!*

The Ancient Spectre hissed in anger. More moths dived out of the sky, this time headed straight for the flaming Serpent. They flew into its gaping jaws...

...and came out the other side.

There was no sickening sizzle. No explosion of moth-wings. It was as if the Spectre weren't there at all.

If the fire is real, they will land anywhere but...

The Doctor was apoplectic. *"MAAAAAAA!!!!!!"* he screamed.

He ran across the Ledge, heading straight for his mother. A hundred Breedies fell on him and pinned him to the ground.

Jamie couldn't explain Creaky Nan's change of heart, but she took the opportunity she'd been given. This was her one chance.

You must reject the Image at the water's edge...

She stood up and ran towards the Ancient Spectre.

The Spectre eyed her hungrily.

"JAMIE TUFF!"

The crowd screamed, and the Spectre's flames blazed brighter.

"IT'S THE GIRL WHO WANTS TO RUIN EVERYTHING."

The Spectre's voice shook Dancing Ledge, knocking the Islanders off balance. They cried and moaned in terror, stumbling back towards the cliff. But at the tip of the Ledge, just a few yards from the Serpent, Jamie's feet were planted firmly on the ground.

"YOU THINK YOU'RE A MATCH FOR ME? YOU THINK I'M POWERLESS BECAUSE THAT OLD HAG DEPRIVED ME OF MY FEAST? THEIR SOULS ARE NOTHING COMPARED TO YOURS. THOSE CHILDREN WON'T JOIN ME IN THE UNDERWORLD. BUT YOU WILL!"

"There *are* no Children of the Underworld!" Jamie shouted. "They—like you—do not exist!"

The Spectre lunged. Its jaws opened... And snapped shut over Jamie.

Jamie looked at the astonished crowd from inside the Serpent's fiery jaws. The Spectre withdrew, and then tried to grab her again. And again. But each time its jaws passed straight through her.

It roared with rage.

"You *see!*" said Jamie to the crowd. "The Ancient Spectre's powerless! Look at the moths. Look at me! The Spectre can do you no harm unless you believe in it!"

The Spectre came for her with even more fury, but again it passed straight through her, its ghostly flames no hotter than a summer's breeze against her skin.

As the Ancient Spectre showed itself unable to harm Jamie, the Islanders' fear started to evaporate. And as the scales of their fear fell, something sizzled in the air above them: the Serpent's tail.

Denied its final sacrifice, and with the Islanders' belief working against it, the souls it had already consumed were now too few to sustain it. The Spectre was being eaten up like a candlewick, starting from its tail.

The beast's screams echoed across the Island as its body vanished. Soon only its screaming head remained. The head warped and melted until it was no longer a head at all but a raging fireball, which smoked and hissed and sputtered, and finally blew itself out.

And then there was nothing but the deep Great Sea and the Blanket of Stars.

At once, Jamie was surrounded by whooping and cheering Islanders. Some of them were yipping and trilling their teeth. Max and her father pushed their way through the throng and hugged her, and wouldn't let go.

"I don't know how you did it, but *these*," said Max, cricking his neck to the sky, "are the best fireworks I've ever seen!"

Jamie stared across the water. Bright white spheres of light were shooting out of the Great Sea and racing up to the heavens.

"They're souls," Jamie whispered. "The Spectre's death has released them. They're flying up to the Blanket of Stars."

She smiled at Max. "Where's Billy?"

Max did his best not to look hurt. "He's just back there."

Billy, Charlotte and the other ten juvenites were walking down the cliff path. Jamie ran over to them and launched herself at Billy. "Stop trying to die on me!"

Billy smiled sweetly.

Creaky Nan met them at the bottom of the path with a fistful of moth grubs. "You are each to swallow three of these," she said to the juvenites. "Don't chew them," she added.

Jamie took three grubs from Creaky Nan's palm. "I don't get *why* you did what you did, but you saved us, Nan. Thank you."

"Me, child?" said Creaky. "No! I just bought you time. *You* made the Islanders see the truth. As soon as you exploded their belief in the Ancient Spectre, you destroyed the source of its power. The Turned are now un-Turned, and even the souls the Spectre ate are now travelling up to their rightful homes."

"But... I thought you were on the Doctor's side."

Creaky Nan shook her head. "We had to make sure our son was fooled. When we found out about our Kingsley's plan, Old Cott and I discussed how best to stop him. My husband was quite prepared to take the fall."

Jamie remembered the sound of Old Cott's body thumping to the ground. Her heart stung with the pain.

"Girl?" A hand fell on her shoulder. She spun round.

The old man was wheezing after the exertion of climbing down the uneven cliff path. But other than that, Old Cott seemed to be in the best of health.

"What?" he said. "You think Creaky's Burrowers only cure souls? What about your leg? Nan, where's Kingsley?"

"My name is the Doctor. And I am behind you."

The Doctor was on his knees just yards away. Nesbitt and ten other Crackpots were holding guns to his head.

Evelyn spotted her son and waved. "That's my boy!" she said proudly, as she walked up to the congregation with Miss Humfreeze. The two women gave Jamie a hug, and then fixed the Doctor with the Goddess of all glares.

"Where's dad?" Nesbitt asked.

"If he isn't here," said Evelyn sadly, "I'm afraid he must be dead." She surprised herself with the tears she produced.

"Don't be so 'asty!"

Ray Crackpot walked down onto the Ledge, leaning on George for support. His head was covered in the Ticklers' surgical spiderweb. The uncaged Crackpots followed behind them.

"It was close," said Ray. He slapped George's back. "But this one 'as brains!"

And then Ray saw just whose gun was held against whose head. "Nesbitt! I don't know what I'd have done if I'd lost you as well as T—"

His sentence died as a falcon dived towards him. It landed neatly in front of the gobsmacked man and swiftly made the change.

"T—Tom—Tommy?"

"Yes!"

Ray whooped. "Ha haaaaaaa! Tommy, I don't know *what* you are, but you're alive! My son's alive!" he yelled. "Didn't I say 'e was alive, Evelyn?"

Evelyn gave her husband a slobbery kiss. "You did a few times, yes!"

The Islanders didn't know whether to gasp or cheer. They settled on a mixture of both.

After all she had been through, Jamie had little surprise left for a bird-turned-Tommy, though the sight of him gave her hope. She wondered if the golden hawk circling above them might be Seveny. She desperately wished it so.

She was about to ask Tommy when Empu Salim joined them, Kai in one hand and Maria in the other.

Charlotte flung herself into her brother's arms. "Kai!" she said. "I hope someone's been looking out for you!"

"Funnella did!"

"Funnella?"

The Headmistress was perched on a rock near Ella's unconscious body, looking out to sea.

"What happened to her?" said Charlotte. "She looks quite gentle!"

"Yes," said Kai. "She is."

Jamie wondered if the whole world had gone mad. But the Headmistress *did* look changed. And what about that punch she'd given the Doctor before he had summoned the Ancient Spectre? But curious as Funnella's transformation was, Jamie was a lot more worried about Ella.

Magnus hadn't left Ella's side. He'd been joined by Violet Last.

"What will happen to Ella?" Jamie asked Miss Humfreeze.

"Now that the danger's over, we can travel back to Little Sea and retrieve her soul. I've a talented team of Crackpots and Brainticklers who'll help me."

Jamie smiled. The world hadn't ended, the Doctor had been brought to his knees, Miss Amina was flanked by two leather-clad warriors with drawn swords, and the whispering of the crowd suggested that even the Establishment had been dethroned.

So why doesn't it feel over?

Jamie stared at the Doctor. She expected his face to be twisted with anger. But his eyes were elsewhere. He seemed to be concentrating on something....

On Ella.

Ella Rose Last was starting to move.

"Ella's back!" yelled Evelyn.

Miss Humfreeze frowned. "If the Spectre's death had freed her she would have woken up immediately. Someone else has done this." She glanced at the Doctor. His eyes were focused yet vacant. "And if Ella's soul is still Turned..."

Ella leapt to her feet and began to sprint. Jamie gave chase, but couldn't catch her in time. Ella toppled over the Ledge and into the Great Sea.

Jamie dived after her. She had no trouble seeing Ella: her shimmering blonde locks were a beacon in the black water. Jamie grabbed hold of her and dragged her back to the surface.

Ella gasped for breath.

"Ella Rose Last, you are loved!" said Jamie, looking deep into her friend's eyes.

But it wasn't Ella who looked back. Her hands flew to Jamie's throat and *squeezed*. The two girls sank beneath the water, and as they sank deeper and deeper, the water pressed against them in a crushing embrace.

Jamie was barely holding onto life when she realized what she had to do.

Dreamweave.

* * *

She landed in Ella quickly and discovered she had company. Ella's soul was back in her body, but it was very weak. It was another soul that had its hands round her throat.

The Doctor's.

Jamie had to improvise, and fast.

When the Fiend's upon you...

She imagined a sun in front of her and allowed its rays to feed Ella's fragile soul. But as her sun filled Ella with warmth, the Doctor filled Jamie with lead. And his darkness was relentless. The Doctor was far stronger than her. And as he squeezed Jamie's soul, Ella's hands squeezed her throat.

Jamie tried to throw his soul-grip as Miss Mackadoo had so often done to hers. But as she pushed back against his darkness her sun dimmed, shrank, and finally disappeared.

Through Ella's eyes, she saw the last bubbles of air leave her mouth and her muscles begin to spasm. Soon, she would have no body to return to.

...do not fight! But flood it out, your soul ablaze with Golden Light!

All but exhausted, Jamie thought of those she loved—alive, dead or lost. And as she focused on them, she stopped battling the Doctor. And her soul swelled until she was filled with a Golden Light so bright that there was no space left for darkness.

And the Doctor's soul was gone.

Jamie possessed Ella, forced her hands open, and left.

* * *

Back in her own body and with no air in her lungs, she grabbed Ella's hand and tried to swim upwards. But they had sunk too deep. They would never make it to the surface.

Seveny was high in the sky when her friends disappeared under the waves. Without a thought, she cocked her wings and plunged after them. And then, quite suddenly, she was somewhere else.

* * *

A million faces curiously examined her.

"Who are you?" she hawkthought.

"Farseers. Your family. Look after your sister."

Look after your sister?

The faces faded.

* * *

Seveny hit the water. She shape-shifted everything but her hawk eyes, realising she would need them to see through the black brine.

She took a deep breath in and dived.

The girls had sunk so deep she could hardly make them out. And they were still sinking.

"Seveny!"

She looked up towards the Great Sea's surface. The outline of a falcon hovered over the water.

"You've got to save them," Tommy hawkthought. "I can't swim!"

"What do I do?"

"Mindmove."

Seveny had never Mindmoved a living thing before. But there wasn't time to worry. She focused the power up through her spine and out between her eyes. The line of force stretched down into the darkness. But it didn't reach her friends.

She sent out another line, one she hoped was strong enough to touch but not hurt them. It found Jamie's hand. She gently pressed the line through the hand to hook it, and felt another hand. Jamie was gripping Ella! She could haul them up together.

She pulled the line in and the girls began to rise. Their weight felt like a never-ending needle stabbing into her mind, but she kept her focus and dragged the girls up through the depths.

They were just yards away when Jamie's grip on Ella slackened.

Seveny yanked the line with all her might. It snapped back into her brain, and the girls shot to the surface.

Something enormous crashed into the sea near them. A giant pair of talons grabbed Ella and tore her from the water.

"Quick!" Tommy hawkthought. "Get Jamie."

Following Tommy's lead, Seveny shape-shifted into the biggest eagle she had ever attempted. She scooped up Jamie in her claws, and with one sweep of her enormous wings they were in the air.

The giant Halfhawks flew for Dancing Ledge.

Seveny released a coughing Jamie into Geoffrey Tuff's arms, and Tommy laid Ella, who was gasping for breath, in front of Violet Last. The Halfhawks shape-shifted back to their human forms.

"Help! He's gone mad!"

Everyone turned towards the shout.

Nesbitt had Miss Amina pinned against the cliff-face. His gun was pressed to her chest.

"Please, don't!" she begged. "Please!" She looked into the Crackpot's eyes—and her own eyes widened. "Daddy? Daddy! Please, Daddy! Noooooooooooooooo!"

A shot rang out. Miss Amina fell to the ground.

Her soul slipped from her snake-toothed mouth.

It was a dull, misshapen thing, quite unlike the shining stars of the juvenites. It travelled out across the bay, hovered uncertainly for a few moments, and then disappeared under the Great Sea.

"Well!" said Nesbitt. "Ella's soul may have escaped my Master, but another has taken her place." The Doctor hadn't bothered to copy Nesbitt's stutter. "And such a soul! The Spectre will feed well on its darkness."

"You killed our daughter!" cried Miss Humfreeze. "And years of torture at your hands have Turned her soul."

"The Spectre must be fed, Humfreeze."

"The Spectre does not exist!"

"And yet you all saw him." Nesbitt, possessed by the Doctor, aimed his gun at the crowd. "Did you, or did you not, see the Serpent?" He looked out to the Great Sea. "I call forth the Ancient Spectre!"

But nothing happened. The crowd's fear was broken. The only thing troubling the ocean was its waves.

But something was rattled. Max gripped his sword.

As Max realized the implication of his blade's vibrations, Nesbitt strode towards the group. His gun was aimed at Jamie.

Geoffrey Tuff bent over his daughter, trying to shield her. Max ran in front of them both and raised his sword.

"Don't come any closer!" he said. "Or I'll—"

Nesbitt fired.

Max and Geoffrey, with Jamie in his arms, crumpled to the ground.

Evelyn wrestled the gun out of Nesbitt's hands and Magnus pushed the possessed hansum to his knees.

Nesbitt's puddle-eyes blinked. His gun was in his mother's hands. His arms were locked behind his back. A look of confusion crossed his face. "What ha-ha-have I missed?"

He discovered the heap of bodies in front of him.

"Oh Goddess, what ha-ha-have I done?"

"You've done nothing," said Miss Humfreeze. "Bring the Doctor here!"

Fira and Striker marched the Doctor over. He looked tired. Defeated.

Creaky Nan reached into her pocket and took out a small pot of foul-smelling paste which she smeared across the Doctor's forehead. "There'll be no more Dreamweaving for now," she said darkly.

"You just killed your own daughter," said Miss Humfreeze. "*Our* daughter. And for what? Your 'Children of the Underworld' are still alive, and your Ancient Spectre's dead! And you tried to kill these three, but not a soul between them has set sail."

A flash of light erupted from the bloody heap. A solitary orb shot up to join the stars.

Empu Salim gently separated the bodies. Jamie had suffered a shot to her chest, Geoffrey Tuff a wound to his neck, and Max was covered in blood.

One of them was dead.

"Nine Lives!" George ran to his blood-soaked friend and shook him.

"Still eight lives left!" croaked Max. "Did I save Jamie?"

George looked anxiously at Creaky Nan, who'd set to work on the girl. Though Creaky Nan looked grave, she nodded.

"She'll be fine." said George.

Violet Last gasped and ran to Geoffrey. Empu Salim let her have a moment, then whispered something in her ear. Violet cradled Geoffrey's body in her arms and kissed him. And then she did something that made not the slightest bit of sense.

She looked at Funnella and beckoned her over. The Headmistress joined her, and Violet took her hand.

"Geoffrey loved me," Violet said, "but he never stopped loving you. Your place is here."

Violet Last stepped back, and Funnella Fitzgerald knelt down.

What the Headmistress did next shocked everyone, especially the Doctor. Funnella kissed Geoffrey tenderly on the lips, then softly stroked Jamie's hair.

"How *dare* you," said Miss Humfreeze. "Isn't it enough you tried to put Jamie Underground? Isn't it enough you kidnapped Kai and were so cruel to him he wouldn't speak? Isn't it enough that Seveny—"

"I could speak." Kai pushed through the quiet crowd. "But Charlotte was gone and I didn't see the point, and Funnella said not to tell anyone, but she was *always* good to me, and she wanted to save me from the Tombland Gang, and when she wasn't with me, Herbert was."

"Then why did you run away?" George asked.

"Funnella told me to. She told Herbert to take me to the Library, and before we left she told me that I had to lose him and find you. And I did as I was told."

"It still stands, Funnella, that you drove Seveny off a cliff!" said Miss Humfreeze.

"If she hadn't, I wouldn't be a Halfhawk Mortal." Though Seveny was wearing a donated coat, she was violently shivering. "I don't know why she did it, but I really think she freed me."

Jamie opened her eyes at the sound of Seveny's voice. She looked at her best friend and managed a smile. Then her grey eyes turned steely. "Funnella." Her lungs crackled with the blood inside them. "You ordered the Gang to kill me."

"I did. Because if I hadn't the Doctor would have killed you himself. I sent the Gang on what I'd planned to be a wild goose chase. You were never meant to reach the Gravel Pit. I was going to escort you home. I tried to stop you leaving school—"

"Oh my Goddess," said Miss Humfreeze, remembering the headlock she'd given her. "So you did!"

"So... When did you stop being evil?" said Max.

"Funnella hasn't." The Headmistress addressed the crowd. "I was employed by the Farseers, powerful spirits who watch over you all, to take over the Headmistress's body until Jamie embraced her Gift. I Dreamweaved into Funnella, stayed hidden for a week so I could study her behaviour, and possessed her body in the assembly following the April Taking. It was my decision to house Kai, to push Seveny to the brink, to Call Ella and to put Jamie on *G and D*—I had to appease the Doctor and the Establishment or else I'd have raised suspicion. I laughed Jamie out of this very body when I thought she'd be discovered by the Doctor." The Headmistress looked back down at Jamie.

"Didn't you find it claustrophobic when you Dreamweaved into Funnella?"

Jamie nodded. It had been quite a squish.

"So if you're not Funnella," said George, "Who are you?"

"I'm Gloria Tuff. Jamie's mother."

Jamie couldn't believe what she was hearing. She wanted to scream but she hadn't the strength. Miss Humfreeze, however, could read her mind.

"You're lying!" she cried on Jamie's behalf.

The Doctor smirked. "No, she's right. You remember the day your mother died, don't you, Jamie? When you opened the door to me? 'My father's at work,' you said. 'It's just me in the house.' But that rash of yours was spreading up your face. I pushed you out of my way and went up to the attic—and found *her* lying there. Surely you remember me ripping your mother from her bed? And her screams..."

His smirk turned into the cruellest smile.

And for the first time, Jamie remembered.

The screaming, and the crying, and the tearing, and the begging. Having to tell her dad that his wife was never coming back. He hadn't got angry with her, even then. He'd just got sad. No, he'd never blamed her for what had happened that day. But *she* had. She'd blamed herself.

And then she'd buried it.

"You killed your own mother," said the Doctor.

Yes I did, thought Jamie. *With my inability to lie. With my rash.*

Tears rolled from her eyes.

"You are a fighter, Jamie Tuff!" yelled Funnella.

Only my mother used to say that!

"Mum?" said Jamie, choking on the blood in her lungs.

She tried to sit up. And that was when she discovered her father lying next to her. Unmoving.

"He's up there, now," her mother said, looking up at the Blanket of Stars.

Jamie lay back down. The blood rattled in her lungs. Her eyes closed.

"You had *no* part in my death, you hear me?" said Gloria Tuff. "Don't let the Doctor have a part in yours! He wants you dead because your Gift is greater than his. But his fears are no reason to hide your light. Nor to give up fighting!"

Jamie Tuff's eyes sprang open. "Kingsley Cott," she said, her voice as sure as molten metal. "I shall *never* let you win!"

Her words provoked an extraordinary response: the Doctor started to cry.

"I think it's time you went Underground," said Miss Humfreeze. "You've made your prison, you should lie in it. Evelyn? Frank? Would you escort the Doctor to the Spider Chamber? And George, perhaps you could find a way to fix the trap so he can't escape."

The sobbing Doctor was hauled to his feet and dragged through the door in the cliff.

Miss Humfreeze and Magnus joined Creaky Nan and Empu Salim in treating the casualties. Max had a gunshot wound to his leg, Jamie a punctured lung, Ella was half drowned, and Seveny had gone fully into shock.

"Sam!" yelled Miss Humfreeze. "We need Tickler assistance!"

Sam O'Brady, Barry, and a hundred thousand other Brainticklers swarmed across the Ledge.

The No-Placers and Breedies had pretty much the same reaction as the Crackpots had on their first encounter with the Ticklers.

Miss Humfreeze put her fingers in her mouth and whistled. "Anyone who isn't ill or a Tickler, please leave the Ledge. And watch where you tread!"

Once the Ledge was evacuated, the Ticklers set to work on the casualties, armed with rolls of surgical spiderweb. As they started to work on Jamie, Gloria Tuff—in possession of Funnella's hands—cradled Jamie's face.

Jamie looked into Funnella's eyes and felt unparalleled joy. For through those eyes she saw thick bobbed hair that didn't quite cover pointy ears, a little upturned nose and slate-grey eyes. It was her mum as she had known her. Her mum before she died.

"You're about to leave me, aren't you?" said Jamie, speaking to her mother's soul.

"I have to. But you mustn't think of us as gone. Your father and I will always watch over you, for souls can never be destroyed."

"And you'll look after Dad?"

"With my entire being."

Jamie smiled through her tears. "Then you'd better catch him up."

Gloria Tuff kissed her daughter.

And one last star shot up to the sky.

Chapter Fifty-one

The Quiet After

After the battle on Dancing Ledge, Miss Humfreeze couldn't let Jamie end up in the Orphanage, so she asked her if she could be her guardian. She didn't have to ask anyone else's permission.

After what had happened at the Summer Sacrifice, the Establishment hadn't dared try any governing. With their fraud and frailties so thoroughly exposed, they were finished and they knew it. They'd slunk back to their expensive homes and shut the doors. No Place no longer had a ruling committee.

Nor did Pity Me School have a Headmistress.

After Jamie's mother departed, the real Funnella woke up. When she discovered the Doctor had gone to prison, she almost cried. When she heard the Deputy had been burned to a crisp, she looked personally wounded. And when she discovered the date, she nearly fainted.

"June?" she screeched. "It's not. It's April!"

And then she saw the Brainticklers. Deciding Funnella looked in thorough need of a tickle, they swarmed towards her in their thousands. She jerked like a cat with fleas as they boarded her head, and she ran away over the cliffs, screaming.

That was the last anyone had seen of her.

Without Funnella running the school, support for the Pity Me Perfects had collapsed. They were now doing their damnedest to be as nice as Honeydew to everyone. For the first time in their lives, in fact, they were trying to be perfect. Even the Tombland Gang had lost some of their swagger after seeing things much deadlier than them on Dancing Ledge.

But with no one ruling No Place, there were many things that needed working out. Large things involving housing and money, and smaller things such as whether or not to maintain the tradition of the festivals.

After Empu Salim's speech in the school field, the No-Placers' belief in the Great Goddess had wavered. The majority still believed in her existence and thought the festivals were a fitting tribute. The rest decided it would still be nice to welcome in the seasons. They all agreed the festivals brought them together, and that was something special. So they had voted to keep them, but to change the way in which they were celebrated.

"What do you think will happen at the Autumn Harvest?" asked Jamie, running her tense fingers through Loopy's whiskers.

"Nothing," said Miss Humfreeze, who was making a large pot of tea to go with their fish dinner. "Who'll call people Overripe now? Now the Establishment has been overthrown, no one will ever be sent Underground again."

Jamie smiled. "Good. I don't know what I'd do if I lost you, too."

"Ahem!" said a husky voice. "I know we've only been house-mates a month, but you'd still have me."

"True, but you're not so good at helping me with my homework!"

Magnus laughed. "Mother has the edge, but she *is* a teacher. And she hasn't spent her whole life Underground with the

Doctor!"

Magnus had meant to be funny, but Miss Humfreeze's heart ached. "Every day I wonder," she said quietly, "whether if I'd done things differently you'd both be up here."

"I know, Mum," said Magnus gently. "But you do have me and Jamie. Miss Amina's not suffering any more. And I'm free. We're all free of *him*."

Miss Humfreeze sighed. "That's true. He's safe Underground. And he won't be Dreamweaving again."

George had made a comfortable, inescapable cell for the Doctor out of his own spider-trap. And Creaky Nan's magic had ensured that the Doctor was trapped in his own body for good.

"Talking of Dreamweaving," said Miss Humfreeze, "how have you been sleeping, Jamie?"

"I haven't Dreamweaved since Dancing Ledge," said Jamie, her eyes not leaving the cat. "I'm glad, really. I don't think it's right, visiting someone without their invitation."

The schoolteacher empathized. Though she'd re-embraced most of her Gift with pride, she refrained from mind-reading for the same reason. But Miss Humfreeze didn't need to be a mind-reader to know that all was not quite right with Jamie Tuff.

For the girl's red rash was snaking up her face.

Acknowledgements

I would like to thank my mum Juliet, my dad Paul and my
two sisters Chioma and Sophie for housing me, loving me...
and not staging an intervention.

Joel, my fellow clumsy. All the thank yous in the world.

In memory of Hadar Shalgi. She had the Golden Light.

About the Author

Holly grew up in a small, sleepy village in Suffolk. The acting
bug hit her at age nine, when she was asked to play Baboushka
in the school nativity. That same year she played the lead role of
a naughty black poodle in a pet parlour themed ballet, and she
thought she had made it.

Years passed, but the acting bug didn't. She went to
Goldsmiths, University of London to study Drama, after which
she completed her actor training at Arts Ed.

Writing a book was never part of the plan. But life's full of
swerves and surprises and ideas dropping into people's heads.
Holly had an idea drop into hers, and that idea became The
Summer Sacrifice, and The Summer Sacrifice became the first
book of the Master Game Series.

For more information please visit:
www.hollyhinton.com

6727101R00190

Printed in Great Britain
by Amazon.co.uk, Ltd.,
Marston Gate.